Myeong-seong Seunim:

The Bright Star above Unmunsa Temple

MYEONG-SEONG SEUNIM:

THE BRIGHT STAR ABOVE UNMUNSA TEMPLE

Written by **Ji-sim Nam**
Translated by **Rei Yoon & Seung Suk Lee**

Bulkwang Publishing

Prologue

It has been over thirty years since I became a lay disciple of Myeong-seong Seunim (*Seunim* is the Korean title of respect for both Buddhist monks and nuns). This is by no means a short period of time in the scale of a human life. I have only received and have given back nothing to my teacher. I have organized the life story of Myeong-seong into a biographical novel. It is only now that I feel that I have a much deeper understanding of her. The deeper I understand, the more grateful I am.

I had two preconceived notions about Myeong-seong Seunim. One was that she was exactly same on the inside and outside. Second was that she was flawless. These ideas of her formed in my head through decades of observing her. Now that I am finishing the book, I feel she deserves another title – "worthy of praise." Indeed, her life and life's work deserve to be praised by all sentient beings, Buddhas and Bodhisattvas of the human world and of Heaven.

I chose this format of biographical novel because small

pieces of imagination were helpful in providing the big picture. However, an overwhelmingly large portion of the book is biographical and is based on facts that objectively record the life of this great teacher. I have come to recognize the historical significance of this task, which is why I have included most of the material in its raw form.

For historical background, I have quoted much from Sun-seok Kim's *What happened to Korean Buddhism in One Hundred Years?* Much of the history about Bhikkhuni is from Chun-saeng Ha's *The Sangha of Korean Bhikkhuni.* I thank both of them for their generous permission to borrow from their work. Their books have been instrumental in composing this novel.

One of the happiest things in life must be meeting someone you respect. I, for one, have surely enjoyed this privilege. I hope that readers will be able to share in this blessing through this book. I bow three times in the direction of Bamboo Forest House (*Jungnimheon*) where Myeong-seong Seunim resides. I have received an undeserved amount of merit; may it be spread out and shared among other beings.

Ji-sim Nam

<u>Notes</u>

1. The book generally follows the Revised Romanization of Korean (2000).
2. With a few exceptions, Sanskrit was preferred for expressing Buddhist terms. Exceptions include bhikkhu, bhikkhuni, and sangha. Diacritical marks were generally omitted.
3. Effort has been made to explain the meaning of the Korean instead of only transcribing the sound. For example, Examples include Bamboo Forest House (*Jungnimheon*) and Pavilion of Profound Lectures (*Seolhyeondang*)
4. The sutras are described using their common names in English, as well as Sanskrit and Korean expressions. For example, Heroic March Sutra (Śūraṅgama Sūtra or *Neungeomgyeong*).
5. The two-syllable Dharma names of monastics and ordinary people are rendered using hyphens between the two syllables. For example, Myeong-seong, Myo-eom, Dong-hwa Kim
6. Chan/Zen/Seon (禪) is rendered as "Seon" following the Korean usage.
7. Translator's notes were added when deemed necessary to aid in the English-speaking public's understanding. For example, Guksa (teacher of the nation)

Contents

Chapter 01

A distant
memory
of father

It was still cold. Spring had arrived on the calendar but not on the skin. Trees were still grey, dried-up grass covered the fields. Only the warmth of the sun in the blue empty sky signaled spring. Spring was here, only people had not yet noticed.

Im-ho was standing outside, waiting for her mother. Her skin was white and her eyes sparkled brightly. She was wearing a black cotton skirt and purple silk jacket with a white silk scarf around her neck. She was well-dressed for a young girl from the countryside.

"Hurry, Im-ho is waiting for you," urged Im-ho's aunt. Mother soon appeared. She was wearing the same jade green coat that she wore on the day she was married. She had the same white silk scarf around her neck.

Im-ho's aunt spoke as she bent down and gave her a hug. "Im-ho, you are starting school today. I am confident you will be the best in your class. You finished the one thousand basic Chinese characters faster than anyone." Im-ho gave back a shy smile.

"Let's go," said Mother as she held Im-ho's hand.

"Take this money. Get some warm rice-soup somewhere before you return. It will be well past lunchtime when you get home." Her aunt handed some money to her mother.

"Thank you." Her mother put the money in her pocket and recaptured Im-ho's hand.

"Hurry and go now. Im-ho, have a great day at school." Sadness appeared on her aunt's face. She was thinking of Im-ho's father, and how he was absent.

Im-ho's father's name was Jae-yeong Jeon, and her mother's name was O-jong Jeong. Her father was from Bonggang Village of Waeseo Town in Sangju County. Her mother was from Usin Village of the same town. Im-ho's father was a descendant of Jeong-won Jeon and his family originated from Okcheon. His ancestor, Jeong-won, was a civil servant who belonged to the Yeongnam School. He was born during the rule of King Myeongjong and passed away during King Injo's reign. During the reign of King Gwanghae, Jeong-won served as a judge in Ulsan City and as governor of Jeolla Province. When he saw that King Gwanghae was not a virtuous leader, he resigned and returned to his hometown. Injo, the next king, appointed him to yet another government position. He became secretary of the Interior Ministry, Royal Adviser, and Director of the Royal Library and Archives. He was posthumously designated Prime Minister.

Jeong-won came back home in his old age but he declined the gift of land that the king had endowed to him. Rather, he retired to a poor town in the mountains called Bonggang. He was a great scholar, and together with Gyeong-se Jeong and Jun Lee, they were the three great stars of the Yeongnam School.

Im-ho's mother, O-jong Jeong, was a descendant of Gyeong-se Jeong. Gyeong-se was a disciple of the famous scholar Seong-nyong Ryu and his family originated from Jinju City. He started as a third secretary during King Seonjo's reign. During King Injo's reign, Gyeong-se became the Deputy Director of the Royal Library and Archives, governor of Jeolla Province, Director of Audits, Minister of Interior, and Minister of the Royal Library and Archives. He was an expert in neo-Confucianism and adhered to the "Principles and Energy" theory of Yi Lee. He was particularly well-versed in the study of proper social decorum and thus became a member of the Proprieties School together with Jang-saeng Kim. Gyeong-se, after retiring from public service, returned home and settled in the mountainous village of Usan, and further devoted himself to continuing his studies.

Both Im-ho's mother and father were descendants of great scholars of the Joseon Kingdom. Their ancestors, Jeong-won Jeon and Gyeong-se Jeong, together with Jin Lee, were called the Three Wise Men in the Mountains. So already, the ties between the two families were deep.

Both Jae-yeong and O-jong were fifteen when they got married. When Jae-yeong turned nineteen, he asked his wife, "Do you want me to go out into the world, get higher education, and become a great person or do you want me to stay at home and just be a farmer?"

O-jong replied without hesitation, "Of course I want you to learn more and become a great person."

"Then do as I say. Go up in the attic. There will be a white vase where my father hid some money. Pretend you are cleaning the house, take out that money and bring it to me. Then I will leave home to go study."

O-jong did as she was told, hoping that her husband would return as a successful person. Jae-yeong left the house as soon as he got the money. This was in the 1920's, before Im-ho was born. For many years, Jae-yeong was not to be heard from. His parents felt sorry for their daughter-in-law, who was raising Im-ho all by herself. They invited her to live together with their family and that is how Im-ho and her mother went to live with Im-ho's aunt, Jae-yeong's sister. Im-ho was seven years old when she first saw her father. That was the first and last time she had seen him.

It was April, but winter was still lingering. Old men in *gat* (a traditional horsehair hat) and fathers with their hair tied up in traditional *sangtu* fashion were wandering around in the playground. Children were gathered at the centre.

"Go in there and join the others," Mother spoke as she let go of Im-ho's hand. Im-ho glanced at her once and walked over to the group of children. Mother looked around to find a place to wait. Most of the adults present were men, which made her feel uncomfortable. She found a tree and hid behind it.

Shortly after, five or six teachers came out to the playground. One of them made the students stand in two lines: one for boys, one for girls. The boys' line was about three times longer than the girls' line. The principal went up to the podium to give a welcoming address.

"Boys and girls, congratulations. You are now students of the Great Empire of Japan. Every single one of you must study hard and become a great person. Please grow up to be a patriot for your nation. Become pillars of your family. That is the only way we can survive."

The principal continued with his speech. He was obligated to mention his allegiance to the Japanese Empire as a formality. Everything that he said afterwards was from his heart. Inside his heart, he wanted the students to grow up to be great people so that they can one day save their nation, Korea. The students were only ten years old at most. They had no idea what he was talking about. Regardless, he continued, in the hopes of planting the tiniest seed within them.

Im-ho listened to the principal's speech with eyes full of curiosity. Her face was white and round, lips firmly closed. She certainly stood out from the crowd. Her mother looked at her from behind the tree. She had been thinking of the day Im-ho was born. Im-ho's grandfather had been waiting for the baby, anxiously looking at the clock. It was an auspicious hour, which meant that someone born at that particular cosmic hour would grow up to become a great scholar who could return honor to the family. However, he was greatly disappointed when he learned that the baby was a girl. He taught little Im-ho the basic Chinese characters before passing away.

After the principal's remarks, teachers led the students into their classrooms. Parents were left outside. Naturally, they grouped together to chat. They mostly knew each other, having come from the same village. As all close people do, they had a lot to chat about. Im-ho's mother, being an outsider, still felt uncomfortable standing alone under the tree and decided to go out of the gate. She decided to visit a shop to buy sugar candy for Im-ho.

When she came back, students were rushing out of the classrooms. They all carried textbooks they had just received from school. On their chests were attached ribbons that read "Use Japanese Only."

All the textbooks they received were in Japanese. April 1st, 1938, the day Im-ho entered school, happened to be the day the Japanese imperial government in Korea had announced the New Education Policy and started a systematic campaign to eliminate the use of Korean as a language.

"Im-ho is the only student who got a perfect score in arithmetic," said her teacher while looking at her proudly. "Im-ho, your Japanese is as good as a Japanese student. You even excel in math."

The students had to write from 1 to 100 and only Im-ho got them correct. All the other students looked up at Im-ho with envy, which made her feel strange. 'If you know how to write from 1 to 10, then why can't you write from 1 to 100?' she thought to herself.

As the school day ended, the teacher told the students, "That is it for today. Today is Saturday. Do not come to school next week. From Monday through Saturday, all students have been mobilized to go catch pine caterpillars in the mountains, but you have been excluded because you are too little. Students with clean-up duty, stay behind to clean the school. The rest of the students are dismissed."

As the kids left the classroom, they were joyful and noisy because there would be no school for one week. The Japanese imperial government was ruling Korea under semi-wartime martial law. They mobilized the student's labour for all kinds of government needs, including pest control.

Im-ho walked back home alone. There was a boy from the same village who attended her school, but he walked much faster and they never walked together. Im-ho had to wrap her books in a cloth and sling it across her shoulder. Walking three miles across two hills was not easy for small Im-ho, but she never disliked learning. Everything new she learned was amazing and fun. One week of spring break didn't bring her joy like the other kids.

She entered the village and approached her house with small footsteps. Her house was at the highest point in town, with a roof decorated with black tiles. As she neared, she sensed excitement throughout the house.

'What is going on?' Im-ho wondered. An elder spoke to her as he was coming out of the house.

"Your uncle is here. Go in and pay respect to him."

The smell of food filled the air. Relatives and friends had gathered to see the long-missed visitor. Im-ho's usually quiet house was buzzing with excitement. Im-ho's cousin shouted at her, "My dad is here! Go and bow to him!"

Her cousin's face was beaming with excitement. Im-ho did not reply as she went up the stairs and entered the living room. Many adults from the neighborhood were present. Uncle was telling them of the outside world that he had seen in his travels. He was the older brother of Im-ho's father. She did not know what work he was doing, but from what she had heard, he was a busy man who mostly stayed in Seoul and visited Japan and China frequently. Her uncle returned to his hometown only once or twice a year, but he'd stay for a few months when he did come. For Im-ho, he felt more like a father than her real father.

Im-ho untied the book sack and entered. Her uncle spoke first, "My darling Im-ho, it is so good to see you." Im-ho bowed deeply and knelt in front of him. "I have brought a gift for you. Try it on outside." He handed her something wrapped in newspaper.

"Thank you." She received it with both hands. She bowed again and went outside. She overheard an elder speak to her uncle as she was leaving.

"Have you heard any news from your younger brother? It seems he is alive but then why does he never come home? That is not right. Look at that girl, she is growing up without a father. What of her mother?"

She shook her head in an effort to forget such thoughts and concentrated on the gift she had just received. It was a beautiful pair of rubber shoes embroidered with flowers. The shoes were red with white and yellow chrysanthemums blooming all around it. Green leaves appeared in between the flowers. She hurriedly tried them on. They felt slightly big, but were so pretty. She wanted to show them to her mother, so she went to the kitchen. Her cousin saw her again and yelled, "Are those shoes from my dad? Wow, you are lucky today!"

Im-ho ignored him again and hurried to find her mother. In the kitchen were two ladies who had come to help. Her aunt was busy leading the whole team while her mother was nowhere to be seen. Im-ho's face stiffened. Her mother was outside, washing the vegetables alone. Her head hung low. Im-ho knew she was crying.

Im-ho quickly turned away so that her mother would not know that she had seen her. Even at her young age, Im-ho knew why her mother was so sad. Im-ho leaned against the wall and slowly sat down. Her father's distant face came to her memory. It was clear sometimes, but mostly not. She drifted into a happy daydream. She had seen her father just once. Whenever she remembered her father, she was blanketed with a sense of great happiness.

It was a day in spring, many years back, when Im-ho was around seven years of age. A strange man had come to her house. The whole house sprang into life and everybody from the village came over. Im-ho sensed that the man was her father. An elder spoke to him, "How could you have disappeared for so long? Your daughter is now seven years old. Im-ho, come here. This is your father."

Im-ho's heart pounded rapidly with a sense of excitement. In the future, she would always feel the same emotion whenever she thought of her father. Her father had returned home after eight years and stayed for ten days. He gave Im-ho and her mother a once-in-a-lifetime gift by taking them to Seoul. The two were overwhelmed at the sight of the city. Father wanted to offer this to his wife, who had lived such a lonely and difficult life.

Im-ho boarded the train with her parents. She was wearing a white dress embroidered with orange maple leaves. It was their first time to ride a train. Suddenly, the huge piece of metal started moving! She was amazed. She looked around busily with curiosity. Her father was sitting by the window, with Im-ho in middle and her mother by the aisle. As the train picked up speed, rice paddies and mountains started to fly by. It seemed that the landscape was moving, not her.

"Do you want to have a better look?" Her father lifted Im-ho and put her on his lap. She pressed her nose to the window. Her heart was pounding, not because of the scenery, but because her father was hugging her. She was shy but happy. She had never felt such a feeling.

"Come down now, Im-ho. It's hurting your dad's knees." Her mother spoke in a low voice.

The three came all the way to Seoul as if in a dream. For her entire life, Im-ho's tongue remembered the taste of the boiled egg and caramel candy that she had for a snack on the train. What of the warm broth in the streets of Seoul, bread and milk from the bakery, cherry blossoms at night in Changgyeong Palace, and all the pretty little things at the Hwashin Department Store?

As soon as Im-ho's thoughts reached Hwasin, she remembered the small girl. Im-ho had been excited in the department store, looking here and there, in her dress with the embroidered orange maple leaves. Im-ho's hair was cut short in the style of imperialist Japanese students.

A small girl entered the store holding her mother's hand. She must have been a rich girl from Seoul. She stuck out her lips and murmured to her mother. "Mother, look at her. She must have come from the countryside. Look at her hair. It looks like she put a bowl on her head." Im-ho was embarrassed. She looked up carefully at her father because she was more worried that her father would be embarrassed of her.

All in all, however, it was a happy time spent together as a family. Im-ho asked herself, "Where is my father? Why does he not come to see me?"

Im-ho's father was actually a Buddhist monk. His Dharma name was "Gwan-eung" Seunim (*Seunim* is a title of respect given to Buddhist monks and nuns). He was an expert in the Mind-only (Yogachara) school. He was one of the greatest Buddhist scholars of his time, and also a Seon (or Zen) master who had completed six years of meditation in the Gateless Gate (*Mumun Gwan*). Indeed, he was one of the few Korean monks of the twentieth century who had mastered both theory and practice. To understand Gwan-eung better, one would need to look into the historical background of the time. It was the era of the Japanese colonization of Korea, and education within the Buddhist community had taken strange turns because of this.

Gwan-eung joined the path of renunciation with Tan-ong Seunim as his Master when he turned twenty, in 1929. Tan-ong resided at the Namjangsa Temple of Sangju county. Gwan-eung studied in a Buddhist college that belonged to Jikjisa Temple. Jikji was a Head Temple that had many temples beneath it, including Namjang. He then moved to the Yujeomsa Temple in the Geumgang Mountains and finished college at the age of twenty-five, in 1934. At the age of twenty-nine, he graduated from Hyehwa College. Four years later, when he was thirty-three, he graduated from Ryukoku University in Japan. For thirteen years, he had faithfully studied the inner curriculums in Buddhist colleges, and outer curriculums at Hyehwa and Ryukoku. He grew into a Buddhist scholar while he was still young, during the time of Japanese rule.

Wonheungsa Temple had been built during King Gojong's reign in 1902 to pray for the peace and prosperity of the kingdom. This temple had authority over all the other temples in Korea. Four years after the founding of Wonheungsa Temple, progressive monks came together to organize the *Buddhism Research Society* (*Bulgyo Yeonkuhoe*) and founded the Myeongjin School within the temple. This school was the first modern Buddhist school. However, the Japanese Buddhist sect of Jōdo-shū seemed to have been behind the founding of this school, for Japan wanted control over Korean Buddhism and they knew that control began with education. The leader of Jōdo-shū, Hiroyasu Sinsui, had mentioned as much in his congratulatory remarks on the founding ceremony of Myeongjin School.

"The renaissance of Buddhism lies not in the building of more temples but in the advancement of knowledge. To develop knowledge, we must first improve the social status of monks. We must allow their free travel into the palace area and build a Buddhist school in the capital to educate them."

Japanese Jōdo-shū established the *Buddhism Research Society* in order to introduce a new education system for Korean monks. Japan's plan was to educate the elites among the monks and turn them into collaborators for them. Despite being tainted with Japan's desire for control, progressive monks in Korea also felt the need for innovation in the education system for Buddhist monks. Myeongjin School was the product of a strange balance between Japan's conspiracy and the needs of Korean monks. In order to open the eyes of the monks to the changing world, the school introduced a lot of subjects that were compatible with secular schools and were not related to Buddhism.

Myeongjin School introduced missionary studies, foreign languages, world history, land survey, agriculture, mathematics, science, library studies, manufacturing, sports, and the like. The school taught more secular subjects than Buddhist subjects because only monks who had already graduated from Buddhist colleges were allowed to enter. The school produced eighteen graduates by 1909. Among them were Yong-un Han, a Korean monk who was one of the most well-known independence fighters against Japan, Sang-no Gwon, who went on to become the first President of Dongguk University after Korea was liberated from Japan, and Jong-uk Lee, who served as the Chairman of the Board of Dongguk University and as a member of the National Assembly.

Myeongjin School was established under the influence of Japanese Jōdo-shū, however, it was Korean Buddhists who ran the facility and tried to modernize Korean Buddhism in step with the rapid changes happening in the world. Nonetheless, the process of setting up a proper Buddhist education system was not easy and there was a lot of confusion owing to inexperience. The leadership change from the Buddhist Research Society (*Bulgyo Yeonkuhoe*) to the Central Religious Affairs Centre (*Wonjong Jongmuwon*) added to the confusion.

Myeongjin School changed its name many times: Buddhist Academy (*Bulgyo Sabeom Haggyo*), Buddhist Senior College (*Bulgyo Godeung Gangsuk*), Central Students Club (*Jungang Hangnim*), Buddhism Transmission School (*Bulgyo Jeonsu Haggyo*), and Hyehwa College (*Hyehwa Jeonmun Haggyo*). Finally, after liberation from Japanese rule, it became Dongguk University, which continues to this day. Gwan-eung was in the middle of such changes. He had studied in Buddhist Colleges in Jikji and Yujeomsa Temples, which were part of the traditional system, and continued on to study in Hyehwa College and Ryukoku University in Japan, which were part of the secular curriculum. Buddhist elites knew that they had to learn both traditional and secular in order to survive, let alone thrive.

It was after Gwan-eung had just finished studying in Yujeomsa Temple and before entering Hyehwa that he took his wife and daughter to Seoul. That was eight years after becoming a monk. Gwan-eung had always felt sorry for his family. He was twenty-seven years old when he saw his seven-year-old daughter for the first time. He wanted to give them something memorable. A trip to Seoul was precisely that. It was also the first and last family event that they had together.

Im-ho's teacher spoke after school had finished. "I have to make a disheartening announcement. Im-ho Jeon is moving away to Yecheon and will no longer study with us. She is the vice president of the class and also the best student in academics. You should all be sad, but I am no less saddened. We wish all the best for Im-ho in her new school." All her classmates looked at her with sorrowful looks. For the first time, Im-ho felt the grief of separation. She tried to grasp the meaning of departure but remained silent.

Im-ho blushed as everybody's eyes fell on her. She was sad to leave. For three years she had not skipped one day of school. She was the top in her class. As vice president, she helped her teacher with the classroom chores. She had become vice president because girls were not supposed to be president at that time.

Her friends saw her off. She came out of the school and walked the hilly road back home. Many thoughts came to her mind, for adults were telling her that she would now go live together with her father. Im-ho's aunt gave her a big hug. She congratulated Im-ho for finally uniting with her father and told her that she should continue to do well in her studies, but Im-ho's grandaunt was not at all impressed.

"I am not sure I can trust your father. He is a person who does not understand the meaning of a wife and his own child."

She was definitely not a fan of Im-ho's father. Her aunt attempted to defend him.

"What do you mean? He is a kind person."

"Kind? How kind is it to just leave his family behind without ever sending any news?"

"Well, that's because he became a monk..."

"Can you just stop? Do not even mention the word 'monk' in front of me. I have seen parents send their children to the temples in extreme poverty when that was the only way to feed them. Never have I seen a proper person with a proper mind voluntarily become a monk. Why would they want to become low class? He is from a rich family with a proud history. His family even had two servants. Why would he demote himself to such a low status? Not to mention that he is a married man with a wife and daughter."

Grandaunt shook her head in disapproval and turned away. Im-ho felt uncomfortable and puzzled. Do monks really belong to the low class? Then why would father voluntarily choose to become one? Was he not well-educated?

Since when did monks belong to the low class in the Joseon dynasty? This was something that started around the eighteenth century. The *Book of Prohibition*, published during the rule of King Yeongjo, stipulates that if a monk enters the palace area without permission he shall be punished with one hundred beatings on the buttocks and be permanently demoted to slave class. This measure marks the beginning of when monks became regarded as the lowest class.

Why did the Joseon dynasty restrict them from entering the palace area? The ruling class promoted Confucianism and suppressed Buddhism. However, queens, concubines, and wives of the aristocracy continued to practice Buddhism. Such support kept Buddhism alive. Even some of the Confucian elites were fascinated by Buddhist theories and established relations with Buddhist monk-scholars. The rulers of Joseon finally decided to ban monks from entering the palace area altogether and demoted them to slave class.

Joseon officially withdrew the ban on April 3rd, 1895. It is written in King Gojong's Records that "Prime Minister Hong-jip Kim and Interior Minister Yeong-hyo Park pleaded and obtained royal permission." Why did Kim and Park want to banish this age-old law? It was because of a Buddhist monk named Dong-in Lee who introduced the modern world to them.

Dong-in Lee was a heroic monk of the late Joseon period. He kept a close friendship with the leading reformers of the time, including Og-gyun Kim, Yeong-hyo Park, and Jae-pil Seo. Monk Lee would gather these people at Bonwonsa Temple outside the West Palace Gate and Hwagyesa Temple outside the East Palace Gate and teach them about the West and the modern world.

Due to systematic oppression and mistreatment by the kingdom, the social status of monks was as low as it could be.

They were mobilized to build mountain forts, to make paper for Confucian students to write on, and to offer foodstuffs like honey, herbs, and straw sandals to the Confucian ruling class. They were sometimes even forced to carry on their shoulders the carriage for ruling elites when they went on picnics. They would also prepare food and liquor for such outings.

After centuries of maltreatment, monks were no different from the servant class in the eyes of ordinary people. Gwan-eung's choice to become a monk confronted this reality. How could anyone from the family understand him? They had no regard for choosing a life in pursuit of the truth. They were indignant that Gwan-eung had insulted the family tradition by entering the Buddhist order.

When Im-ho arrived home, she found her belongings already packed. She was really going to live with her father. She was happy, sad, and confused all at the same time. Her aunt quickly came to her side and urged her to go in. "Come on, Im-ho. Let's go eat." Im-ho looked around but could not find her mother. Without being asked, her aunt explained.

"Your mother has gone to pay her farewells to the elders of the family. Don't worry. I prepared chicken soup for you. Go eat."

Im-ho untied the book sack from her shoulders. Looking around the house and preparing herself for departure, Im-ho slowly came to realize the meaning of separation.

Chapter 02

Growing up in the bosom of Mountain Odae

When she was eleven, Im-ho and her mother left her hometown of Sangju and moved to Yeonbangsa Temple in Yecheon. That is where her father, Gwan-eung Seunim, resided, and together with her mother they rented a house near the temple. Im-ho entered the third grade at Yecheon Elementary School. It was 1940, which also happened to be the year when the Japanese imperial government in Korea initiated the ludicrous programme of trying to replace every Korean's name with a Japanese name.

The imperial government maintained that the "Creation of Surnames and Changing of First Names" should be done in accordance with will of the Korean people and that they should create a way for Koreans to become part of the great subjects of the Japanese emperor. However, three months after the policy's implementation, only 7.6 percent of Koreans had changed their names. The Imperial government was not impressed. They started to take forceful measures by banning children from school, making employment impossible, and not issuing any government certificates to people who did not change their names. They simply made it impossible for people to live a normal life.

The changing of names swept across the Buddhist land all the same. Anybody who held a position, such as the abbots of the thirty-one head temples, scholars, and leaders of organizations, was not allowed to continue their work without changing their name. At first, only a few pro-Japanese monks took part, but, not long after, all monks and even laypeople had to change their names. Truly, this was a difficult period, but still, many Buddhist organizations did not cease their efforts to defend their identity. Monks like Yong-un Han and Yong-seong Baek translated traditional Chinese Buddhist sutras into Korean.

The Yeonbangsa Temple and Dharma Propagation Center were established by Yongmunsa Temple. The Temple decided to invite Gwan-eung Seunim to be the Dharma teacher as part of the effort to maintain the identity of Korean Buddhism. Despite being under the jurisdiction of Jikjisa Temple, Yongmunsa Temple was still a very big temple with a large influence. It decided to open an urban teaching centre to answer the needs of the time. Why did Korean Buddhists become interested in spreading their teachings to the people? The lifting of travel bans that had prevented monks from going to the palace region played a role. The greatest mind-changing influence, however, came from visiting Japan.

The Japanese Imperial Government organized a number of tours for Korean Buddhist leaders to visit Japan. Abbots, renowned monks, scholars, journalists from Buddhist newspapers, and the like were sent to Japan as part of organized tour groups. The idea was to show them how developed Japan was and to convince them that Korea would be better off under Japanese rule. Visitors were given extraordinary treatment. They visited the head temples of many different Japanese Buddhist Orders, department stores, the cities of Kyoto and Osaka, universities, middle schools, high schools and even kindergartens. They were particularly impressed with the many charity organizations. Not a single visit left them unamazed.

One member of the tour group, Sang-no Gwon, recorded his impressions: "The eleven-story Mitsukoshi Department Store is like a mountain. The elevators and escalators make me feel like I have visited Tushita Heaven and the Pure Land."

Gwon remarked how everything that he saw made his jaw drop. These visits were the deciding factor that made Korean Buddhist leaders feel that drastic innovation was needed. Adding to the difficulty was the 500-year legacy of suppression of Buddhism by the Joseon dynasty and the demoted social status of monks. The establishment of Dharma Propagation Centers became part of their action plan, and they began to set up teaching centres in the cities.

When Im-ho entered Yecheon Primary School, she was also the top student in her new school. She was particularly good at arithmetic and Japanese, and her friends would learn from her. Students with low scores were kept behind after school so the teacher could help them catch up. Im-ho would also stay behind to help the teacher tutor her classmates in arithmetic and Japanese. Her father, Gwan-eung, was impressed and told her to attend his class on basic Chinese characters at the temple. Gwan-eung taught Buddhist scriptures to monks, but he also taught the *Thousand Character Classic* to children. Im-ho started going to the Propagation Center after school to learn the thousand Chinese characters from Gwan-eung.

Im-ho had actually studied the *Thousand Character Classic* already with her grandfather. Naturally, she was a quick learner. Her grandfather had only taught her how to read and pronounce the characters. Now Gwan-eung taught her how to write them. He also explained the meanings and stories hidden behind the characters. Im-ho found it more difficult, but also more fun.

Im-ho, with her brilliant and intelligent eyes, started to develop a special relationship with Gwan-eung. Not only were they father and daughter, but now they were becoming teacher and disciple. Every day after school, Im-ho would run to the temple to study the thousand Chinese characters. At the temple, she would also naturally hear stories of the Buddha.

As she spent more time at the temple, she became accustomed to all the rituals and ceremonies. She learned how and why worship, prayer, and offerings were done. Slowly, she started to realize the enormity of the Lord Buddha. She would do chores for the monks. Im-ho would clean the halls without being told to. She eventually became an inseparable part of Yeonbangsa Temple.

Im-ho liked Yeonbangsa Temple. For one thing, it was more spacious than the room that her mother had rented for them, but more than that, Gwan-eung Seunim was there. She never called him "father", but that did nothing to negate the fact that he was her father. He was the Dharma Teacher and was always teaching others. He taught both monks and laypeople. Initially, he taught the *Thousand Character Classic* to children, but, not long after, teenagers and adults also came to learn. His teachings were popular because they were different from the ordinary teachings offered by traditional Confucian teachers.

When teaching the Characters, Gwan-eung would introduce all kinds of stories from the history of China and Korea. He talked about the saints and sages. He told students how big the world was and how fast it was changing. He spoke of the many different countries in the world and how they came to be. The teachings encompassed history, geography, science, philosophy, and politics. Underlying his passion for teaching was his desire to educate young people to be proud Koreans who would serve the nation.

People respected him for his knowledge and sincerity. Im-ho respected him and was also proud of him. Two years after Im-ho came to Yeonbangsa Temple at Yecheon, Gwan-eung left for Japan to study after being chosen by Haeinsa Temple's scholarship program. Im-ho's mother became noticeably anxious. She was being left all alone again without a husband in a town where everybody was a stranger. The fact that she was also pregnant at the time added to her anxiety.

Gwan-eung went on to study and graduate from Ryukoku University in Japan. He was invited to be a Dharma teacher at the Buddhist College of Woljeongsa Temple in Gangwon province. At Woljeongsa resided Han-am Bang Seunim, the greatest Seon master of the time, and the patriarch of Korean Buddhism. Han-am wanted Gwan-eung to come teach the monks so that they may broaden their views. Gwan-eung also relished the opportunity to teach in the temple where the greatest master resided.

Gwan-eung left for Woljeongsa Temple the same year Im-ho graduated from primary school. Again, Im-ho followed her father and attended Pyeongchang Middle School, which was located near the temple. Room and board was arranged in Pyeongchang City. She lived in a house with a young girl named Yeong-ae, who went to the same school. They quickly became close friends.

Gwan-eung had two teaching positions, Dharma teacher at the Buddhist College in Woljeongsa Temple and Head Instructor at a Dharma Propagation Center in Pyeongchang City. He traveled back and forth to teach. At Woljeongsa Temple,

Gwan-eung taught the sutras and Ui-beom Won taught Sanskrit, Buddhist history, and subjects other than the sutras. Another hero of modern Korean Buddhism, Tan-heo Seunim, also resided at Woljeong. He was a disciple of Han-am. Historically, though it was a dark and tragic period of Japanese rule, nestled within Odae Mountain were Han-am, Tan-heo, Gwan-eung, and Ui-beom Won, who together radiated the light of Dharma.

Im-ho excelled at Pyeongchang Middle School as well. She was the top in her studies and was always well-behaved. The Japanese principal was impressed and praised her whenever he saw her. Gwan-eung knew about all of this and his expectations of her grew. One day, when he was at the Dharma Propagation Center, Gwan-eung called for Im-ho. There were guests present when Im-ho arrived.

"Im-ho, bow to these men. This is professor Kato, who teaches the early history of Buddhist sutras at a Buddhist university in Japan. Here is Myeong-gi Jo, who completed his studies in a university in Japan and currently studies Won-hyo Seunim at the Religious Studies Department of Gyeongseong Imperial University," Gwan-eung explained to Im-ho.

Im-ho gathered both hands and bowed politely. She was an eye-catching girl with fair skin, brightly shining eyes, and lips firmly closed. She displayed both intelligence and elegance.

"Is she your daughter?" asked professor Kato with a smile.

"Yes," Gwan-eung answered.

"She looks very bright. She will grow up to be someone

great."

"I have asked Mr. Jo to purchase biographies of great historical figures for her." Gwan-eung's reply to Kato implied that he already expected his daughter to become a great person.

Myeong-gi Jo looked at the child with a smile. Jo would go on to become the greatest scholar of Buddhism in Korea and, later, the President of Dongguk University. This is how the two great spirits met for the first time.

Im-ho brought home the ten biographies of great historical figures that Jo had given her. Her heart was pounding so fast she could hardly breathe. She also thought of the last words that professor Kato said to Gwan-eung.

"I envy you, Gwan-eung Seunim. You are with Han-am Bang Seunim, one of the greatest monks of our time. Even I cannot come to this temple whenever I want to see Han-am."

Im-ho repeated what Kato had said. It felt weird because, to Im-ho, Han-am did not seem much different than an ordinary grandfather. Whenever Im-ho would leave, Han-am would follow her down the stairs to see her off. He always told her to keep reciting "Gwanseeum Bosal." (*Gwanseeum Bosal* is Avalokiteshvara Bodhisattva)

"Was he that great of a monk?" She murmured. Then, she immediately began silently reciting Gwanseeum Bosal. She told herself that she would try harder to do whatever Han-am asked of her. Im-ho had grown up in a different environment compared to her peers. Having her father become a monk and leave the house was not an easy matter for her mother nor for her. However, precisely because her father was a monk, she had the privilege of having many experiences that her peers could not. The greatest blessing was that she had come to know the Lord Buddha and that she had also met great teachers.

The ten books had stories of fifty people. They included saints, politicians, artists, philosophers, and scientists. She felt so happy to have those books. The first thing she did was to call her friend Yeong-ae. Im-ho explained how she got the books and suggested that Yeong-ae and she could read them together. The books were written in Japanese and published by a Japanese publisher in Seoul.

"You can read from book one and I will start from book ten. We can meet at book five. Let's see who gets there faster," Im-ho suggested with a beaming face.

"No, you should read from book one. They are your books. I will start from book ten and read backwards."

"It makes no difference. You can start from book one." Im-ho wanted to offer something nice to Yeong-ae because of how kind she and her mother always were always to Im-ho.

"Your Japanese is so much better than mine. You will be reading book five long before me," Yeong-ae joked.

The stories of individuals were all so inspiring. Im-ho felt as if a fire was burning inside her when she read about Joan of Arc and Saint Francis of Assisi. While France and England were engaged in the Hundred Years War, Joan of Arc prayed to God that her country may win so that the French people could live in peace, which was when she heard God's voice tell her, "You shall go to war to fight the enemy."

Only sixteen years old, Joan of Arc left her hometown and went to the battlefields. She liberated Orléans and helped bring France to victory. However, she was then captured by the enemy and taken to England where she was burned at the stake as a witch. After about twenty years, an inquisitorial court, authorized by Pope Callixtus III, examined the trial, debunked the charges against her, pronounced her innocent, and declared her a martyr.

The life of Francis of Assisi was so great and holy that Im-ho felt it indescribable. Divine energy filled her when she thought of the perfect joy that he knew. One day in winter, Saint Francis was traveling with Brother Leo to Saint Mary of the Angels. He was suffering greatly from the cold, which is when he described to Brother Leo what perfect joy was. Having read this, Im-ho realized for the first time what it meant to have faith. Reading about his life, Im-ho felt she could understand why people, including her father, would choose to be the disciples of Buddha. They wanted to join the path of the divine.

Im-ho was particularly drawn to the stories of Joan of Arc and Francis of Assisi because of her country's own circumstances. Korea had been colonized by Japan and she knew how the Japanese were exploiting her country. Gwan-eung's Woljeongsa

Temple had borrowed money from the Japanese Oriental Development Bank to build a Dharma Propagation Center in Gangneung City. Im-ho had heard that the bank nearly took possession of the temple because of that debt. Because she knew how her country was being victimized by Japan, she was most inspired by Joan of Arc, who had fought to save her country. The life of Francis of Assisi helped her to better understand her father.

The ten books that Gwan-eung had given her made her realize how great a human being could become. She realized that greatness could be achieved only when one strives for divinity. She was not to live a life of pleasure, wealth, or self-interest, but instead a life dedicated to the pursuit of divinity. This was why some men and women left their homes to become monks and nuns. Perhaps Im-ho had been blessed by Manjushuri of Odae Mountain. Already, from this early age, she knew what kind of life she wanted.

When Im-ho was sixteen and in ninth grade at Pyeongchang Middle School, news of the Japanese Empire's defeat rang out on radio broadcasts throughout the nation. People were crying and hugging. In every town, parties and celebrations ensued. Japanese people in Korea now had to risk their lives to escape the country. Some particularly nasty Japanese and Koreans who had collaborated with them were rounded up and beaten.

Im-ho watched all this happen as the victors and losers switched roles. She realized the presence of a power that ruled this world. This power was related to violence. Japanese rule was characterized by violence against the Korean people, and now some Koreans resorted to violence to punish the Japanese.

"What would Gwanseeum Bosal have done at a time like this?"

Im-ho was still a small girl, but she had begun pondering such questions. What she saw going on in the world was definitely not what the Buddha had taught us.

After liberation, Woljeongsa Temple became more active. The temple decided to reach out to the people to spread their teachings and to help those who were disadvantaged. The Christian community had been active, even under Japanese rule. They had set up hospitals and schools as part of their missionary work. Many young people had become Christians and many attended schools in the United States with support from American missionaries. The monks of Woljeongsa Temple knew that this was a growing trend. They decided to start a kindergarten and established it within the Dharma Propagation Center in Gangneung City. Gwan-eung Seunim was asked to become the Dharma Teacher of the Gangneung Dharma Propagation Center and to also become the president of the kindergarten.

The Gangneung Dharma Center had been established in 1922 using a co-investment from the three main temples of Gangwon province, namely, Yujeomsa Temple of Geumgang Mountain, Geonbongsa Temple of Goseong, and Woljeongsa Temple of Odae Mountain. The next year, in 1923, the centre established Geumcheon Kindergarten because they felt that it was important to teach children from a young age to practice compassion and appreciate Buddha's teachings. This was the first kindergarten in Korea. It was also the aspiration of Buddhists in Gangwon province to see the Gangneung Dharma Center and kindergarten develop. Gwan-eung Seunim was chosen as the best person for the job due to his solid background in traditional Buddhist teachings that were augmented by his studies in extra-Buddhist curriculum at Hyehwa College and Ryukoku University in Japan.

Since Gwan-eung Seunim was assigned to the Gangneung Dharma Center, Im-ho naturally followed him and entered the ninth grade at Gangneung Girl's School. Gangneung Girl's School was a renowned school in the region. Some students came all the way from Pohang or Yeongdeok to study at the school. All the students took great pride in their school. When Im-ho left for her new school, her friend Yeong-ae accompanied her and the two girls again boarded together.

The first thing that surprised Im-ho was the above average education level of the students in the new school. Im-ho had always been the top student in Pyeongchang, Sangju, and Yecheon. She thought she was the smartest student in the world, but Gangneung Girl's School was different. There were many students who were more studious than Im-ho. They would stay late every day at the library to study. The intense competition shocked Im-ho. She doubled and tripled her efforts in studying. Fortunately, not long after, Im-ho began to excel. After about six months, she solidified her position as the top student again. After school, not only did Im-ho study, but she also read numerous books in the library. Many of the books were not available in Yecheon or Pyeongchang. She felt blessed that there were so many books for her to read. Books were like magic to her and she vividly remembered the ecstasy that the ten biographies had brought her.

Im-ho liked to read biographies and literature. Stories of great people always stirred something in her. She wanted to be one of them. Literature made her understand more about life. She understood the beautiful love between woman and man. After all, she was a girl with a natural curiosity for boys.

Gwan-eung Seunim would visit Gangneung Girl's School from time to time to give special lectures. The principal of the school, Hong-gyun Won, was friends with Gwan-eung. He frequently invited Gwan-eung as a well-known and respected figure in the region. Whenever Gwan-eung came to visit, students would glance at Im-ho, because they all knew that she was his daughter.

Im-ho felt both pride and pressure when she was the centre of attention. She received special treatment because Gwan-eung was her father. The other monks, laypeople, teachers, and friends all treated her differently because of their immense respect for Gwan-eung. So, while Im-ho was proud of her father, she always had to be well-behaved, decent, and stay out of trouble. Constantly having to avoid making any mistakes left her feeling tense all the time. It was a lot of pressure.

When Im-ho was in the eleventh grade, Gwan-eung Se-unim came to her school to give a lecture after summer break. He spoke of how everybody should act according to their roles. Teachers had to act like teachers, students had to behave like students, fathers should be like fathers, mothers should be motherly, children should do their duties, farmers should be faithful to their role as farmers, and government officials had to follow the rules of conduct as officials. Gwan-eung said that that was the best way to live a life. He gave many examples to deliver his point. The students, deeply moved, sat and listened quietly.

However, a question arose from deep within Im-ho's heart. She remembered her mother's face. A husband should be like a husband. But where was her mother's husband? When Im-ho moved to Gangneung, her mother got a small piece of land on which she planted potatoes, corn, cabbage, and radishes. They ate what they grew. Her mother's life was as tough as tough could be. It always broke Im-ho's heart to see her mother suffer. To her mother, Gwan-eung was simply her husband. She was married at fifteen. She believed that a wife should follow her husband, so she moved many times to unfamiliar places, but Gwan-eung was living his life as a monk, not as a husband. To her mother, Gwan-eung's life as a monk was very difficult to accept.

Im-ho had observed their relationship since she was a very young child. That is why she thought of her mother's face when she heard "A husband should do what a husband should do." She also thought of her little brother. Was Gwan-eung a true father to him? As Im-ho listened to Gwan-eung speak, she felt a painful love for her mother and brother.

When Im-ho entered the twelfth grade, she became the head of the disciplinary team. The disciplinary team was meant to oversee students so that they did not cause trouble. She wore an armband and went around with the teacher to supervise other students. Her main duty was to point out those students not following the dress code. Sometimes she would scold students who went places that they should not go or did things that were not allowed. Without even realizing it, she began taking on an air of authority about her which made the other students shun her. One day, however, it was Im-ho who ended up at the centre of trouble.

Im-ho's best friend, Yeong-ae, whispered to her one day, "There is a music festival at Gangneung Agriculture High School this Saturday. Do you know the band leader, that cute guy? He will be playing the saxophone. Let's go check it out." Yeong-ae continued talking about the program in an attempt to persuade Im-ho.

"What about our *Thousand Character Classic* lesson?" Im-ho asked. Every Saturday they attended the Chinese character class taught by Gwan-eung.

"Forget about that. Let's skip it just this once. The class is every week. This festival happens only once," Yeong-ae pleaded and, even though Im-ho felt uncomfortable, she decided to accompany her friend to the music festival.

She too wanted to see the handsome boy playing the saxophone. Gangneung Agriculture High School was a famous school in the region and was ranked the top boy's school in the province, just as Gangneung Girl's School was ranked the top girl's school. Many students wanted to study at these schools. It was only natural that the students from these schools would be attracted to one another. They were boys and girls just beginning to become curious about each other. Students from each school knew who at the other school was cute, who was pretty, who was good at studying, and who was good at sports. It was no surprise that many boys and girls found themselves falling in love, though mostly unrequited.

The band leader was one of the most popular boys at the school. He was tall and good looking, with dark eye brows. Girls found themselves mesmerized when he played the saxophone on stage. Many girls aspired just to see him play music from afar. Im-ho also felt a strange sensation in her heart. She decided to dare to skip her father's class and go to the festival.

When Gwan-eung taught the sutras, his only students were monks, but when he taught the *Thousand Character Classic* at the Gangneung Dharma Center, monks and laypeople alike would come to learn. His lecture was famous, not to only laypeople, but also to teachers and civil servants who would come to listen. Gwan-eung's explanations could go on and on about just one character. When explaining the character "天", which literally means "heaven" or "sky", he would incorporate all kinds of cosmological and philosophical discourses. His talks would range from Buddhist theory to Confucianism, from Western philosophy to ancient Indian thoughts. Students learned about history, politics, contemporary issues, human nature, laws of the universe, and so much more. That is why Gwan-eung's lectures attracted so many people, including scholars.

Even though Im-ho and Yeong-ae were supposed to be in that class as well, it unfortunately overlapped with the music festival. That Saturday afternoon, Im-ho went to the festival instead of her father's class.

The next day, Im-ho was summoned by Gwan-eung. He told her to bring her stamp. Im-ho felt extremely worried and knew something was terribly wrong. She went to the Dharma Propagation Center and when she arrived, Gwan-eung gave her a letter and told her to stamp and sign it. The letter stated that Im-ho wished to voluntarily quit school.

Im-ho was so shocked that she began to cry. She begged him to forgive her, but Gwan-eung did not budge. His face remained ice cold. Soon, other people of the Center came together to beg on her behalf, but it was of no use. When Yeong-ae heard what happened, she rushed to the Center, knelt down in front of Gwan-eung and begged for his forgiveness. She confessed that everything had been her fault, but still, Gwan-eung was adamant. Even Im-ho's teachers from the school came to beg him to forgive Im-ho, but nothing seemed to change his mind. Im-ho cried and begged and stopped eating. On the third day, Gwan-eung summoned Im-ho. He took back the letter and spoke with a touch of softness.

"If you are hurt, you should show your injury to the doctor instead of hiding it."

To Im-ho, this sounded like Gwan-eung was telling her she should have come to him to ask if she could go to the music festival instead of just skipping class. It was a hard-learned lesson. She decided she would be honest and brave about all things that she would do. From then on, she always tried to be frank and open.

Time went by and Im-ho's graduation was approaching. A few days before the graduation, an art teacher came to the class, handed out a blank sheet of paper to each of the students and told them to draw "the mark of a bird that has flown by." Some students drew clouds, or the trajectory of the bird's flight, or something that they thought of from their school days. Im-ho looked at the blank paper and then handed it back to the teacher, blank, for a bird leaves no mark behind. The teachers and the students stared at her in surprise.

Im-ho received the most honorable award at the graduation ceremony, but she felt lonely. Neither her father nor mother had come. She was closing the chapter of her life as a girl. Now she was to start her next chapter as a woman.

After the graduation, Im-ho first went to the Dharma Propagation Center. She wanted to show her father her certificate of graduation and her award. Gwan-eung greeted her as if he had been waiting for her. He looked at her with pride.

"Congratulations on finishing school. I bought these books in Japan. I've kept them so that I could give them to you for your graduation."

Gwan-eung then pointed at a volume of books. As Im-ho looked with curious eyes, Gwan-eung picked up one of them and handed it over to her. On the cover was written "The Truth of Life" in Japanese.

"The Truth of Life?" Gwan-eung nodded as she mouthed the title.

"It is a very good book. It will help you understand the religions, cultures, and philosophies of the world. The author wrote this masterpiece so that people would understand the truth of life. Since you are now an adult, you should make an effort to understand it as well."

It felt as if Gwan-eung was taking her through a ceremony of adulthood. Im-ho listened carefully to every single word he said.

"There are twenty-one books. They will not be easy to finish, but once you get a taste, I'm sure you won't be able to put them down."

"Thank you." Im-ho reached out to take the books.

"Take the books tomorrow. First, go see your mother. She must be anxiously waiting for you."

She looked up at Gwan-eung without speaking. Something inside her was in turmoil. She wanted to cry and let all her agony melt away. She clearly felt her father's love for his wife. That was his style. That was how he loved, as a monk. At that moment, Im-ho had the answer to the question she had felt in Gwan-eung's lecture.

Im-ho put her palms together and bowed. She stood up to leave.

"Take both the graduation certificate and the award."

She knew that he wanted her to show them to her mother.

The joy of liberation from Japan was short-lived, and the world soon fell into chaos. Intellectuals, workers, farmers, students, and all different groups of people became divided into right and left. They busied themselves with hating and blaming one other. Few had any clear idea of what "right" and "left" meant, much less the ideologies that they consisted of. The Soviet Union's military began its occupation of the northern half of the Korean peninsula. American forces came to the south. The period of military rule began.

The reason that Korea was not able to become an independent country after Japan's defeat was because it did not achieve independence through its own power. The allied forces had defeated Japan and Korea had not been a part of it. Gu Kim, who led the provisional Korean government in Chongqing, China, knew how important it was for Korean armed forces to participate in the war against Japan. He had trained a special unit of Liberation Forces to do precisely that and they had only one week left to join the allied forces when the emperor of Japan announced their surrender. It is said that Gu Kim collapsed and lamented at the news. If Korea's Liberation Forces had joined with the allied forces, Korea would have been part of the group of winners and able to secure its position in the post-war discussions. This was yet another misfortune befalling Korea.

In September of 1945, US Forces based in Okinawa docked in Korea through Incheon Port. People welcomed them as the liberators. The U.S. military had complete authority over the southern part of the Korean peninsula. Naturally, they needed English-speaking Koreans to help them. Many Protestants and Catholics who had studied in America with the support of American missionaries saw their opportunity. Commander Hodge asked Bishop Gi-nam Roh to provide him with a list of Korean leaders. Roh made a list of sixty leaders and sent it to the US military government. That is how Christians gained influence so quickly in South Korea.

Beginning in March of 1947, Christians used Seoul Broadcasting Company, a public broadcasting station, to air missionary programs every Sunday throughout the country. They designated Christian pastors as correctional officers in eighteen prisons. They were able to preach from a secure position as government officials. There were many assets left behind by the Japanese Imperial government. Many of the assets that should have been returned to Korean Buddhists were actually given to Christians. Christians who had studied in America, like Chang-geun Song, Jae-jun Kim, and Gyeong-jik Han were some of the people who unfairly received assets that belonged to the Japanese Buddhists of "Cheoligyo", securing a basis for the development of Christianity in Korea.

On August 26, 1946, Joseon Buddhism Central Headquarters sent a report to the Finance Minister of Gyonggi province. It stated that out of over forty "Japanese Buddhist assets" in Seoul, only eleven were transferred to Korean Buddhists. Tragic as it may be, no one in the Korean Buddhist community had realized how critical teaching and learning the English language would be. That Korean Buddhism, with a millennium-old history, would be overshadowed by Christianity was the last thing anyone expected. This was occurring during the period when Im-ho was attending Gangneung Girl's School.

One day, after Im-ho had graduated, Gwan-eung called her to the Dharma Center. He asked her, "Now that you have graduated, how do you feel about becoming a school teacher? I can refer you to a few places."

There were only a few women who were educated at that time. Most of them were able to find jobs as teachers in elementary schools.

"I also want to be a teacher," Im-ho replied without hesitation. She needed a job. She needed to support her mother and brother. After graduation, Im-ho had left the boarding school and returned to live with them, and this experience convinced her that she needed to help take care of them.

"I will find a place for you," Gwan-eung replied. He seemed to understand what was going on in her mind. Gwan-eung was expressing and implementing his love for his family in his own way. After about ten days, Im-ho was assigned to Gang-dong Elementary School. The school was about five miles to the east of Gangneung City. Her mother and brother moved with her so she could be near the school.

She was initially charged with teaching a second grade class. There were over forty boys and girls from nearby fishing villages. Their faces were sunburnt, but their eyes shone bright with innocence. Im-ho thought they looked like baby chicks. She felt like a mother hen who would raise and protect them. She was happy teaching in the school. She taught from text books, played the organ and sang with the students, exercised together with them on the playground, and sometimes taught them ping pong. Im-ho was good at ping pong and she had fun when playing with the tall and stronger students.

Im-ho told the students stories of the great people that she had read about. She told the stories vividly, as if reading from a story book. The children loved to hear them. Im-ho could recite them as if they were her own stories because of how deeply immersed she had been when reading them. She had learned a lot from each individual hero and heroine. Her students were less than ten years old, and could surely not understand the points she was trying to make. Nonetheless, she knew that the stories would embed themselves deep into their memories and would one day become a compass that would direct them down the right path, just as her grandmother's old stories, which resided deep within her, had taught her right from wrong.

Im-ho started to become engrossed in *The Truth of Life* books that she had received from Gwan-eung. The books explored in detail the religions of the world. They had stories of saints, philosophers, and thinkers. These stories included history, science, and cosmology. She felt like she was sailing through a vast sea of knowledge in search of her own truth.

The twenty-one volumes were a majestic journey in search of the truth. She read it over and over again. She realized why Gwan-eung had wanted her to read them. It caused her to recognize the ultimate value of life and how to best live in order to actualize it. Just as a map is needed to find a destination on the road, the same is needed in life. If one follows the right guide, one's eyes will be opened to the ultimate meaning of life. Im-ho treasured the biographies and *The Truth of Life* books that her father had given her. They made her realize what a noble life was. She wanted to walk a noble path as well.

For the first time in her life, Im-ho was able to understand what achievement felt like. She did her best in her duties and work. She learned that if she did her best and remained honest, she would be rewarded. It was also tremendously satisfying to see her mother and brother living a relatively stable life with what small money she earned. That was no less satisfying than teaching the students.

A few months after Im-ho started working, she had her first summer break. She packed a few clothes and her twenty-one books about the truth of life and went to Seven Star Hermitage (*Chilseongam*, currently Beopwangsa Temple) in Gujeong county. She decided to spend a month there. Cheong-u Yang Seunim, the abbot at the hermitage, was a close friend of Gwan-eung. Gwan-eung and Tan-heo had stayed at Chilseongsa Temple together. The three monks were very close. One day, Cheong-u Yang would teach the Diamond Sutra (Vajracchedikā Prajñāpāramitā Sūtra or *Geumganggyeong*), the next day Tan-heo would talk about the Flower Garland Sutra (Avataṃsaka Sūtra or *Hwaeomgyeong*), and then Gwan-eung would lecture about Yogacara Buddhism on the following day. When one spoke, two listened. After each lecture a discussion followed. They would sometimes have leisurely chats and sometimes heated debates. No matter how much their views conflicted, they always seemed happy. Im-ho watched them and thought, 'That must be Dharma Delight.'

To Im-ho, the three monks exchanging knowledge, giving and receiving lectures, and immersing themselves in profound discussions looked like they were in heaven. She did not fully understand what was being discussed, but she would still sit beside them to listen. It brought her immense joy, regardless.

One day, after the early morning Buddhist ceremony, Im-ho took one volume of *The Truth of Life* and climbed above a rock in the valley. The morning sun was just striking the fog and the whole place filled with a tranquil energy. Im-ho was reading the book while listening to the creek flow and, without any thought, she looked down beneath the rock. What she saw made her sit up straight and she fixed her eyes on it as it approached. It was a snake, and it was slowly approaching her. Rather than feeling scared or disgusted, she felt a deep sense of sympathy. She wanted to save the snake.

She spoke to the snake in a low voice, "I will read this book to you. Please listen carefully so that you may escape the world of the animals and enter a path that seeks the truth."

Im-ho read from the book out loud. After a while, when she looked back down at the snake, it was lying on the ground without any movement. Its body was becoming stiff. Im-ho was shocked and began reading with even more sincerity. After she finished reading, she came down from the rock, entered the Dharma Hall, and offered three prostrations to the Lord Buddha.

That night, Im-ho had a most auspicious dream. In the dream, she received a shining bead from Jijang Bosal (Ksitigarbha Bodhisattva). She was standing in the back of a crowd that was gathered at the Main Hall. Jijang Bosal extended his arm and gave the prayer bead to her. It was mysterious and deeply moving. The next morning, when Im-ho woke up, she hurried to see the snake. It lay where it had been the day before, dead. That occurrence remained a mystery to Im-ho for the rest of her life.

'Did the snake really die because of the book I read to it? Did the snake depart from suffering and reach its blessing as I had prayed for? How was Jijang Bosal able to give me the bead when I was standing all the way at the back?'

This was Im-ho's first religious experience.

A year after Im-ho started working as a teacher in Gangdong Elementary School, on June 25, 1950, the Korean War broke out. The North invaded the South and declared war. The war destroyed numerous Buddhist temples, relics, and cultural assets. Many monks were either abducted by the North or killed. The North Korean military advanced quickly. On June 28, they had already seized control over the West Gate Prison and released leftist monks such as Sang-bong Jang, Yong-dam Kim, and Seo-sun Gwak. Hae-jin Kim of the Buddhist Youth Party had followed Gu Kim to the north to attend the South-North Negotiations in 1948 and had decided to stay in the north. He returned south with the North Korean People's Army. He summoned leftist monks and took over Taegosa Temple (currently Jogyesa Temple).

They established an organization called the South Joseon Buddhists League, and Yong-dam Kim became the chairman.

The League supported North Korea during the war. They held political classes to convert the public, organizing a reading club that gathered every night at Taegosa Temple where they studied and discussed communism and the role of Buddhists. They taught people songs that praised communism and North Korea, and implemented their best propaganda.

They seized sewing machines from people, put the machines in the temple office, and used them to make military uniforms. Taegosa Temple was converted into a military factory and no longer performed religious functions. Numerous uniforms were produced there daily. However, when the forces of the United Nations (UN) Command landed in Incheon in September 1950, the tables turned against the communists. North Korean troops were now being pushed back by UN forces. Many UN and Republic of Korea (ROK/South Korea) soldiers were wounded in battle trying to reclaim Seoul, the nation's capital. Jungdong School became a military hospital. ROK military authorities needed more space and sent wounded men to Taegosa Temple, too. The main hall, shrine, living quarters, and offices, were all filled with wounded men, as there was no other place for them to go. Taegosa Temple, once used by the North Koreans was now serving South Korean troops. The irony of war was well demonstrated here.

Odae Mountain did not escape the chaos, either. Hanam Seunim had foreseen the war coming. He had all the monks transferred to a safe place, while he, himself, remained in Sang-wonsa Temple. His disciples urged and begged for him to leave, but, like a large rock, he did not budge. Only Hi-chan Seunim, Hi-seop Seunim, and Pyongdeungsim Bosal (*Bosal* means bo-dhisattva but is also a title for female Buddhists) stayed behind in Sangwonsa Temple to serve Master Han-am. Beom-nyong Se-unim had fled for safety, but then returned to stay by Han-am's side. He considered it more meaningful to protect their great master than to try to escape and save his own life. Most of the monks thought the same, but Han-am ordered them to leave. Tan-heo Seunim, in particular, could not imagine leaving his teacher behind. He lied to Han-am, saying that he would head for the south when, in reality, he stayed in nearby Chilseongsa Temple in Gangneung. He was determined to be at his teacher's side should anything happen.

Other than Tan-heo, there were a few other monks from the Odae Mountain family, including Gwan-eung, who stayed in Chilseongsa Temple. When the war broke out, Gwan-eung told Im-ho to bring her family to Chilseong too. At first, the UN's participation in the war gave some much needed relief to South Korea, but things quickly escalated to heavy fighting. The people of Chilseongsa Temple had to escape southward in the middle of winter. The monks and Im-ho's family each took a loaf of rice cake and began walking south. Much to Im-ho's dismay, Gwan-eung was not part of the group. He had left for Chilseong, saying he would be back after a few days, but had not returned by the time everyone had to evacuate. Im-ho's family had no choice but to leave without him.

It was bitterly cold. Winter was not an ideal season for walking and sleeping out on the road. They would walk during the day and seek food and shelter at night. It was difficult for everyone to remain at the same pace and find shelter together. Therefore, naturally, the group split after a few days.

One day, Im-ho's mother suggested, "Let's go to our home town. We should find some help there."

Im-ho agreed, and they continued walking toward Sangju. Im-ho and her mother would take turns carrying her brother. After an exhausting journey they arrived in Sangju, where, much to their delight, they learned that Gwan-eung had arrived at Namjangsa Temple in Sangju. The family was reunited.

Gwan-eung began searching for a way to support his family. He decided to become a teacher at Sangju Public School for Agriculture and Sericulture. Sangju was famous for sericulture and the Japanese had established this school to train professionals. The school had an opening for a history teacher, so Gwan-eung was invited to begin teaching history.

Not long after, Im-ho was also invited to teach at a nearby elementary school and she accepted the offer. It was a war-time school and facilities were very poor. Gwan-eung and Im-ho were grateful for those who worked so hard to keep the school running so that they could teach the children. They taught as best as they could and, despite the meager salary, they managed to keep the family fed.

One day, after about six months had passed, Gwan-eung called for Im-ho. She went to Namjangsa Temple where a small Buddhist college had been set up to educate a few monks. Gwan-eung was teaching them the sutras. The secular schools had not given up on teaching the next generation, and neither had the Korean Buddhists. They were doing the best they could to provide an undisrupted education for the monks.

Im-ho bowed to Gwan-eung and knelt down. Gwan-eung began to speak, "I have thought about this for a long time. I feel I cannot wait any longer. I think it would be best if you became a nun. What do you think?"

Im-ho was startled.

"There are many paths that a person can take. I believe this is the most noble. If it were not a good life, I would not be suggesting this to you."

Im-ho closed her eyes in deep thought. Her mother and brother came to her mind first. But soon, they were replaced by the Lord Buddha. His own life seemed to offer her the answer she sought.

'Buddha became a monk, renouncing all duties as a prince, didn't he?' She had made up her mind. "I will take that path."

"Very well. I will make the necessary preparations."

"Yes, please."

"Before joining the Buddhist sangha, read this book. Becoming a monk or nun is a search for the truth. This book objectively describes what the truth is. It will guide you."

Gwan-eung put a book in front of her. The title read *Truth*. She picked it up carefully and put it on her lap. This is how Im-ho became a nun. Gwan-eung had probably been thinking of this all along when he gave her those biographies of great people, and especially *The Truth of Life*. Those books certainly inspired Im-ho to aspire to a noble life.

That day, after returning home, she had a dream. She was using all her strength to try and climb up a steep cliff. Suddenly, two bodhisattvas appeared and stood beside her. They helped her climb up the remainder of the cliff. After reaching the top, she took a deep breath and looked down. Thousands and thousands of people were gathered below. They were bowing at Im-ho with their palms together. They were bowing with such respect that it seemed they were worshipping Buddha. When Im-ho awoke, she was shaken. She could not understand the dream, however, delight was beginning to swell in her heart.

A few days later, Im-ho left for Haeinsa Temple. For her father, Im-ho's decision to become a nun made him very proud, but for her mother, the decision was a heartbreaking shock. Im-ho was twenty-three years old.

Chapter 03

Read quietly,
Myeong-seong

"Bang, bang, bang!"

Gunfire shots rang out nearby. Im-ho, now a postulant (*haengja*), opened her eyes at the sound. It must have been the partisans, the communist soldiers who evaded capture by hiding in the mountains. Every now and then, she would hear the sounds of gunfire in the middle of the night. People said that this was the communist guerillas firing their guns.

Im-ho looked out the window. It was still dark, but she knew it was time to rise. She cleaned her bed and went outside. It is said that the night is darkest right before sunrise, and the temple was shrouded in a velvet of black. Im-ho stared at the stars for a moment then hurried to the *haeuso* (toilet, literally "place for relieving one's worries"). The other nuns were still asleep, but it was time for Im-ho to start her day. After visiting the *haeuso*, she washed her face at the creek and went to the kitchen.

With no starlight to help illuminate, the kitchen was even darker than the outside. Im-ho used her hands to find the matches and lit a lamp. Objects started to reveal their shape. She searched for the basket where she had put cooked barley the night before. Much to her surprise, the barley was gone. Communist guerrillas must have taken it during the night.

They hid and lived in the mountains. At night, they would sometimes come down to the village to steal food. They would occasionally visit Haeinsa Temple, as well. At first, the temple locked the gate to prevent any theft, but after a discussion, decided to leave it open. So, the large monastery of Haeinsa Temple did not lock the gate; all other small temples and hermitages followed. They left the door to the kitchen unlocked. They worried that if the guerillas could not find food, they might resort to threatening or hurting people with their weapons.

Im-ho stared at the empty basket, but what was gone was gone. 'How can I prepare breakfast for everybody? If I tell the Seunims what happened, they'd understand. However, I cannot just let them go hungry.'

She thought for a moment in the dark. An idea came to her. She picked up a basket and a hoe and went out to the garden. It was still not the summer solstice, and the potatoes had not yet been harvested. Still, they should have reached a good size by now.

She went out to go harvest some potatoes, but as she headed towards the field, she grew afraid. It was still dark. Guerillas seemed to be hiding around every corner, ready to jump out at her. The darkness itself felt like a guerilla. She was so scared that she became unable to move her feet. However, she took a few deep breaths and began reciting "Gwanseeum Bosal." She raised her voice so that Gwanseeum Bosal would be able to hear her.

"Gwanseeum Bosal, Gwanseeum Bosal, Gwanseeum Bosal..."

As soon as she started speaking out loud, her heart seemed to light up. Her eyes could suddenly make out the path and the potato field. Morning was rushing in, pushing out the darkness. Im-ho kept reciting as she started digging. Potatoes began exposing themselves one by one. She continued repeating Gwanseeum Bosal as she harvested the potatoes and put them in the basket, which quickly filled up.

She grabbed the basket and stood up. The path was clearly visible now. The fear that had paralyzed her had vanished. Im-ho returned to the kitchen with peace of mind. She washed the potatoes, put them in an iron pot, poured a bucket of water, and started the fire. Although the temple was in the middle of the mountains, they did not have enough firewood. Because of the guerillas, the Seunims were not able to go deep into the forest to collect firewood. It was early summer, so firewood was particularly scarce. She had to use wet branches; the only kindling that was available nearby. These branches normally produced so much smoke that Im-ho would shed enough tears to fill a sauce bowl whenever she got a fire going.

This morning was different. The green branches caught fire as if they were dry. She put a few more branches on the fire and cooked the potatoes with ease.

'Now, I have to prepare food for the elder Seunim.'

No matter how severe the food shortages were, she always prepared white rice for the elder Seunim. Im-ho had buried a jar of white rice out of sight of everyone from where she would get the rice for the elder. She washed the rice, put it in a small pot, and waited for the burning branches to turn to charcoal. Wet branches produced too much smoke and soot. So, after making the first fire, she collected the charcoal to cook the rice for elder Seunim.

While Im-ho was busy making breakfast, one by one, nuns began emerging to prepare for the morning ceremony. Somewhat flustered, Im-ho sped up with her cooking. A while later, the sound of chanting came from the Main Hall. Im-ho went there to join them. She went to her spot and offered triple prostrations to the Buddha.

After the ceremony, the nuns left as silently as they had entered. Im-ho was left alone. She put her mat a little closer to the Buddha and began her 108 prostrations.

"Please help me be faithful to my duties as a postulant. I shall live another day to its fullest. Let me be worthy of being your disciple." After bowing down and touching her forehead to the ground 108 times, she quickly returned to the kitchen. She had to finish preparing breakfast for everybody.

At breakfast, she told the seunims about the missing barley and how she had to go out to the field to harvest potatoes.

Hearing her story, the seunims smiled in approval. They knew that it would have been completely dark when she went out. After breakfast, Im-ho washed the dishes and prepared for lunch. She then cleaned her teacher's room as well as the room of the elder Seunim, which was right next door. Next, she grabbed the book "Gate of the Renunciate" (*Chimun*) and headed off to the main monastery at Haeinsa Temple.

While walking from Gugiram Hermitage to Haeinsa Temple, she practiced memorizing what she had learned the previous day. The Gate of the Renunciate class was all about memorization. She had to remember the text by heart. Im-ho was top in her class. After all, she had studied the *Thousand Character Classic* multiple times and, having grown up in the temple, was familiar with Buddhist teachings. She had received a high school education, which was uncommon among female postulants at that time. She also had worked as a teacher.

After the Gate of the Renunciate class, she came back to Gugiram Hermitage. Every single step of the way, she would recite "Gwanseeum Bosal." She wanted to make good use of every second. As soon as she returned to Gugiram, she changed her clothes and prepared lunch. It was war time, and there were shortages of everything, but she did the best with what she had.

After lunch, she washed the dishes, then headed off to the vegetable garden with some other nuns. In the garden grew grains and vegetables that fed everyone, and Im-ho and the nuns had to tend to them. They would pull weeds under the heat of the sun and then pick greens for dinner. Collecting the leafy greens was Im-ho's task. After the other nuns finished pulling weeds and had left, Im-ho stayed behind, moving around the garden in a squatting position. Having to prepare enough greens for dinner, as well as the following day's breakfast and lunch was not easy. Sometimes she thought the nuns who left her alone to work were unkind. But she knew that controlling such feelings was part of the training. She tried to bring her mind back to a wholesome state.

After coming back from picking greens, she had to pound barley or rice in a mortar to hull it. If there was a small amount of grains, she used the mortar. If there was a lot, she used the person-powered treadmill. Without the use of any machines, these were the only ways to produce edible grains. She worked with the mortar alone, but other nuns had to help her when she used the treadmill.

It was summer and they mainly had barley to pound. Barley was too rough to the tongue if was only cooked once. It had to be pre-boiled and then cooked again. At that time, her battle with the green branches began again, accompanied by the tear shedding from the smoke. Im-ho was occupied with her work when suddenly something fell on the floor. She looked down and saw that the framed image of the Kitchen God (*Jowang*) had fallen onto the kitchen floor. Im-ho thought it was lucky that, despite the fall, the glass had not broken. Im-ho put the picture back on the wall and continued with her work. At dinner, she told the others the story.

"The Kitchen God knew you were doing a great job and wanted to praise you." The senior nuns interpreted what had happened in this way. Im-ho felt happy, believing that perhaps this is what the senior seunims had wanted to say themselves.

After dinner was the evening worship. After that, Im-ho had some free time, during which she would read the ten books of *Truth* given to her by Gwan-eung. The moment had she received the books, she had promised herself that she would read them ten times.

She had to do her homework at night, which meant she had to light a lamp. This was not easy, however, since the lamps used kerosene, which was expensive. Also, because the seunims feared that the lamp would attract the partisans, they did not allow using lights at night. It was the pattern of the senior seunims to attend the evening worship before it got dark and go straight to bed afterwards. What bothered Im-ho was not the physical work she had to do but the fact that she could not read at night.

She was doing her best at whatever task she was given. She was faithful and diligent about her duties as a postulant. However, deep inside her, there remained a skepticism that she couldn't erase.

'I want to study the sutras in a great monastery. How can I do that?' She decided to express her desire through her prayer. She prayed to Gwanseeum Bosal, asking for an opportunity to be given to her so that she may go to a great monastery to study the sutras.

The next day, she was coming down the hill after finishing her class. As always, she was reciting "Gwanseeum Bosal" as she walked. She spotted her teacher standing under a tree. She could sense that her teacher was waiting for her. 'What could it be?' Im-ho felt slightly nervous and quickened her pace. Her teacher also started coming toward her, waving her hand to signal Im-ho to come faster. When Im-ho got to her, she spoke quietly and with a sense of urgency.

"Your mother is here to take you. She is not going to go away easily this time. She even brought your clothes." Im-ho's head bowed down in silence. She felt a twinge of heartache.

"Your mother will not give up easily. Why don't you stay away for a few days? I will find a place for you." Her teacher did not want the two of them to meet.

"I will do as you say, teacher." Im-ho answered with her head facing downward. She knew that if she were to go on to become a nun, it was best not to meet her mother at all. That hurt even more.

"Go to the main monastery for now. Meanwhile, I will find a place for you." Having finished, her teacher turned away. Im-ho briefly watched her walk away, then turned and reversed her course to go back to where she had come from. She headed back to Haeinsa Temple's main monastery, away from Gugiram Hermitage. She did not feel comfortable. Her mother was left in the savage world all alone, raising her son by herself. She tried not to become emotional, tried to suppress thoughts of sympathy, guilt, and worry. Her heavy heart sank with each step of the way.

While staying at the main monastery, she was ordained as a novice nun (*samini*) by the abbot of Haeinsa Temple, Beom-sul Choi Seunim. She received the name "Myeong-seong" as her Dharma name. "Myeong" meant bright eyes, while "Seong" meant star. Im-ho Jeon had completed her training as a postulant and was now Myeong-seong Seunim. This was in 1952, and she was 23 years old.

A red sun was rising above a sea of clouds. It reminded Myeong-seong of the dream she had had the night before. In this dream, she was standing with her two feet on the clouds. She had the sun and the moon in each hand. She threw them at the Buddha, and the Buddha would throw the sun and moon back at her. It felt as if they were playing a game of catch. At first, she was not sure who her partner was. She could not see clearly. She just knew that there was someone who would catch the spheres and throw them back. When she realized it was the Lord Buddha, she was so surprised and humbled that she put her palms together and bowed deeply.

Myeong-seong went into the grotto and used a dry towel to wipe the platform clean. She organized the tools and looked up at the Buddha. The stone Buddha was looking down at her with a serene smile. Almost unknowingly, Myeong-seong smiled back. It was an exchange of warmth and love. She felt like she had become family with the Buddha. It was something she had never imagined before. The feeling was so strange and humbling that she put her palms together and bowed again.

By then, Myeong-seong had been relocated to Mireugam Hermitage, which belonged to Dasolsa Temple in Sacheon City. Mireugam Hermitage was a nun's temple, and Myeong-seong was given the role of head of kitchen. She prepared porridge, kimchi, and pickled wild greens and put them in the refectory. When the other seunims came in, they put the food in their bowls and ate in silence. After they left, Myeong-seong would wash the dishes and prepare food for lunch. Porridge was for breakfast and rice was for lunch, so she needed to prepare soup and other food to accompany the rice.

Myeong-seong finished working in the kitchen and went to her room. She had homework to do, which she had given to herself. She would pray, read from the *Truth* books, and work on memorizing Gate of the Renunciate in its entirety. She would busy herself with these tasks until it was time to prepare for lunch. Then, she would go back to the kitchen to make side dishes and vegetable soup to eat with the rice. Again, she had to use wet branches, so she would shed a sauce bowl's worth of tears in front of the fire.

After lunch, she went out to the garden to tend to the greens, then she pounded rice in the mortar, and washed and ironed the clothes of the other nuns - the chores seemed to never end.

Not long after Myeong-seong had come to Mireugam Hermitage, Bon-gong elder Seunim joined her there. Bon-gong was one of the greatest Seon master nuns of the time. Gwan-eung had originally wanted to send Im-ho to learn from her, but Bon-gong was not accepting any new disciples. She did, however, make her favourite disciple become Im-ho's teacher. That is how Myeong-seong began her path as a nun under Seonhaeng Seunim, a disciple of Bon-gong. Regardless, Myeong-seong was happy to see Bon-gong. Bon-gong had finished a Seon retreat before coming to Mireugam to stay. Myeong-seong dutifully washed and mended Bon-gong's robe.

After dinner and the evening worship, Myeong-seong was able to have some time to herself. She did the same thing she had done at Gugiram Hermitage. She was getting used to the daily repetition of life. Then, Gwan-eung Seunim arrived at Mireugam Hermitage. Gwan-eung had heard about how dedicated his daughter was to her duty as a postulant. He also knew that Myeong-seong had moved from Gugiram to Mireugam because her mother had come to take her. All in all, he wanted to come see how she was doing.

Myeong-seong went to meet Gwan-eung. He was chatting with Bon-gong. As soon as she heard his voice, her heart began pounding. After taking a deep breath, she spoke.

"Seunim, it's Myeong-seong." Myeong-seong overlapped her hands in a polite manner and bowed her head down.

"Come in." Bon-gong replied. Myeong-seong took off her shoes and entered. Both Bon-gong and Gwan-eung looked at her. Gwan-eung's eyes seemed to shake with emotion.

"Let me bow." Myeong-seong bowed deeply.

"Have a seat." Bon-gong pointed to a seat in front of her. Myeong-seong knelt down. She put her hands on her knees and lowered her eyes. Her movement was elegant; her posture was confident. After looking at her for a while, Gwan-eung finally spoke.

"Where is your mind?"

"It is inside the Buddha's heart."

"Where is your body?"

"Inside the Buddha's house." Myeong-seong answered without hesitation.

"Is it not uncomfortable?"

"My mind and body are both well."

"That is good." Gwan-eung smiled in relief. After a moment of silence, Gwan-eung asked.

"What is it that you desperately want?"

"I wish to study the sutras."

"I can help you with that," Gwan-eung offered.

Bon-gong interrupted. "Seunim, please stay in Mireuk to teach the sutras. I will organize a Dharma class."

"Please do so. I will give a lecture on Self-Admonition for Beginners (*Chobalsim Jagyeongmun*)."

That is how Gwan-eung started teaching Self-Admonition

for Beginners at Mireugam for Myeong-seong. All the postulants and seunims attended Gwan-eung's class. Bon-gong attended too. Bon-gong had made all of the postulants and seunims attend Gwan-eung's class as a way of being considerate. She did not want people gossiping about the father-daughter relationship between Gwan-eung and Myeong-seong.

Gwan-eung's lecture was profound and elegant. It was like a deep flowing river. Self-Admonition for Beginners consisted of three parts. First was Ji-nul Seunim's *Beginner's Mindset*, which provided new Buddhists with detailed instructions on how to conduct themselves in speech, bodily action, and mental activities. Second was Won-hyo Seunim's *Cultivation*. Third was Ya-un Seon Master's *Admonition*. Gwan-eung wanted to teach his daughter, with all his heart, on how a nun should live and conduct her body and mind. This was the book that taught her that.

When the giver and receiver agree, happiness abounds in the exchange. Myeong-seong was so happy throughout the entire lecture. When Gwan-eung finished the lecture and was leaving, he gave her his copy of Self-Admonition for Beginners and told her. "Read this ten thousand times. It will benefit you."

Myeong-seong received the book with respect and gratitude as if it had been given by the Buddha and Bodhisattvas themselves. She also resolved herself to read it ten thousand times.

When Gwan-eung left Mireugam Hermitage after finishing his lecture, Myeong-seong stood behind the fence and watched him walk away for a long time, until he was no longer in sight. Tears came out uncontrollably. She cried and cried. Knowing that he had come to Mireugam and organized a class because he wanted to teach his daughter, she felt fatherly love from him.

Gwan-eung left and Myeong-seong was alone. She studied intensely. She was determined to finish reading Self-Admonition for Beginners ten thousand times. It takes a lot of time to do that, but with all the kitchen work she had, making time was not easy.

She checked the homework she had given herself. She would soon complete reading *Truth* ten times. Then she would be done with that. She had fully and perfectly memorized the Gate of the Renunciate from beginning to end, so she was done with that task as well. Her other task was praying. That was something she was unable to stop doing. If she were to become a good nun, the Buddhas and Bodhisattvas would have to look after her. She couldn't stop praying to them.

Two tasks remained for her homework: praying and reading Self-Admonition for Beginners. She would pray whenever she could, or during the short time she had before going to sleep. She read Self-Admonition for Beginners when she could fit time in between other tasks, or when she finished her daily routine and had some time of her own. Everyday was full and compact. She did not have a moment of idleness. She was not tired though, but rather, full of happiness and a feeling of fulfillment.

Time passed, and summer went with it. When the mornings and evenings started to bring a cool breeze, Bon-gong Seunim summoned Myeong-seong. Myeong-seong went to Bongong's room and knelt down. Bon-gong opened her mouth.

"Gwan-eung Seunim will teach Four Collections at Yeonhwasa Temple in Jinju City. Go there and learn. I have to leave here now and go to a Seon temple for meditation."

At that moment, Myeong-seong realized that Bon-gong had come and stayed at Mireugam in order to look after her. Myeong-seong was deeply touched. She felt the strong bond of family within the sangha.

"I will do as you say."

It was hard not to cry. Myeong-seong looked into Bongong's eyes. The old nun smiled at Myeong-seong. To Bon-gong, Myeong-seong was a precious new hope. She murmured to herself. 'She is a pearl. A large brilliant pearl that has fallen right into the bosom of the Buddha.'

Green sprouts will grow even in the most degraded of soil. It was a tough and dark period in Korean history, but the Buddhists continued to work to raise the next generation. They nurtured and watered the new sprouts. Wherever they were, senior monks and nuns taught the Dharma to postulants. It was war time, and their effort to keep the flame of Dharma burning was truly super-human. Gwan-eung's teaching of Four Collections (*Sajip*) at Yeonhwasa Temple in Jinju City was one example of such efforts.

Four Collections refers to Letters, Introduction, Summary, and Essence of Seon. Only after studying all four and receiving the basic knowledge are monks and nuns ready to study the sutras. Gwan-eung had taught Self-Admonition for Beginners at Mireugam and now Four Collections at Yeonhwasa Temple. He would never admit it, but his choice of subject matter was most likely influenced by his desire to teach and guide Myeong-seong. Whatever the reasons, this continuous teaching of the Dharma maintained the transmission of that knowledge.

Myeong-seong could already read and understand difficult Chinese-character sutras. She was full of desire to study the sutras. She absorbed everything that Gwan-eung taught like a sponge. As a teacher, Gwan-eung was also delighted. There is a sense of rapture when a teacher gives and student receives and both share a passion for the knowledge. Gwan-eung continued his teachings, finishing Four Collections in six months.

On the last day of his lecture, Gwan-eung called Myeong-seong to see him. "I will write a letter to Un-heo Seunim. Go and study at the Monastic School in Tongdosa Temple." After training her about the basics, Gwan-eung was now connecting his daughter with new teachers.

Un-heo had started off as an independence fighter. After fighting against Japan, he realized that education was the most important job for saving the nation. He built many schools and taught numerous students. His faith did not change after becoming a monk. He set up schools belonging to Buddhist foundations. He was especially interested in the education of Buddhist nuns (*bhikkhuni*). He knew that if they were unable to provide an education for nuns, there would be no future for Korean Buddhism. He met with the leaders of Korean Buddhism at that time, namely Hyo-bong, Cheong-dam, Seong-cheol, and Hyang-gok. He explained the importance of bhikkhuni (fully ordained female Buddhist monks) education. Everybody agreed and encouraged him to go on and start the initiative.

One day, by coincidence, Un-heo had come across Deog-yun Song Seunim, the abbot of Donghaksa Temple. Deogyun was a married monk. As soon as Deog-yun heard of Un-heo's dream, he invited him to come to Donghak to teach the nuns there. That is how Korea's first modern Bhikkhuni College was born. Gwan-eung wanted Myeong-seong to meet and study with Un-heo because of his advocacy. In fact, Un-heo was one of the three top scholar-monks of the time. Gwan-eung and Tan-heo were the other two. Un-heo was also a distant cousin of the great writer, Gwang-su Lee, who had written *Monk Won-hyo, Dream, Soil,* and *Love.*

When Myeong-seong went to Tongdo Monastery, monks such as Wol-un and Ji-gwan, and nuns such as Myo-eom and Myo-yeong were studying under Un-heo. Wol-un would later go on to become the greatest lecturer among Korean Buddhists.

As soon as Un-heo read Gwan-eung's letter, he allowed Myeong-seong to join the class. Myeong-seong lived in Bota Hermitage with Myo-eom and Myo-yeong and visited Tongdo Monastery everyday to attend Un-heo's lecture on the Heroic March Sutra (Śūraṅgama Sūtra or *Neungeomgyeong*).

Everything was in chaos right after the war. It was very difficult to run a proper school. Senior monks would hold classes in whatever conditions the situation allowed. Young monks would join with a passion to learn. For Un-heo's class at Tongdo, ten monks from Tongdo and three nuns from Bota Hermitage had joined to study the Heroic March Sutra and Awakening of Faith (Mahāyāna śraddhotpādaśāstra or *Gisinron*). Nuns and monks were not allowed to sit together, so Un-heo would first teach the monks and then repeat the lesson for the nuns.

The Heroic March Sutra was a very difficult sutra. Students called it the "Rock Hard Sutra", because no matter how hard they studied, they could not understand or crack it. The classroom was a marvelous scene, where monks and nuns all gathered together under Un-heo to study the sutras amidst the chaos of the post-war period. Many of these students would, in the future, grow into the leaders of Korean Buddhism.

Un-heo was satisfied with the passion of the students. As a staunch supporter of bhikkhuni education, he believed that meeting Myo-eom, Myo-yeong, and Myeong-seong was a blessing from the Buddha. The three heroines would be future leaders, and Un-heo's plan was to train them so that they would become the trainers themselves.

The outside world continued on with its samsara of entanglement. Armistice brought a ceasefire, but that was after the war had already taken its toll on Buddhism. Numerous temples, monasteries, and cultural relics had been burnt down or destroyed. Lost were precious relics thousands of years old. Forests had been devastated, and temples stood in solitude on desertlike mountains. While things were visibly broken on the outside, there was even more chaos happening within. The ideological and political struggle between left and right had also permeated Buddhism, dividing it into two.

Because of this chaos, Un-heo had to stop his Awakening of Faith lecture. He had just begun teaching it after finishing the Heroic March Sutra. On the last day of his lecture, Un-heo announced that he was moving to Yeonhwasa Temple in Jinju City and would continue the lessons there. Myo-eom and Myeong-seong followed him to Yeonhwasa Temple. For Myeong-seong, the temple was full of memories, for it was there that she had studied Four Collections under Gwan-eung.

Awakening of Faith is the work of Asvaghosa. Asvaghosa explained that the One Mind is divided into Two Aspects. This is truly the core and foundation of East Asian Buddhism. It was not long after Un-heo moved to Yeonhwasa Temple that the "Buddhist Purification Movement" began in Seoul. Un-heo had to stop his teaching and go to Seoul to take part. Most of his students accompanied him, Myeong-seong and Myo-eom being among them.

After the Sino-Japanese War of 1894, Japan proceeded with its plans to annex Korea. They made detailed plans for every sector of society, including Buddhism. By the time Japan announced the annexation of Korea in 1911, six Japanese Buddhist Orders – Jōdo Shinshū, Jōdo-shū, Nichiren-shū, Sōtō-shū, Shingon-shū, and Linji-shū – had already established an astonishing 167 centres and branches in Korea. At first, Japanese Dharma-teachers started working around the ports through which the Japanese entered Korea. However, it did not take long before they made their way deeper inland into various regions. With support from their headquarters in Japan, they set up kindergartens, schools, and vocational training centres, working to win the hearts of the Korean people.

On June 3, 1911, the Japanese Imperial government declared the "Temple Order Decree." According to this law, thirty large temples would become the "Head" temples to which the other smaller temples in the region would belong. The designation of abbots for the head temples had to be approved by the Japanese Government-General, and the abbots of the smaller, affiliated temples had to be approved the Provincial Governor. Very soon, Korean temples were inundated with pro-Japanese monks. These monks started to follow the Japanese Buddhist tradition; they took wives and ate meat. Later, Hwaeom Monastery was added to the list of head temples, bringing the total to thirty-one.

The new law obligated the abbots to report, within five months of their appointment, an inventory of the land and forests belonging to the temple, along with all the buildings, statues, sculptures, stone artworks, ancient scriptures, old paintings, bells, sutra rolls, and all sorts of Buddhist relics and tools. This list was submitted to the Government-General. The moving or modification of any of the declared items had to be reported within five days.

Japan was attempting to eradicate traditional Korean Buddhism. However, Korean Buddhists would not go down without a fight. Seunims like Yong-seong Baek and Yong-un Han, who had been among the thirty-three national representatives in the nationwide anti-Japanese movement of March 1, 1919, joined forces with laypeople in a united effort to protect and preserve Korean Buddhist traditions. Many organizations and societies were formed. The Joseon Buddhist Seon School, or the Seon Practice Centre (*Seonhagwon*), was the result of these efforts. This school was formed without the assistance of the Japanese government. Life was tough for these pioneers, but they tried to protect Korean Buddhism while still living their lives as practitioners.

When Japan finally lost the war and Korea was liberated, the Korean War broke out. Chaos followed chaos, and destruction followed destruction. The monks of the Seon Practice Centre were in the most destitute of conditions. They belonged nowhere and had no place to keep their begging bowl or robe. In 1952, they asked the patriarch Man-am Song Seunim to provide them with a space where they could stay and practice. He took the request seriously and ordered his staff to review it. After several discussions, the staff decided to hand over eighteen temples to the monks, including Dongwha, Jikji, Bomun, Sileuk, and Naewon. The monks were infuriated that out of the 1,200 temples in the country, they were offered only 18. Moreover, these did not include any of the Three Treasure Temples (Tongdo, Haein, and Songgwang, the three major temples in Korea each symbolizing Buddha, Dharma, and Sangha).

On May 20, 1954, President Syngman Rhee declared that married monks should leave the temples. President Rhee had visited a temple by chance and saw a lady drying her laundry, which included baby diapers and women's clothes. Rhee asked why a woman would be washing clothes in a temple, and was told the historical background of how married monks had taken over all the temples nationwide with the support of the Japanese government.

Furious, President Rhee immediately issued a special order. "Erase the Japanese influence in all Korean temples."

This triggered a bloody battle between the minority of non-married traditional monks and the married Japanese-influenced monks. This battle would later be called the "Buddhism Purification Movement." Un-heo had gone up to Seoul precisely to support this movement. Myeong-seong, Myo-eom and other followers accompanied him.

From June 24 to 25, 1954, a month after the president's order, the "Committee to Prepare for the Order Purification Movement" was established. From December 10 to 13, a national convergence of monks and nuns was held. They initially gathered at the Seon Practice Centre, but the building could not accommodate all the people. Some people rolled out blankets and slept outside the Main Hall of Jogyesa Temple. It was the middle of December, and the monks and nuns were sleeping outside in the Korean winter cold. Myeong-seong and her fellow nuns were together with them. They slept outside in the yard at night and prayed to Lord Buddha all day. They prayed that Korean Buddhism would be restored to its original purity.

One day, Sung-san Seunim hurried to the temple. He was the secretary of the committee. There was an urgency in his voice.

"Six monks are about to kill themselves in front of the court!"

A court was to rule on the conflict between the non-married vs. married monks, and six monks had decided to disembowel themselves to demonstrate their determination to the court. A large group of monks and nuns began walking over to the court. Their hearts were heavy with grief as sleet fell from the sky. As they were walking, a truck stopped in front of them. People from the truck shouted at the monks and nuns to get in the truck. The seunims assumed that the truck was going to take them to the court. However, they soon discovered that the truck had brought them to the Yongsan Police Station. All the seunims who had been walking to the court had been taken to the police. They were detained there for three days. Myeong-seong was one of the eighteen nuns who had to sleep in a cold cell. Ja-ho Seunim, secretary of Sunamsa Temple, brought porridge to them everyday.

When the national convention of monks and nuns ended, Myeong-seong moved to Gaeunsa Temple. Geum-gwang Seunim was the abbess of this temple. Her original Dharma name was Geum-nyong, but she was commonly called Geum-gwang ("gwang" meaning light) because her body had been illuminated with an auspicious light while she was teaching the Nirvana Sutra (*Yeolbankyeong*) at Sorimsa Temple in Busan. Her body appeared just like the Buddha's, with light radiating in all directions. The audience was deeply moved, while people from the village at the bottom of the mountain hurriedly brought water to the temple, thinking that it was on fire. Myeong-seong knew about Geum-gwang Seunim and respected her, so she was happy to stay at Gaeunsa Temple.

While Myeong-seong was staying at Gaeunsa Temple, the three greatest Dharma-teacher nuns of the time opened a Lotus Sutra (Saddharma Puṇḍarīka Sūtra or *Beophwagyeong*) class. They were Geum-gwang, Su-ok, and Hye-ok. It was called the Lotus Sutra Forest Gathering. Geum-gwang Seunim was known for having radiated light during her lecture on the Nir-vana Sutra. Su-ok was an elite nun who had studied in Japan. She was particularly good at writing traditional Chinese poems. She was so good at it that she could converse in Chinese poems with Gyeong-bong Seunim, one of the greatest Seon masters of the time. Hye-ok was another legend; she is said to have gone up to the Dharma seat and lectured on Self-Admonition for Beginners when she was fifteen. It was said that people were so moved by her ability that they bowed to her. Myeong-seong and Myo-eom were there to learn from these three great nuns. The two would later go on to become among the greatest bhikkhu-nis in Korea.

When the three Dharma-teachers were finishing their lecture, they had Myeong-seong and Myo-eom teach the last part of the Lotus Sutra. To be certain, the two young nuns had already been recognized by the three teachers. One of the other student nuns who was studying together with them was Il-yeop Kim Seunim, who had studied in Japan and was one of the top writers of the time.

It was on one of these days that a woman with the Dhar-ma name "Dae-bo-hwa" Bosal organized a workshop on the Lotus Sutra at the Seon Practice Centre. She was the owner of the Seongnam Hotel and also the president of the "Maya La-dies' Club." Too many people gathered to attend, so they had to transfer the workshop from the Seon Practice Centre to Jogyesa Temple. The organizer asked Myeong-seong to teach the Lotus

Sutra. Myeong-seong found herself speaking at the Main Hall of Jogyesa Temple. While she spoke, Cheong-dam, Il-ta, and Dong-san Seunims came in to listen to her. These were very senior monks. Strangely, Myeong-seong did not feel nervous. On the contrary, the senior monks felt like Dharma-guardians to her. Her Dharma talk that day was impeccable.

When she finished, she received praise after praise. Never before had a novice nun, only twenty-eight years of age, given a Dharma talk on the Lotus Sutra in the Main Hall of Jogyesa Temple. The president of the Buddhist Followers Society, Hyeon-u Geosa (*Geosa* is a title for male Buddhists) commented on this occasion.

"There was a nun called Seonhwaja during the Silla kingdom who studied astronomy. Her documents are kept at Tongdosa Temple. Today, seeing Myeong-seong speak reminds me of Seonhwaja. Such nun teachers appear once in 500 years. My heart is overjoyed."

The Dharma talk that day was a big success. President Seo-un Seunim presented Ja-ho Seunim with an award to recognize her efforts in helping support Myeong-seong's studies.

In 1953, the first Bhikkhuni College was set up in Donghaksa Temple, on Gyeryong Mountain. Gyeong-bong Seunim (a different Gyeong-bong from the Seon master at Tongdosa Temple) was appointed head instructor. Myeong-seong had also studied at Donghak College initially, before moving to Seonam College.

The curriculum of a Buddhist college consisted of a Novice Nun class (*Saminigwa*), Four Collections class (*Sajipgwa*), Four Sutras class (*Sagyogwa*), and Flower Garland class (*Daegyogwa*). In the Novice Nun class, students would study Self-Admonition for Beginners, Novice Nun Rules and Decorum, and Introduction to Studies. The Four Collections class consisted of Letters (*Seojang*), Introduction (*Doseo*), Summary (*Jeoryo*), and Essence of Seon (*Seonyo*). The Four Sutras refer to the Heroic March Sutra, Awakening of Faith, Diamond Sutra, and Complete Enlightenment Sutra (*Wongaggyeong*). For the final class, the nuns study the Flower Garland Sutra. Myeong-seong and Myo-eom couldn't help but excel, considering how many novice nuns were actually illiterate at that time. The two had already studied the curriculum at Seonamsa Temple before coming to the monastic school. Myo-eom had been ordained as a novice nun by the famous Seong-cheol. She was the first nun to take part in the historic Bongamsa Temple Association. Afterwards, Myo-eom had studied Letters, Introduction, Summary, and Essence of Seon from Un-heo at Donghaksa Temple, and then followed Un-heo to Tongdosa Temple to study the Heroic March Sutra.

When Myeong-seong had completed the entire Four Collections under Gwan-eung, Myo-eom had finished the same course under Un-heo. The two had met at Tongdosa Temple while studying the Heroic March Sutra. The two nuns followed Un-heo to Yeonhwasa Temple in Jinju City to study the Awakening of Faith. Now, they came back to college in Donghaksa Temple. Their level of attainment simply surpassed all other students.

After the armistice was signed, the gunfire ceased. Buddhism, however, fell into utter chaos. The movement to rid Korean Buddhism of Japanese influence had begun. Many conscientious monks dedicated themselves to this cause. There were frequent legal battles in the courts with few signs of resolution.

The outside world was chaotic, but education had to continue. The teaching of nuns at Donghaksa Temple continued. Gyeong-bong Seunim was particularly fond of Myeong-seong. He was going to make a great teacher out of her. When Myeong-seong read the sutra out loud, he would stop her.

"Myeong-seong, Myeong-seong, read quietly! Do not use your voice too much. Save your vocal cords; you have a lifetime left to use them."

Senior monks and nuns held high expectations of as well as affection for Myeong-seong. They even wanted to take care of her vocal cords. They knew she was the future, and they would do their best to nurture her.

One day, Ja-ho Seunim contacted Myeong-seong and suggested that they study the Flower Garland Sutra together at Seonamsa Temple. Ja-ho was the secretary at Seonamsa Temple at that time and took a liking to Myeong-seong. Despite her new appointment as class leader for the following day, Myeong-seong actually ran away from the temple and went to Seonamsa Temple. She did not ask for permission because the senior monks were like parents, and would not allow such an outing. When she got on the bus, she felt a kind of liberation, the sense of freedom that comes from escaping a routine. This may have been the first and last time in her life when she felt such freedom.

There are two theories on the history of Seonamsa Temple. One is that it was built by monk A-do during King Jinheung's reign in the Silla dynasty. The other is that it was founded by Do-seon Guksa (*Guksa* means teacher of the nation) during the rule of King Heonkang. Scholars believe the latter to be more probable. The temple was greatly renovated by Euicheon from the Goryeo kingdom. During the Joseon kingdom, when King Jeongjo was unable to have a baby, he requested Monk Nul-am to offer a one hundred day prayer at the Hall of Circular Wisdom (*Wontongjeon*). Not long after the prayer, Jeongjo had a son, Sunjo. Sunjo knew of this fact since he was young. When he became king at the age of twelve, he immediately endowed Seonamsa Temple with a large plot of land and a plaque that read "Hall of Great Merit (*Daebokjeon*)." Seonamsa Temple grew to an enormous size, with over one hundred halls and shrines.

As with all other temples at that time, Seonam was also in the middle of the conflict between traditional monks versus married monks. On the east side of the Main Hall was located Simgeom Dang, where the nuns resided. On the west, married monks lived in Seolseon Dang. The reason why the nuns were located there was probably to avoid any physical confrontations. Nevertheless, Seonamsa Temple had an operating traditional Buddhist college. Classes were offered for nuns living in the east wing. When Myeong-seong and Ja-ho first started attending, a married monk called Man-u was the lecturer. He taught the Flower Garland Sutra. However, he soon had to quit teaching and move to another temple because other married monks attacked him for teaching the nuns as a married man.

Seong-neung Seunim succeeded to Man-u's position. A student of Han-yeong Park Seunim, he was quite knowledgeable. He had taught at the Buddhist colleges of Tongdo and Haeinsa Temples. Seong-neung taught the Flower Garland Sutra. This Sutra was the supreme sutra, directly explaining the world of enlightenment. Myeong-seong invested all of her energy into studying it. She studied before and after class, a habit that she had acquired in elementary school. Moreover, the Flower Garland Sutra was a lot of fun. It was profound, and it fully satisfied Myeong-seong's intellectual desires.

When the Buddha taught the Flower Garland Sutra, his top disciples Subhuti and Maudgalyayana are said to have sat speechless, dumbfounded like dumb or deaf men. The Sutra is notorious for its difficulty. Teachers would teach only as much as they could and students received only as much as they were able to, but they did so in great earnest.

Two years had passed since Myeong-seong had moved

to the college in Seonamsa Temple. One day, after the lecture, Seong-neung Seunim pulled out the cushion from beneath him and handed it over to Myeong-seong. It was a lectureship transmission ceremony; the passing down of the Dharma-seat.

"From now, you take over."

A few days later, Seong-neung left Seonam. He told the others that he was too old and sick to continue.

After Seong-neung left, Myeong-seong started teaching the students. Ja-ho was the secretary, and Myeong-seong was the treasurer of the temple. Myeong-seong's workload suddenly doubled. It was the first time for Myeong-seong to officially transition from being a student to a teacher. As it had always been monks who taught the nuns, it was quite a curious thing for a nun to be teaching the monks. Myeong-seong was thirty years old.

Because Seonamsa Temple housed both nuns and married monks, nuns at the temple had to set an example. Apart from studying the sutras, the nuns lived according to strict discipline. Myeong-seong trained and taught her students to stay away from ill-will and bad conduct. Religious leaders had to follow a strict lifestyle. Myeong-seong lived her life in constant tension as she tried to live up to the precepts, continue her prayers and study the sutras.

After Myeong-seong became a teacher, her accommodations were moved to the Hall of Circular Wisdom. When Myeong-seong read out loud the Six Hundred Scrolls of the Diamond

Sutra, which was recorded in the Tripitaka in the Circular Wisdom Hall, monks, including married monks of the Taego Order as well as visitors, all came to listen to her voice, rapt with ecstasy. When Myeong-seong gave Dharma talks on the Diamond Sutra on first day of the month, on a full moon, in the Pavilion of Eternity (*Manseru*), monks, nuns, laypeople, and even young students came to listen. She was certainly a rising star, receiving respect and love from all directions.

As treasurer, Myeong-seong had to be in charge of the temple's financial matters. Tens of bhikkhuni-students were living together, and the financial situation could hardly get any worse. Myeong-seong found herself having to squeeze out every last bit of effort in order to make ends meet.

Five years passed. One winter day, the snow flakes started to grow in size until it looked like huge balls were falling from the sky. Myeong-seong was resting after lunch when Tae-gyeong Seunim rushed in and spoke.

"Seunim, these people seem to be making charcoal again. We should go there immediately."

"Yes, let's go."

Myeong-seong quickly rose and put on a thick winter coat. There was a furnace on top of Seonamsa Temple for cooking charcoal. People would cut down trees that belonged to the temple and burn them to make and sell charcoal. This was a financial matter, and so it was up to Myeong-seong to address it. The two nuns put on rice-straw slippers, which made it easier to walk in snow, over their black rubber shoes and hurried up the mountain. Tae-gyeong Seunim cleared a path with a stick and Myeong-seong followed.

Everything in creation was white. The white mountain path brought a sense of liberation to Myeong-seong. The air felt cool. Things felt fresh. Both her body and mind became as light as snow flakes as she moved higher up. Soon, the nuns arrived at a small charcoal furnace and a hut. They could hear people speaking. The hut was deep in the mountains, covered in white, where the trees and grass all vanished within the snow. There, a small family was living together.

Tae-gyeong Seunim went in first and told them that Myeong-seong was here. A small man came out of the hut. He was covered in charcoal from head to toe. His black color stood out in stark contrast to the surrounding white. The hardship he was undergoing could be no clearer. His face was perplexed and apologetic at the same time.

"Seunim, I am sorry." He put his palms together and bowed.

"You know this is wrong. You shouldn't keep doing this." Myeong-seong reprimanded him.

"This is all I can do." The man replied. "Please come in. It's snowing so heavily."

Tae-gyeong Seunim went in first, and Myeong-seong followed. The hut was tiny. The man's wife and three children peeked out at the nuns with worried faces. They knew they had done something wrong. But was it not poverty that had driven them to this situation? Myeong-seong's heart ached deeply as her eyes met theirs. She looked around the hut at the knick-knacks the poor family had lying around. She saw a brass basin on top of the fire. It was producing steam. Myeong-seong felt her eyes getting red. In winter, her mother would put a basin like that on the fire to warm the water so that she and her brother could wash their faces. In this bitter white cold, where would her mother be? Where would her brother be, and how would they be getting by? Her mother and brother would be living by themselves, supporting each other, with no one helping them. Tears were already streaking down her face.

"Stay here for the winter. In the spring, you will be able to find another job. Then you won't have to rely on making charcoal here." Her voice was shaking as she turned away.

In early spring of 1961, Myeong-seong left Seonamsa Temple and moved to Cheongnyongsa Temple. She had lived in Seonam for five years. She had to move because the traditional monks had lost in the lawsuit against the married-monks. The battle between the traditional monks and the married-monks had begun in 1954, following President Syngman Rhee's order to eliminate Japanese influence from Korean Buddhism. The battle never showed any signs of settling, as violence and lawsuits continued in a constant cycle. After the Revolution of April 19, 1960, the Democratic Party seized power. After this, all pending lawsuits were ruled in favour of the married-monks. This was influenced by politics, as the new administration automatically opposed any decisions made by President Rhee, who was labeled a dictator. Buddhism fell into deeper and deeper confusion. That was why the bhikkhunis had to leave Seonamsa Temple.

Chapter 04

Teacher of humans and devas

After leaving Seonamsa Temple, Myeong-seong decided to go to Seoul. She wanted to study more in Seoul. She had always wanted to broaden her knowledge. When she was teaching at the college in Seonam, she frequently felt that she could do a better job if she knew more. As a child, Myeong-seong had seen Gwan-eung go to Ryukoku University in Japan to study extra-Buddhist curriculum, and she was influenced by her father's educational path.

Monks and nuns are said to be the teachers of both humans and heavenly beings. It was not only people, but also devas who needed deliverance. Monks and nuns have to be supreme in everything: from their conduct to knowledge, from their actions to wisdom. Only then would they be qualified to save others. It was becoming increasingly difficult to make a claim of superior knowledge having only studied a Buddhist curriculum. They had to learn what the outside world was learning. Myeong-seong decided to enter university.

She made her home at Cheongnyongsa (Blue Dragon)

Temple in Sungin neighborhood, Jongno District. Cheongnyongsa Temple is where Queen Jeongsun, wife of King Danjong, had lived until her death at eighty-two years of age. She had been banished from the palace when she was fifteen. She spent her final night together with Danjong in the temple's Uhwa pavilion. After separating from Danjong at the Bridge of Permanent Separation (*Yeongligyo*), above Cheonggye creek, she lived in the temple as a bhikkhuni. She dyed fabric to earn a living. Occasionally, she would climb up the hill behind the temple and look longingly toward the east, in the direction of Yeongwol, where Danjong had been exiled to.

Yun-ho Seunim was the abbess of Cheongnyongsa Temple. Bon-gong and Yun-ho Seunim were close friends. Myeongseong was a Dharma grand-daughter to Bon-gong, so Bon-gong asked Yun-ho to arrange a place for her to stay. Cheongnyongsa Temple was established during the Goryeo dynasty. From the founding, it was a royal temple. Royal concubines and ladies of the court stayed there and cultivated themselves. That is why, at one time, it was known as Karma Purification Temple (*Jeongeopwon*).

Because Myeong-seong was known for being a Dharma-teacher, after she arrived at Cheongnyongsa Temple, seunims from Cheongnyong, and even seunims from outside the temple, gathered to learn from her. Naturally, a class was organized. More than ten bhikkhunis wanted to learn the curriculum that was taught in a Buddhist college. Myeong-seong began by teaching them Self-Admonition for Beginners. It was the very book that Gwan-eung taught her when she was still a postulant at Mireugam Hermitage. On the day of his lecture, Gwan-eung had advised Myeong-seong.

"Read this ten thousand times. It will benefit you greatly."

Myeong-seong had succeeded in reading it three thousand times. She had memorized every single letter of it. Her lecture was highly knowledgeable. She explained in detail what the text was trying to convey, while at the same time she tried to explain the proper physical, verbal, and mental action that a se-unim must master in order to become a great teacher of humans and heavenly beings. She told them how seunims should eat, sleep and conduct themselves, and how to continue being faithful to the vows. She repeated the message over and over so that it would sink for everyone.

She was not just delivering knowledge. She was a guide and a friend, for they were all walking down the path of becoming teachers of heaven and earth. She was accompanying them on this path. The bond between teacher and student got stronger and stronger. Few women attended school at that time, and it was common for bhikkhunis to have little formal education. Myeong-seong made time to teach the illiterate students how to read and write both Korean and Chinese. This was necessary in order to study the sutras.

Myeong-seong entered Dongguk University in 1961, fulfilling her dream of studying extra-Buddhist curriculum in

Seoul. She went into the Department of Buddhist Studies. She was the third bhikkhuni student; the first two being Gwang-u and Wol-song. Dongguk University had been established by a Buddhist foundation, so assuredly, the Department of Buddhism was at its heart. Some of the students that Myeong-seong studied with included Hongpa Seunim, president of the Gwaneum Order, Buddhist scholar Ik-jin Go, professor Pyeong-nae Lee, professor Seon-yeong Park, Jae-ho Jo, Jeong-seop Han, and Seong-suk Hong. Seong-suk would later become Myeong-seong's lay-disciple.

Myeong-seong became a university student at the age of thirty-two. She studied with her natural diligence and dedication. She was a university student, but at the same time attended all the Buddhist ceremonies and worship and even taught students at the temple. She was busy with many tasks at once, but she excelled, for studying diligently had been her habit since elementary school. She got straight A's in all her subjects.

She was taking on the roles of four people. She was always short on time. Just a single miscalculation in time wreaked havoc on the rest of her schedule. Myeong-seong made a timetable that she abided by to the minute. She never stopped praying. Since walking and praying could be done at the same time, she would recite Gwanseeum Bosal when she was walking to and from school in order to save time.

It took 40 minutes from Cheongnyongsa Temple to Dongguk University by foot. Myeong-seong took neither the train nor bus. She would have to transfer if she took the train and the buses were always too full. In the early 1960s, buses were packed so tightly with people that buttons were often torn from people's coats. One would find one's arms and legs twisted awkwardly and neatly ironed clothes would often come out all wrinkled and dirty after riding the bus. Riding the bus was a difficult experience that would drain one's energy.

Myeong-seong chose simply to walk. Another reason for this was to save money. Cheongnyongsa Temple paid for about half of Myeong-seong's tuition fees. But she needed to save every cent of that. She had to pay for the tuition, buy books and other school supplies. She always packed her own lunch. Walking 80 minutes round-trip was a precious time for her, which she spent reciting the name of the Buddha or practicing new English vocabulary.

Myeong-seong was not an easy friend for her fellow students. First, she was much older than the other students. She was also a nun. She already had a high level of academic achievement. It wasn't easy for other students in the same department to approach her or make friends.

One day, Myeong-seong quietly went up to another student.

"Seong-suk, please follow me."

Curious, Seong-suk Hong followed her. Myeong-seong took her to an empty classroom and sat down.

"Have a seat."

"What...?"

When Seong-suk sat down, Myeong-seong put a book down in front of her and opened it.

"I saw that you did not understand this part during class. Let me teach you."

Seong-suk suddenly remembered that Myeong-seong had been sitting beside her in class. They were studying Buddhist texts written in Chinese. Seong-suk had been sitting blankly because she did not understand what was being taught.

"Nobody knows what they have not yet learned. If you haven't studied Chinese, of course you cannot understand Chinese texts. There is no reason to be ashamed."

Myeong-seong pointed at the writing that had been covered in the lesson and started teaching her, one character at a time.

After that, Myeong-seong became Seong-suk's teacher. Whenever Seong-suk had something she did not understand, she followed Myeong-seong around, asking her to help. Every time, Myeong-seong would take her to an empty classroom and explain the content in detail. Other students began to gather around and Myeong-seong ended up becoming a teacher among her fellow students. It seemed as she was destined to teach wherever she went.

Seong-suk Hong started to find school more and more interesting. Myeong-seong was a charismatic figure, fully armed with a high level of knowledge of Buddhist texts. Even the professors felt nervous around her. Seong-suk was excited that someone like Myeong-seong was her private tutor. She went home and told her mother about this. This delighted her mother, a devout Buddhist, and she prepared snacks for them both. Later, she even started packing a lunch for Myeong-seong. Seong-suk would bring two lunch boxes to school everyday. She was having fun in her school life, and gradually began to enjoy studying as well.

Cheongnyongsa Temple was situated outside of Seoul's East Gate. It was an old, traditional bhikkhuni temple with many members. They offered a Dharma-teaching on the first day of the lunar month and the full moon, but always found it hard to get quality teachers. The temple asked Myeong-seong to teach these lessons. As a result, she now had a new job teaching lay-people in addition to teaching other nuns. She started teaching the Diamond Sutra to laypeople.

She was teaching nuns in the temple, studying in university as a student, and teaching laypeople who came to the temple. She had to juggle all these tasks and stay on top of everything. She strictly managed and kept to her schedule. Everyday was fully packed with things to do. Mistakes were unacceptable. Living up to this situation, Myeong-seong had to become even more reason-oriented and not allow herself to be vulnerable to emotions. She did not have the luxury of feeling depressed, empty, or tired. That would distract her from her tasks.

One year passed like this. Her report card showed straight

A's in all subjects. Fortunately, she was granted a scholarship from the Gwaneum Club. Starting from her second year in school, she did not have to worry about tuition.

It was now winter break, and she had more time for herself. One day, she saw an article in the newspaper about a calligrapher named Yeo-cho Eung-hyeon Kim. He and his brother, Il-jung Chung-hyeon Kim, were the top two greatest calligraphers of the time. Myeong-seong's heart raced. She had always wanted to learn calligraphy but had never met the right teacher. She sensed that this was the opportunity she had been waiting for.

After lunch, Myeong-seong headed towards the calligraphy school that she had read about in the newspaper. It was by Cheonggye creek. The creek had not been covered, and small huts made from wooden boards had been built along the edge in long, destitute rows. This was where the poor farmers from the countryside first came to live as they looked for jobs in Seoul. The water was filthy and the whole place had a foul smell. Children were playing with a kicking toy (*jaegi*) by the water. Myeong-seong stared at them for a while with a sad look, then turned the corner to where the calligraphy school was. It was on the second floor of the building.

On a wooden plaque was written "Eastern Calligraphy Training School (*Dongbang Yeonseohoe*)." The smell of India ink filled the air. Over twenty students were standing or sitting in two neat rows, practicing their writing. They were holding the brush perpendicularly, concentrating on each and every stroke.

Looking at them, Myeong-seong was filled with joy. This was an artform that she yearned to know! She met Yeo-cho and told him that she wanted to learn.

"Where are you now?"

Yeo-cho was interested in the new student. A few bhikkhus had come to learn before, but it was the first time for a bhikkhuni to come asking to learn.

"I am staying at Cheongnyongsa Temple, in Sungin neighborhood."

Yeo-cho was only three years older than Myeong-seong, but she was already treating him with the respect fit for a teacher.

"That is not very far. But do you think you have time to learn with all your studies at school?"

"This is something I have wanted to learn for a long time."

"Have you practised writing with a pen?"

"Yes. I have practised pen-writing with some books."

"That's good. Having practised with a pen will make it easier to learn with a brush."

Thus, began Myeong-seong's study of calligraphy in the school of Il-jung and Yeo-cho. Yeo-cho was a very popular calligrapher known to have mastered all styles of writing, and who incorporated all the best aspects of traditional Chinese writing into his own style. He was said to have "unified the mind and hands." That was a high level to attain, being able to express through his hands what is in his mind. Yeo-cho was even called "second only to Chu-sa", who was the best calligrapher in the history of Korea. The brothers, Yeo-cho and Il-jung were the two great mountains of Korean calligraphy. They had continued the lineage of Chu-sa Jeong-hi Kim – Jae-hyeong Son – Hi-gang Yu. Yeo-cho was an intellectual who had graduated from the elite Whimoon High School and Korea University with a major in English literature.

Myeong-seong was thrilled to finally learn calligraphy. She went to Insa-dong to purchase brushes, India ink, inkstone, and seal stone. She did not buy traditional paper because that was expensive; she would practice on newspapers and buy traditional paper later. She contemplated walking all the way back to Cheongnyong to save money, but decided that saving time was more important and took a train from Jonggak to the East Gate. Joy was springing out of her heart.

As soon as Myeong-seong got back, she remade her daily schedule. She figured that she would need to devote at least two hours a day to calligraphy. She decided to practice for one hour at the calligraphy school and another hour back at the temple. Adding two hours to an already hectic schedule meant that she had to take away two hours from somewhere else. Myeong-seong looked hard at the schedule but could not find an answer. Finally, she realized that there was time between classes in school. She decided to use that time to finish reviewing and studying what she had learned that day at school.

A single day had only twenty-four hours. Now it was even

more packed with things to do. She would rise at 3 am, attend the early morning worship, teach sutras to the students, eat breakfast, walk to school for 40 minutes while reciting Gwanseeum Bosal, attend classes in school, and study what she had learned during the empty times between classes. Even her free time, however, was not actually time for herself. Her classmates would track her down and follow her with questions, asking for help with their studies of Chinese texts. After her university classes, Myeong-seong hurried to the calligraphy school to learn. Then, on her way back to the temple, she would memorize about ten English vocabulary words daily.

When she arrived at the temple, she had dinner. After dinner, again, she taught the sutras to students for an hour. She spent all her time during the day learning, and in the evening, teaching. Only when it was 8 pm would she have any time of her own. Then, Myeong-seong would practice her calligraphy until she went to bed. First, she practiced how to hold the brush. Then, how to draw straight lines, both left to right and up to down. Next, she started writing characters. She would spread out newspaper and start writing. An hour passed quickly. She wanted to continue writing throughout the night, but the rules of the temple dictated that she go to sleep at 9 pm. Unable to leave the lights on later, she concentrated intensively during that one hour.

One Sunday morning, Myeong-seong was practising calligraphy after finishing her laundry. Just then, a member of the temple came to see her, requesting a consultation. She had asked Myeong-seong for a private consultation the day before. Myeong-seong had told her to come back on Sunday, and she had really come. Myeong-seong decided to try to keep writing as she listened to the temple member. She concentrated her mind on both tasks simultaneously. To her amazement, she found herself able to do it. Her hand, mouth and ears seemed to have minds of their own; each performing their individual roles perfectly.

A student who had been watching her doing this murmured to herself. 'She should practice her writing after the guest has left.'

However, to the student's surprise, Myeong-seong was listening and responding with precise answers, as if she was wholly devoted to the conversation alone. The student was amazed, and after the temple member left, she asked Myeong-seong.

"How can you do two things at once?"

Myeong-seong answered. "I don't know. I only did it because both tasks were things that I had to do."

After lunch, when Myeong-seong was getting ready to teach, a student who Myeong-seong hadn't seen before came to speak with her.

"What brings you here?" she asked.

The girl's head drooped down and she did not answer. After a moment, she opened her mouth.

"I entered Dongguk University to study Buddhism, but

my parents refused to pay for my tuition. I want to become a nun in the future, but my parents adamantly oppose it. They say that they will not pay for my tuition if I study Buddhism."

Myeong-seong realized that the girl needed money. "I see. Wait a moment." Myeong-seong went into her room and brought out enough money to pay for the tuition. It was new, clean currency.

"Pay your tuition with this. Study hard."

The girl received the money, said thank you and left. Myeong-seong did not ask her name, why she wanted to become a nun, why she had decided to seek out Myeong-seong, or any questions for that matter. It was pure coincidence, if indeed coincidences exist, that the money Myeong-seong had in savings happened to be just enough to pay for the student's tuition. This girl would visit Myeong-seong more than twenty years later as the wife of a businessman. She re-paid more than what she borrowed and became a non-shaved disciple of Myeong-seong. Needless to say, she became one of Myeong-seong's strong supporters.

After winter break ended and the spring semester had begun, Myeong-seong asked Yeong-tae Kim and Ik-jin Go to come to Cheongnyongsa Temple to teach. Mr. Kim was studying Korean Buddhist history and Mr. Go was studying Indian Buddhist history. They both belonged to the Buddhist Studies department just like Myeong-seong.

"I do not believe that nuns should be taught only the traditional curriculum. They need to learn what the outside world is learning. Please, can you two come to my temple to teach the nuns Korean and Indian Buddhist history?"

They both happily accepted her offer. Thus began the teaching of modern curriculum at a traditional temple. Such a thing was totally unimaginable in other traditional Buddhist colleges. Ik-jin Go was one of the beneficiaries of the Gwaneum Club along with Myeong-seong. Both Go and Kim would later become great Buddhist scholars and work as professors at Dongguk University.

Dongguk University was established by a Buddhist foundation. The Department of Buddhist Studies was always at the core of the curriculum. Dong-hwa Kim, a senior Buddhist scholar, taught "Introduction to Buddhist Studies." Professor Dong-hwa was close with Gwan-eung Seunim. They both came from Sangju. Dong-hwa had gone to Japan to study Yogacaria and opened a path for Gwan-eung to study at Ryukoku University in Japan. He invited Gwan-eung to study Yogacaria, as Ryukoku University was famous for its Yogacaria program.

Professor Dong-hwa Kim played a vital role in the establishment of Dongguk University after Korea's liberation from Japanese rule. He was also appointed as the first President of the University. Dongguk University started off with just a single department, so the head of that department was equivalent to the head of the university. Myeong-seong got to know Professor

Kim during her second year, when she took "Introduction to Buddhist Studies." She studied Yogacaria from Dong-hwa in her third year, where they firmly established their teacher-student relationship. For Dong-hwa, Myeong-seong was the daughter of his very beloved and respected 'brother' Gwan-eung. He appreciated the fact that Myeong-seong was rising to become the next generation's leader among Korean bhikkhunis. He put great effort and love into training her.

Professor Myeong-gi Jo was also instrumental in Myeong-seong's education at that time. Myeong-gi was the president of the university when Myeong-seong was enrolled. It was not often that a university president would give lectures to students. However, he taught courses on "Cultural History." In fact, Myeong-gi Jo and Myeong-seong had already met many years back when Myeong-seong was studying at a middle school in Pyeongchang. Myeong-gi Jo and the Japanese scholar Kato had visited Woljeongsa Temple together. Gwan-eung was the Dharma-teacher at that time and had introduced his daughter to them. Myeong-gi Jo had been a young man at that time, studying the great thinker Won-hyo at an Institute for Religious Studies, while Myeong-seong had been a young girl from the countryside. Myeong-gi also held a special affection and interest in Myeong-seong and wanted to guide her to become a leader among bhikkhunis.

Myeong-seong's life in school was blessed with love from teachers and respect from classmates. She was very busy, but just as happy.

When Myeong-seong was in her third year, Sung-san Se-unim wanted to see her.

"I am going over to Japan. As I cannot finish teaching The Mirror of Seon (*Seonka Guigam*), can you please take over my class?"

Sung-san was earnest in his request. Now a legend in Korean Buddhism, he would ultimately establish one hundred and twenty Seon Centres in thirty-six countries, spreading Korean Seon all over the world. Myeong-seong had a deep respect for Sung-san, for he had dedicated himself completely to protecting Korean Buddhism as a leader of the bhikkhus during the Purification Movement. Myeong-seong could not help but agree to his request.

The Mirror of Seon is a selection of Seon teachings compiled by Monk Seo-san in the seventeenth century. It is an introduction to the study of Seon. Sung-san had been teaching this to laypeople. Some were lawyers, scholars, and businessmen. They were well-educated and had a good knowledge of Buddhism. Myeong-seong started teaching where Sung-san had left off. It took one year to finish the book. In the 1960s, bhikkhunis still had a rather low status within the Buddhist community. This made it all the more significant that such a respected and knowledgeable bhikkhu like Sung-san had asked Myeong-seong, a bhikkhuni, to teach in his place.

Amidst her busy schedule, Myeong-seong was given yet

another task to do. She was to offer teachings of the Dharma to female inmates at Seodaemun Prison. Though it began later than other religions, Buddhism also joined in the call to provide an education to inmates. It was accepted as one of the social responsibilities of a religion. Wol-un Seunim taught the male inmates; Myeong-seong the females. She visited the prison once a month and told them of the teachings of the Buddha. They had all ended up at that place because of how their lives had unfolded. But Myeong-seong knew that they all possessed the Buddha mind. She devoted herself to awakening their Buddha nature.

She started this service in her third year and continued on until she was a senior. One day, when she was coming out of the prison after finishing her teaching, she saw a boy about ten years old, holding his grandmother's hand. The two were entering the interview room. The boy had a cute round face with clear eyes. He reminded Myeong-seong of her little brother.

"You look smart. What is your name?"

The boy seemed scared. His grandmother answered instead. "His name is Yeong-ho. He came to see his mother."

"What did she do wrong?"

"This boy has no father. His mother was making living selling goods on the street. She got into a fight with another street vendor over space and ended up pushing the other woman. The woman fell and hurt her head. She is still lying in bed. How can his mother be so unlucky? She only gave a light push."

The story reminded Myeong-seong of her own mother.

She had heard a rumor that her mother was leading a very tough life trying to raise her son. After staring at the boy for a moment, Myeong-seong took out all the money she had and gave it to the grandmother.

"This is all I have. Please go and eat something."

As Myeong-seong turned away, the old lady spoke in a soft voice. "I should be giving you offerings. You don't have money either..."

Myeong-seong felt heavy in both her footsteps and her heart.

That autumn, when Myeong-seong had been practicing calligraphy for some time, there was a calligraphy competition organized by Dongguk University. Myeong-seong wrote and submitted the Heart Sutra. She was given the President's Award. The following year, she participated again and was given the highest award, the Chairman of the Board's Award. The president at that time was Professor Seong-uk Baek. In 1966, she wrote the Heart Sutra in the Hiji Wang style and won the contest. Her name was printed in the newspapers. Now she was officially a calligrapher.

Myeong-seong continued to learn from Il-jung and Yeo-cho for years. Practising calligraphy became the most important part of her routine. She taught calligraphy to the students of Cheongnyongsa Temple. All of the students learned it, based on Myeong-seong's belief that bhikkhunis should know how to write calligraphy.

In 1966, Myeong-seong was ordained as a bhikkhuni by Ja-un Seunim at the Diamond Ordination Platform in Haeinsa Temple.

After graduating from Dongguk University, she went on to study further in graduate school. Professor Dong-hwa Kim was her academic advisor. He wanted Myeong-seong to study Yogacaria and follow in his footsteps. Myeong-seong wrote her Master's thesis on Alaya-consciousness. Humans possess eight consciousnesses. Sight, hearing, smell, taste, touch, and thought are the first six. The seventh is manas and eighth is alaya. From this alaya, all beings of this universe came to be.

The Japanese had studied Yogacaria in depth, and the majority of documents dealing with the topic were in Japanese. Under Professor Kim's guidance, Myeong-seong read all of the Japanese material that was available. Alaya-consciousness is a complicated and difficult field of study. Myeong-seong studied meticulously, just as she would do in her meditations. She put much effort into perfecting her thesis, which ultimately passed. She became the first bhikkhuni to have gotten her Master's degree.

She continued her studies, now pursuing her doctorate, and decided to write her dissertation on the Three Transforming Consciousnesses. One day, the older sister of Seon-geun Lee, president of Dongguk University, came to see Myeong-seong. She told Myeong-seong that she was managing an orphanage, and she emphasized the social role of Buddhism. What she said made an impression on Myeong-seong, and she went to go see Gwang-u Seunim. Gwang-u had talked about similar ideas a while before.

"There seems to be a lot of work for us to do as bhikkhunis. We should come together to do something for these issues," Myeong-seong said.

"That is a good idea. Other religions are already doing a lot of this type of work, whereas we have been idly standing by," replied Gwang-u.

In 1967, Gwang-u had built the Jeonggaksa (Right Enlightenment) Temple in Seongbuk nieghborhood, Seoul. She was teaching Dharma to the people. One day, she invited Professor Dong-hwa Kim to give a lecture. They were having tea after the lecture when Professor Kim spoke, "There is no other country than Korea with this many bhikkhunis. There is no other country where this many bhikkhunis are studying the sutras. Bhikkhunis are the daughters of the Buddha. If you all came together and formed an organization to help cultivate each other, there would be nothing that you could not do."

Gwang-u's ears perked up at his words. Such an organization had not yet been formed, but it was probably the most important and urgent task that they could do. That is when Gwang-u went straight to Cheongnyongsa Temple to discuss it with Myeong-seong, one of her closest friends.

The two bhikkhunis agreed to build an organization. One

by one, they convinced other bhikkhunis to join them. Jin-gwan Seunim of Jingwansa Temple, Do-won Seunim of Seunggasa Temple, Myeong-won Seunim of Seokbulsa Temple, and Se-deung and Deok-su Seunims of Tapgolsa Temple were greatly supportive and became the founding members.

The following year, on February 24, 1968, over sixty bhikkhunis gathered in Bomunsa Temple to hold the first ever national bhikkhuni conference. They named the organization Udumbara. In-hong Seunim was designated as the advisor, Eun-yeong Seunim became the first president, and Se-deung the secretary. This organization developed into what is now the "National Bhikkhuni Association."

While Myeong-seong was preparing this, she received an invitation from Unmunsa (Cloud Gate) Temple. They wanted her to become their Dharma-teacher. Unmunsa Temple had become a bhikkhuni temple after the Purification Movement. Geum-gwang Seunim, the nun famous for her radiation of light, was the first abbess. She had founded a Buddhist college for bhikkhunis. The first teacher was Hye-ryeon Oh, who was followed by Jae-ung Lim, both bhikkhus. The two did not last in the position very long. The third teacher was Myo-eom. Myo-eom, however, also resigned from the position, announcing that she needed to do intensive Seon meditation to understand the sutras better. Myeong-seong visited Unmunsa Temple a few times to try to convince Myo-eom to stay, but with no success.

Since the teacher's position was empty, eight senior bhikkhunis came to Cheongnyongsa Temple to convince Myeong-seong to come. The abbess of Cheongnyong, Yun-ho Seunim, strongly protested, "I will never let Myeong-seong go. Over my dead body!" However, with persistent persuasion from the eight nuns, she finally relented.

Myeong-seong was in a dilemma. She wanted to finish her doctoral course, but there was an urgent call for her service in teaching. After deep consideration, she decided to devote her life to teaching bhikkhunis in Unmunsa Temple. She went to Professor Dong-hwa Kim to tell him of her decision. He was very disappointed.

"I was going to have you teach 'Ancient Buddhism' starting this semester. Please reconsider. Studying out there in the countryside is as productive as taking a nap here in Seoul."

Myeong-seong replied, "There are many people who can teach here in Dongguk University. But there is no one to teach in Unmunsa Temple. This is my calling."

Thus, Myeong-seong ended her decade of living in Seoul and traveled down to Unmunsa Temple in 1970. It was the beginning of the third chapter of her life.

Chapter 05

New Winds Blowing in Mount Hogeo

Riding with Myeong-seong on the bus to Unmunsa (Cloud Gate) Temple were over twenty students from Cheongnyongsa Temple. Myeong-seong's class at Cheongnyong had to shut down due to her transfer to Unmun. Then her students at Cheongnyong all decided to follow her to Unmun to continue their studies. In fact, the sutra school of Cheongnyong itself was being relocated to Unmun.

They traveled down a long and winding mountain road, kicking up clouds of dust. The bus arrived at Unmunsa Temple in the evening. When Myeong-seong got off the bus, the nuns of the temple surrounded her, cheering, applauding, and crying at the same time. "Thank you for coming!" They repeated. The history of Korean bhikkhunis was about to change.

Myeong-seong was forty years old. She arrived at Unmunsa Temple with a heavy sense of responsibility. She was determined to build a strong foundation for bhikkhuni education.

Unmunsa Temple had been built in 557 CE, during the reign of King Jinheung of the Silla dynasty. A monk of high spiritual attainment had built it and named it Daejaggapsa Temple. King Jinheung had heard news of a temple that had been built in an auspicious place and designated Daejaggap as his favoured temple. In the year 660, Won-gwang Guksa stayed at the temple and expanded it. Won-gwang Guksa was the monk who came up with the "Five Precepts for the Secular World" and passed them on to Gwi-san and Chu-hang, who were Hwarangs (members of an elite group of young warriors). In 930, Bo-yang Guksa enlarged the temple even further. The first king of Goryeo, Taejo Geon Wang bestowed a plaque on which was written Unmun Seonsa Temple, and bequeathed the temple a vast area of land. From that point onward, Daejaggapsa Temple changed its name to Unmunsa. Won-eung Guksa expanded the temple for the third time in the eleventh century. It became the second largest Seon temple in Korea. Seon Master I-ryeon spent his later years as the abbot of the temple, where he wrote the History of Three Kingdoms.

Unmunsa Temple had originally been occupied by bhikkhus. Due to the Purification Movement in the 1950s, it was converted to a bhikkhuni temple.

After the liberation from Japanese rule, traditional Korean monks and nuns had a long and bloody battle against the influence of Japanese Buddhism. Japanese Buddhism had allowed monks to get married. Thirty-six years of colonial rule resulted in the deep permeation of this culture. The battle that began after President Rhee's order was also called the bhikkhu vs. married monk conflict. A minority of monks belonging to the Seon Practice Centre started the long and hard struggle to purify Korean Buddhism. Bhikkhunis also joined in this battle, contributing a great deal to the bhikkhus' victory. As a gesture of appreciation, Donghwasa Temple was given to the bhikkhunis.

The bhikkhunis were delighted when Donghwasa Temple was designated as the main temple for nuns. Seong-mun became the abbess, In-hong the secretary, Jeong-an the treasurer, and Beob-il the administrator. However, not one year had passed when the bhikkhus decided to take the temple back. They said that bhikkhunis should not have been given such a major temple. They offered Unmunsa Temple instead.

So, the bhikkhunis had to move to Unmun. Geum-gwang was the first abbess. Geum-gwang held the conviction that the bhikkhunis needed a good education system if they were to be treated as equals of the bhikkhus. She founded a Buddhist college within Unmunsa Temple. Sadly, however, Geum-gwang passed away two years after becoming the abbess, in 1956. Su-in, Myo-jeon, and Tae-gu were the succeeding abbesses.

In 1958, Hye-ryeon Oh Seunim from Tongdosa Temple was invited to come and be the Dharma-teacher. Jae-eung and Myo-eom were the second and third teachers. When Myeong-seong arrived in Unmun, she was the fourth Dharma-teacher under the supervision of Tae-gu, the temple's fourth abbess.

Myeong-seong took a look around the temple. Grass was growing tall on the roof of the Hall of the Cosmic Buddha (Vairocana, *Birojeon*). The students attending the Novice Nun class, the Four Collections class, the Four Sutras class, and the Flower Garland class were all staying together in the Main Buddha Hall (*Geumdang*). They were studying, eating, and living together, but there was not enough food. The nuns ate porridge for breakfast. Lunch and dinner consisted of rice and barley with soup, pickled herbs, and kimchi. They had no electricity. At night, they would light candles or lamps. The year was 1970, and South Korea was still a poor nation. A bhikkhuni temple deep in the remote mountains was especially poor, and the temple did not have many followers.

Three days after arriving there, Myeong-seong called upon one representative from Unmun and another from Cheong-nyong. These two nuns had always treated Myeong-seong with respect. They bowed and knelt down in front of Myeong-seong, who spoke, "We became nuns because this is the most noble of all paths. I believe that all seunims, including myself, are divine."

The two students looked at Myeong-seong with curiosity. She continued, "Unmun has endured many difficulties. Six months passed without a Dharma-teacher. Our success or failure to build a bhikkhuni education system will determine the future of Korean bhikkhunis. We must make this a success. Nobody can do this except for us." There was a sense of urgency in her voice. The two students lowered their heads in agreement.

"I will start the lessons from tomorrow. Today, I will organize the classes. Once the classes are set up, everybody will be a student of Unmun and I will be the Dharma-teacher of Unmun. Do you understand?"

She was talking about unity. The nuns from Cheongnyong and Unmun had to join together and become one.

"Yes, I understand." They answered.

"Good. You are dismissed."

The students bowed again and left. There could never be any division between the two groups. The germination of even the tiniest seed of conflict could grow into something catastrophic. If internal struggling broke out, there would be no school, no teaching, no bhikkhuni education. Without Unmun College, there would be no future for the bhikkhunis. This was Myeong-seong's conviction, and the two students understood her point fully.

Myeong-seong was deep in her thoughts. In order to travel somewhere, one has to have a destination and the knowledge as to how to get there. There were more than eighty nuns gathered in Unmunsa Temple, mostly in their twenties. Sixty were from Unmun. The nuns of Unmun had already seen their teacher change three times. Afterwards, they had spent six months in the temple without any teacher. The nuns of Cheongnyong had followed Myeong-seong all the way to this mountain to further their education. They had a dream. They yearned for a quality education just like what was provided to bhikkhus.

Myeong-seong had to be their leader and guide. She believed that the two virtues she needed were fairness and honesty.

She would treat everyone fairly, never allowing herself to be dictated by emotions, and she would stay honest in all things. If Myeong-seong could remain true to these two values, the students would have faith in her. Above all, the captain of a ship needs the trust of the crew. If the crew does not believe that the captain is capable of taking them to their destination safely, then the ship will not sail. Myeong-seong knew this all too well, having been a leader among nuns when she lived in Seonamsa Temple.

There is a saying that it is easier to carry three baskets full of fleas than to lead three monks in a single direction. Fleas jump off in all directions, so keeping them in three baskets would be nearly impossible. The saying goes that leading three monks is even harder. They just will not follow you, being generally strong-headed and not appreciating being told what to do. Here were more than eighty nuns in their twenties; young and full of energy. The living conditions did not make things easier. The nuns had to live together in one building, with very little money.

On her first day of teaching, Myeong-seong asked her students. "Tell me how the previous classes were run."

"The Dharma-teacher would read three or four lines of a sutra each day and explain the meaning. The next day, we would recall and recite the lines and the teacher would check our work," the class leader replied.

"What if you could not remember the lines?"

"Then we would be punished by having to do work or by cleaning or prostrating hundreds of times to the Buddha."

"Your method of learning has been too focused on memorization. From now, we will base it on discussions."

The students were puzzled. They had never experienced discussion-centered learning. The traditional method of learning was for the teacher to explain the lesson and the students to receive it. There was little room for discussion or creativity. Perhaps this was because the texts themselves were written in ancient Chinese, which required extensive explanation by the teachers. Students who learned through this method would later teach using the same method. It became entrenched as a traditional method of learning. Myeong-seong was challenging that tradition. She was going to bring discussions into the lessons.

"Sutras are the teachings of the Buddha. They are like precious stones. However, everybody will have a different impression of the precious stone. A teacher will have one view, but that view cannot explain the full depth of the sutra's meaning. By incorporating discussion into our lessons, we will be sharing our views so that we can have a more comprehensive understanding of the Buddha's words."

The students realized that Myeong-seong was acknowledging the value of each student and their individual views.

Every class had a class leader. The leader would study in advance what was to be taught the next day. During the discussion time in the evening, the leader would explain what they understood to their classmates. Everybody would then engage in a discussion. This was simply to expose them to other views and help them to express their views. Students would say, "This is how I think." This statement held two meanings. One meaning was that students should not blindly follow a given view. On the other hand, the students would respect views that were held in common. Everybody had the right to say whatever they wanted to, but in the end, they were required to accept and follow the view that the majority had agreed upon. It was a kind of democracy in education.

The class leader's role was very important. Previously, only the teachers had taught other students. Now, class leaders had to share in the role of a teacher. This meant, of course, that they had to study very hard. However, since they would always have questions, they frequently visited the teacher's room. In this way, Myeong-seong was training the trainers. It was an exceptional strategy for building up an education system for the bhikkhunis.

Students were happy with the discussion-based method. Before this, all that had been required of them was for them to repeat and memorize what the teacher said like parrots. They were not allowed to do anything else. But now, they were free to speak their minds. This made the act of studying immensely more enjoyable. The whole school came to life, filled with new and hopeful energy. Since Myeong-seong was the only teacher, she had to teach all four classes. After teaching the four classes in the morning, they would have lunch. Then, Myeong-seong would again teach the students Japanese language and calligraphy.

This was all very tiring for Myeong-seong. She would be exhausted after teaching four classes in the morning and then again in the afternoon. Despite her weariness, her heart was filled with joy. Knowing that she was making her students happy brought her happiness in return.

Myeong-seong also organized a system of students tutoring other students. Some of the bhikkhunis who had lived in the temple since they were very young had received no formal education. Some had only graduated from elementary school. Since they had difficulty keeping up in the sutra lessons, those students who had graduated from high school or university were asked to tutor them. Within this process, both students, the learner and the tutor, had to put aside their egos. Slowly, the school at Unmunsa Temple began developing. It would be a school where everyone was successful, a school without dropouts.

It was not easy for eighty people to live together, especially when it came to feeding everyone. Located in a remote and mountainous area, the temple had few layperson members who could contribute financially. Food had to be produced self-sufficiently. The students grew their own vegetables. They picked wild edible herbs and dried them. They even planted rice. When it came to transplanting the rice seedlings, they all worked together in an organized manner. One group would carry the seedling beds, another would hold the string for aligning the rows, one would remove the seedlings from the beds and hand them out, and of course, the last group did the planting. There were not enough boots to go around at that time, so only the teacher would wear boots. Everyone else would roll up their pants, tying them with rubber bands, and go into the mud barefoot.

When this work became strenuous, they would sing songs. Someone would take the lead, and the others would sing along or join in for the chorus. On this day only, the nuns were given the freedom to sing whatever they wanted. They sang out loud at the top of their lungs. On this day, the teacher was generous and allowed them this freedom. For the nuns, the day of transplanting rice was like a festival.

Once they had finished transplanting rice, it was time to thresh the barley. This work created a lot of dust, and afterwards they would itch all over. This meant that being able to wash themselves off was very important. Here again, it was no easy task for eighty people to bathe all at once. They heated up water in a huge pot. The older nuns washed themselves first. Despite having worked the hardest, the younger nuns and students from the Novice Nun class often ran out of warm water when their turn came. Since barley threshing was done in the early summer, nuns were able to wash off in the stream if needed. The threshing of rice was truly unpleasant, since it happened in late autumn. After threshing rice, the nuns would remain itchy all over for days.

Just as important as producing food was securing firewood. They did not have any electricity or gas. Wood was their only source of fuel. Firewood was used to cook three times a day, and was also used to heat the rooms. Gathering and storing enough firewood was a crucial task. They would use straw left over from threshing rice and barley as kindling, and nuns would frequently go to the mountain to collect dry branches. However, they were not able to collect enough firewood on their own, and occasionally required the assistance of some men. In early autumn, Unmunsa Temple would pay men from the nearby village to collect firewood for them. The temple did not have to pay in cash, though. Since these people did not own forested property, they would collect firewood for the temple in exchange for being allowed to take as much firewood as they needed. It was an exchange that benefited both parties. When autumn came, people without wooded property would wait for the temple to ask them for help. Fortunately, Unmunsa Temple possessed a large swath of land in the mountains.

One spring day, a year after Myeong-seong had first arrived at Unmun, class leaders were having a discussion together. They were discussing what to plant where. They decided to do it the same as they had for the previous year. At that moment, an idea came to Myeong-seong.

"Why don't you try sowing the seeds in intervals? Rather than all at once, sow a portion of them every ten days three different times. That way we can eat fresh vegetables for a longer period of time."

The students wondered whether it would be okay to plant that way; each crop had an ideal time in which it should be planted. However, one student quickly replied.

"Yes, let's do that. If we sow them all at once, we have to harvest them all at the same time. Last year, it was a real pain trying to eat all the lettuce at once."

The group burst into laughter. Myeong-seong's idea turned out to be a good one, and the students ate fresh salads throughout the summer.

Summer passed and autumn came, and the mountains turned from green to red and yellow. Five or six student-nuns went down to the neighboring village to pick persimmons. It was a tradition among Koreans at the time to "steal" fruits from other houses. It was thought of almost like a game, particularly among children. This stealing game was a part of the culture. Watermelons, apples, pears, persimmons, peaches, potatoes, even chickens could become the targets. Some people even stole fermenting kimchi from people's houses. Sometimes, people would go out to participate in the stealing game at night, only to return home to discover that their own crops or animals had been stolen.

This activity was considered a game that everybody enjoyed. Those who took part felt no guilt, and caused no serious harm. They knew how to keep it a lighthearted game. The nuns, having grown up in the countryside, were all too familiar with this culture. Some of them went to the village to get some persimmons. They were young, energetic, and hungry. Ripe, red persimmons were just too much to resist. One group stood as lookout as the other group picked and collected the fruit. They returned to the temple with a bountiful harvest.

However, their luck did not last long. The next day, the owner of the tree came up the mountain. He had no intention to be polite toward the nuns. He started yelling at the abbess. The abbess attempted to placate him to no avail. Finally, Myeong-seong stepped in. She summoned the group of thieves and asked them what had happened. She then turned to the owner and made him an offer.

"I will apologize for what happened. Please forgive them. What do you say I buy the whole tree from you? Then, you can pick and bring the remaining fruits to us. I will pay you for that fruit plus the fruit taken by my students."

The owner of the tree accepted this offer. A while later, he actually returned to the temple bearing all the persimmons from his tree. Myeong-seong paid him for the fruit, and he went back home satisfied. Myeong-seong then called all the students together and distributed the persimmons equally among them. Then she called upon the nuns who had stolen the persimmons and spoke to them.

"I have only now realized that our temple does not have edible persimmon trees. I am asking you to please plant persimmon trees in the spring so that all of the students can eat as much as they want."

The nuns who had created this trouble to begin with were deeply touched. They fought to hold back their tears. They had been tormented by the scene of their respected teacher being humiliated by the tree owner, and were deeply moved that, instead of punishing them, their teacher had told them to plant trees. This was a wise way of resolving an issue. If Myeong-seong had scolded or punished the students, the outcome would have been quite different.

From then on at Unmunsa Temple, persimmons would ripen red in autumn and the nuns would pick and eat them. But not many would remember how this came to be.

In late autumn, everyone gathered to prepare kimchi. The nuns boiled and mashed squash and potatoes, mixing in pepper powder to make the paste. The temple had its own rules for making kimchi. First, make a lot of it; second, make it salty; third, use as little pepper powder as possible. The kimchi they made had to last through the winter, and considering their tight budget, this was a natural outcome. Every single ingredient was precious. Even the peppers they used were grown in their garden. Many of the student-nuns longed to eat kimchi that was properly seasoned with plenty of red-hot pepper powder.

Unmunsa Temple had a huge ginkgo tree, beneath which the nuns would often gather to work. Preparing kimchi is a communal affair. People would chat with each other, sing, and occasionally eat the salted cabbage with the seasoning. They would wrap the seasoning in a cabbage leaf and give it to a friend. Myeong-seong, who had appeared to be occupied with the work, suddenly spoke, "Please bring me the largest leaf."

The students seemed puzzled. Why did their teacher want a large leaf when she has such a small mouth? One student rose and brought a huge leaf to Myeong-seong. Myeong-seong added a few more leaves to this and took it to their cow. She placed the leaves in the cow's mouth. She watched the huge animal slowly chew the cabbage and returned to her seat.

"You can just throw the cabbage to the cow. Why did you feed it by hand?" a student asked.

All of a sudden, another student poked her and shouted, "Rice cake!" Everybody understood the situation and laughed. It was during the previous Thanksgiving Day that the nuns had been making rice cakes beneath the tree, just as they were now. Some were making the cakes, some were cooking them; it was a joyful atmosphere. Suddenly, Myeong-seong rose from her seat. She put down a few pieces of rice cake in front of the cow. She wanted to thank the cow for having worked so hard. However, the cow barely seemed to notice them. Rice cakes, apparently, had little appeal to the cow, and had to be thrown away. That is why this time, Myeong-seong hand-fed the cabbage to make sure that it did not go to waste. Such was the teacher's conduct that the students would learn about "gratitude."

There is another story related to cows. In the early days, the student-nuns did all the farming, both rice in the paddies and crops in the fields. There were no machines at all; it was three cows that did the heavy work. The cows were the nuns' best friends. The nuns would collect fodder, boil it in water and feed the animals. One day, a nun who was preparing the fodder-soup forgot about the fire. The fire started crawling up the chimney and into the wall. The building could have burned to the ground, but luckily, the fire was spotted early enough to be put out. The event did, however, leave everyone unnerved.

The rice had been harvested and threshed. The kimchi was prepared and ripening. The last thing to do before winter was to prepare fermented beans (*meju*). Meju is a block of mashed soybeans that ferment over the winter. For days, the nuns would boil the beans, shape them into a brick of meju, and hang them from the ceiling of the Pavilion of Eternity (*Manseru*). With that task completed, the only thing left to do was study. More than eighty nuns had diligently grown their own food since the beginning of spring until the end of fall. They could finally spend the winter engaged in as much studying as they wanted. They could not have felt more satisfied.

There were two more such instances regarding fire. At one time, the Pavilion of Five Hundred Arahans (*Obaeknahanjeon*), and another time the Pavilion of Profound Lectures (*Seolhyeo-ndang*) almost burned down. After the autumn harvest, the storage room is filled with jars of dried persimmons. They were kept there to be used only when important guests visited or for ceremonies. A few nuns, who were close friends with each other, came up with the idea of secretly eating some of these dried persimmons. All of the Buddha statues sat on a platform, and a space would form beneath the platform. Trainee monks and nuns would often sneak into this space to take catnaps to make up for their lack of sleep. It was the same in the Pavilion of Five Hundred Arahans. There was a space under the platform. The nuns made a mat out of rice straw and piled up dried persimmons. It was the perfect place for hiding something. These nuns would sneak in there with a candle and eat the persimmons. One day, the naughty nuns were doing their mischievous deeds when they heard some other nuns enter the Hall of the Cosmic Buddha for the evening service. They hurried out of the platform and ran to their rooms. They had to get their robes on to attend the service.

Another nun who was assigned to pray at the Pavilion of Five Hundred Arahans came up to the statues. She lit the candles and incense and started praying when she saw a bright light coming from the cracks beneath the statue. She opened the door and entered the platform. To her amazement, there were piles of dried persimmons sitting on rice straw, and the rice straw was about to catch fire from a neglected candle. She rushed to get water and put the fire out. This could have burned down the entire building.

A similar thing happened in the Pavilion of Profound Lectures. It was winter break, and the students had returned to their original temples. Myeong-seong went to the Pavilion of Profound Lectures to work on her book. She went to a room that was being used by Gye-ho Seunim, the abbess of Jingwansa Temple. She had her own room, in Piha Hall, but she wanted to avoid her room, as too many visitors would come and distract her from her work. As she did often, Myeong-seong would sip on tangerine tea while writing her book. She had a cold at the time, and the tangerine soothed her aching throat. A student came over to tell her that a visitor had arrived, so Myeong-seong went back to her room to greet her guest. When she returned, she found that the electric kettle she had been making tea with had turned red with heat, and the floor mat had caught on the fire and was starting to burn. She yelled for help, and a student rushed to unplug the kettle and put out the fire. Had she arrived just a moment later, the Pavilion of Profound Lectures would have been burnt to ashes.

After these three close calls in which the temple almost burned down, the students came to believe that the reason they had avoided disaster was because something that Myeong-seong had done. Ever since her arrival at Unmunsa Temple, Myeong-seong had worried about fire. All of the fuel used by the temple was provided by burning firewood. The temple was not small, and people were making fires all the time. Early in the morning on the first day of the New Year after her arrival, Myeong-seong had written the Chinese character for water, "水", four times in red ink and attached the writing upside-down on four different pillars in the four cardinal directions of the temple. A few days later, Il-jin Seunim returned from her temple. When she came to pay her respects to Myeong-seong, Il-jin spoke about a dream she had had.

"Seunim, I had a strange dream some days ago. All the buildings and rooms of Unmun were filled up with water and giving off steam. It made me want to come here to bathe. What could this dream mean?"

Myeong-seong told Il-jin how she had written and attached the Chinese character for water on the four directions of the temple. She told Il-jin to be exceptionally careful about fire. When some students heard about this from Il-jin, they raced around the temple trying to find the characters that Myeong-seong had posted. This is how the story became known throughout the temple.

One day, Myeong-seong was passing by the Main Buddha Hall when she noticed that the shoes that the students had taken off were strewn around in disarray. She went and organized the shoes into even rows. Eighty pairs of shoes were now lined up in a tidy manner. She had told her students that practitioners should keep their shoes, robes, blankets, books, desks, and everything else orderly. She had told them this many times but they were forgetful. Myeong-seong listened to the voices of students reading the sutras and went back to her room, a small space beside the office in the Main Buddha Hall.

Early the next morning, after the morning ceremony, the students went to the Main Buddha Hall to read the sutra. Their voices were loud and clear, resonating throughout the temple. Myeong-seong again looked at their shoes. They were just as disorganized as the day before. Just as in the previous evening, she picked up the shoes one by one to organize them. After finishing this, she went back to her domicile.

Finished with their sutra studies, the students came out of the classroom and were startled to find their shoes so well organized. "What happened?" they wondered aloud. The same thing had occurred the night before but it was too dark for them to fully notice it. There was no time, however, to ponder this mystery. The mornings were very busy, and they each had their roles to do in preparing breakfast.

At the end of the day, the nuns gathered in the room again to review what they had learned. Again, Myeong-seong organized their shoes. She listened to the nuns reciting the sutras and returned to her room. This repeated for three days. Then, during her Novice Nun class, she suddenly posed a question to her students.

"How do you feel if someone treats you carelessly?"

"I feel angry."

"Feeling angry means that you regard yourselves as worthy of being treated with respect, right?"

"Yes."

"Then why do treat the most precious things with carelessness?"

The students were puzzled. What was she talking about? Suddenly, one of the students blurted out, "Shoes!" Then, the students realized what their teacher was getting at.

"Humans are not the only things that are precious. Everything in this world has its role, so everything in existence is precious."

Myeong-seong wanted to teach her students that everything in existence was precious and deserving of respect. It didn't matter whether it was alive or inanimate, human or non-human. She taught her students to be as mindful as possible and to offer respect in whatever daily activity they were engaged in. Whether it was taking off their shoes, hanging their robes, putting away their blankets, setting up their desks, putting away clean dishes or stacking firewood, she wanted her students to be full of awareness. "Treat all things as if they were alive," she taught, and she persistently checked to see that everyone put this into practice.

When Myeong-seong inspected these tasks one by one, she found that most of the time her students were failing to follow her advice. Then she would teach them everything from scratch: how to take off their shoes, how to fold and hang their robes, etc. Everybody had different personalities and habits. It was not easy to organize them into a unified body. Eventually, Myeong-seong assigned a number to each of the students. Their shoes were to be placed according to the number; the same for their robes. The blankets were also numbered and put away. Now, things became more organized than ever. Some students complained that it was too strict, but Myeong-seong insisted on making this an ingrained habit.

Later on, the students would realize that all of this focus on daily chores was actually a practice of cultivation. Paying full respect to everyday things taught them what it was like to fully devote their mind. That was the devoted mind, no different from the mind devoted to Buddha. This mind had to be the same, whether it was directed towards Buddha, towards fellow practitioners, or towards inanimate objects. That was the Way.

And so passed Myeong-seong's first winter at Unmunsa Temple.

It was January 1st in the Western calendar. Though it was not yet the traditional Lunar New Year, the change in the calendar brought excitement to the students. The aroma of cooking oil filled the kitchen. At that time, there was no imported oil extracted from soybean or corn. All of their oil was traditional, mostly from perilla or sesame seeds. These plants had to be grown, the seeds harvested and then pressed by the nuns. Naturally, such oil was highly valued and used sparingly. On this fresh New Year's morning, the nuns had finished reviewing the sutras and were taking their small desks outside. One nun sat in front of her desk, organizing her belongings. The nun beside her picked up the other nun's desk, asking her, "Why aren't you cleaning up? It is time for breakfast."

"Why are you touching my desk?" The nun who was sitting suddenly stood up and snatched her desk away from the other nun. Instantly, they became the focus of attention in the room.

"You are just sitting here when you are supposed to be cleaning up."

The nun angrily responded, "Mind your own business."

Then she sat down and continued with what she had been doing. The two exchanged fierce words; the tension escalating each time. Soon they were yelling and fighting. Finally, the nun who had been sitting stood up and grabbed the other by the throat. At that moment, everybody jumped in and attacked the nun who had been acting violently.

Myeong-seong was waiting for the sound of the wooden gong (*moktak*) to signal that breakfast was ready, but when the sound didn't come, she came out and saw the commotion. As soon as the students noticed that their teacher was looking at them, they stopped what they were doing and went back to their chores to prepare for breakfast. Myeong-seong returned to her room, and did not come out. She neither ate nor drank for the entire day. The class leaders got together and stood in front of Myeong-seong's room, not knowing what else to do. From her room emanated utter silence occasionally dotted with the smell of incense.

The students decided to hold a general meeting to deal with the matter, where they decided that the aggressive nun should be expelled from Unmunsa Temple. That nun was known for her bad temper, and this was not the first incident. Seizing upon this opportunity, the nuns were eager to kick her out. The class leaders would tell Myeong-seong of their decision. One of the nuns opened her mouth in front of Myeong-seong's door.

"Teacher, it's us. Please let us in."

After a long stretch of silence, they heard a voice reply, "Come in." The class leaders went in and stood in front of Myeong-seong.

"We repent. Please forgive us." They bowed three times.

"Sit down."

"Please accept our repentance and forgive us."

"Tell me why you want to see me."

"We held a general meeting and decided to expel that nun. She has caused a lot of trouble with other people at other times as well. She is difficult to study with."

After hearing of the meeting and its conclusion, Myeong-seong thought for a long moment. Then she asked them, "What will become of her then?"

The class leaders just looked at each other, unable to answer. They had only thought about kicking her out for the convenience of the group overall, but hadn't contemplated what might happen to a nun who has been expelled.

"If she leaves this temple, she will have no chance to cultivate herself. Improving upon one's character is part of the process of cultivation. Let her stay and help her to study and cultivate herself." This seemed to be the conclusion reached by Myeong-seong after a day spent in contemplation.

"We will do as you say." The nuns gave another three bows and left the room.

After walking silently for a while, the leader of Flower Garment class spoke, "I now understand why our Teacher taught us to organize our shoes, put away the blankets, and the like. If you truly devote your whole mind to something, anything can be corrected. Let us convince our fellow nuns to let her stay. Let us all devote our minds to study and cultivation together with her. Then, I am sure she will change."

Anything can be corrected if one is wholeheartedly devoted to doing so. Being devoted to others is a way of correcting oneself. Only great devotion can bring about great change. Cultivation is about putting in effort, not seeking a comfortable environment. The nuns had learned a valuable lesson.

Chapter 06

O Buddha,
I have so
much to do

Spring was just around the corner, but cold winds were still blowing at Mount Hogeo. After the morning ceremony, Myeong-seong placed two envelopes into the mailbox for the postman to come and collect. Myeong-seong had written letters to Dr. Su-yeong Hwang and Dr. Chung-sik Jang, asking them to come to Unmunsa Temple to give special lectures on the subject of Buddhist art.

The majority of Korea's national cultural assets are Buddhist artifacts. 77 percent of national treasures and 86 percent of general cultural properties are Buddhist in origin. It was crucial that the monks and nuns residing in the temples filled with these treasures have an understanding of their cultural significance. Statues, stupas, bells, paintings, numerous Buddhist implements of worship, and even the temple itself were historical assets. Monks and nuns needed to know about them in order to take pride in being their caretakers. Myeong-seong understood this, which is why she frequently invited outside experts to teach her students about Buddhist art. This had become a formal part of the school's curriculum.

Apart from classes on art, Myeong-seong also organized foreign language classes. She herself would teach a Japanese conversation class and she invited an outside teacher to provide English lessons. She taught the Japanese conversation class herself because she was perfectly qualified to do so, having been educated during Japanese rule. Another reason for this, however, was so that the Temple could save money. Myeong-seong believed that Korea would soon be having more and more exchanges with foreign countries, and the nuns needed to be prepared for this future. Learning foreign languages also broadened the scope of information that the nuns could access. Foreign language knowledge was essential if one was to study the original Buddhist texts. Myeong-seong not only taught Japanese in person to her students, but also prepared cassette tapes and players for her students to supplement their studies. Cassette tapes were still a rare technology in those days. Myeong-seong also joined in the English class as a student. She was feeling the need to learn English more and more.

Having such programs may seem commonplace and unremarkable today, but this was happening in 1971 in a remote mountain temple in South Korea's North Gyeongsang Province. For a traditional nun to think of this, and furthermore, take action to make it a reality was completely groundbreaking. Traditional Buddhist schools were places where teachers would unilaterally deliver their knowledge to the students. Myeong-seong had introduced the concept of "discussion" into this culture. Now, she was bringing in outside experts to teach non-sutra subjects. She was even teaching foreign languages. In the past, such practices would have been completely unthought of. New winds of change were starting to blow in this remote mountain temple.

Professors Su-yeong Hwang and Chung-sik Jang accepted Myeong-seong's request. Mr. Wan-su Choi, director of the Gansong Art Museum, also agreed to provide lectures on Buddhist art. They would spend a whole day traveling all the way to Unmunsa Temple and put their hearts into their lectures. The students of Unmun were lucky to have such esteemed professionals come all the way to the mountains to teach them.

Myeong-seong was eager to implement these changes because of her conviction that nuns nowadays had to learn many other things besides the traditional inner teachings. These "outer" teachings included many topics and subjects that laypeople would normally study in school. Ordinary people were receiving more education than before and if monks and nuns did not keep up, they would fall behind the times. This is why, ever since she had been at Cheongnyongsa Temple, Myeong-seong had always tried to invite outside experts. She firmly believed that the education of monks and nuns had to change along with the times.

It was springtime, and germinating plants were pushing their heads up through the still frozen ground. The students decided to plant flowers in the garden bed. The temple was so big that planting flowers required careful planning. Students who were studying horticulture gathered to discuss which flowers to plant where. Then they brought the flower seedlings and started to plant. Students brought a long piece of string and pulled on both ends to make a straight line. The flowers were to be planted in perfect straight rows, as if to reflect their very disciplined lifestyle.

At this moment, Myeong-seong appeared. Her face was not happy. "Can't you see that the flowers are upset?" she asked the students. Her stern expression made it clear that she was not joking. The students didn't know how to answer.

"Could you live in straight lines like this? If you couldn't, why would you force it on the flowers?"

Now the students understood her point. They replied, "We thought you would like to see them planted in straight rows. You normally like everything neat, tidy, and straight."

"I never said that I like to see flowers in a straight line. They look like they are being lined up for punishment. The outer boundary should be straight, but the flowers inside should be planted more naturally."

As soon as she finished, a student was already pulling out the flower, "I understand. We will plant it again."

"Please remember that flowers feel the same way as you do." Then she made her way towards the bell tower. She was going to see how the students were doing in the vegetable garden.

Back in the flower garden, the students pulled out all the seedlings that had been planted in straight rows and started planting them in an irregular pattern. When they had almost finished, Myeong-seong came back. The students expected that she would be pleased. Yet, again, her face was not happy.

"How can you plant this way? The front row should not be irregular. Plant it in a straight line. Order and freedom have to co-exist."

As she turned away, a few students began complaining, "Why should we be told how to plant flowers? We are not children."

"It is impossible to please her."

"The flowers will bloom either way, why do we have to keep redoing it?"

Suddenly, one of the students exclaimed loudly, "The outside should be orderly and the inside free. Do you not see that she is trying to teach us?"

The students nodded. The outer boundary must be strict and formally arranged. But the things that exist within should be free, creative, and individually unique. That is the harmony between an individual and society, between one and all. Students learned of Myeong-seong's philosophy through these kinds of life experiences.

After a lecture one day, Myeong-seong was walking past the Hall of the Cosmic Buddha towards the Pavilion of Eternity.

She was about to go on a walking meditation. Inside the Pavilion of Eternity was a broken bell; nobody knew when or how it had cracked. It had been sitting there for a long time. Two students were talking behind the Pavilion of Eternity and were surprised to see their teacher approaching them.

"Why are you so surprised? Are you sharing some secret?" Myeong-seong looked at them as she asked.

"We were just chatting about which temple we will go to to pray during the school break," one of the students answered with a smile.

"It's not good to leave a broken bell neglected like this. Something should be done," Myeong-seong murmured, as if speaking to herself.

"Yes, teacher. We should fix it. My temple also repaired its old bell."

Myeong-seong spoke in a soft voice, "It will cost a lot of money to repair this bell. You know that our temple does not have money."

"We can raise money through donations. That is how we fund big projects."

After that, the students all started talking about funding the project. Soon they agreed to write a letter requesting funds so that they could take the letter back to their respective temples to collect money. The class leaders came to Myeong-seong and sought approval. Now, the broken bell was on its way to being reborn.

The fundraising proceeded smoothly. When people heard that the Buddhist College in Unmunsa Temple was trying to repair its bell, they donated eagerly. The temples to which the students belonged were particularly passionate about helping with the project. Surprisingly, they were able to raise all the money needed by the beginning of the school semester. Myeong-seong found a bell master who was able to recast the bell. This was the first project carried out by the Buddhist College of Unmun. It was somewhat symbolic that their first project was an object that could make great sounds that traveled far and wide.

When spring break had finished, more than one hundred students came to Unmunsa Temple, many of them new. After Myeong-seong had become Head Instructor, the school developed quickly. The number of students was growing. The need for and desire by nuns to be educated increased along with the advances in Korean society. Now, with more than one hundred people in residence, the most urgent problem facing Unmunsa Temple was space.

The Buddhist College was different from secular schools in that the students ate, slept, lived, and studied together. At Unmun, the Novice Nun class, Four Collections class, Four Sutras class, and Flower Garland Sutra class were all held in the Main Buddha Hall (*Geumdang*). The space was already packed to capacity. The lack of space had been uncomfortable enough before, but the influx of new students meant that building new classrooms became a priority. This project would not be finished within a single year, as the number of students would increase with each coming year. The newcomers would soon outnumber those who were graduating and leaving. Expanding the facilities became an urgent and inevitable task. When summer break came, Myeong-seong gathered all the nuns involved in management and went on a pilgrimage of begging for alms.

Since Buddhist practitioners are supposed to have no possessions, they would beg for their food. Monks and nuns would offer the teachings of the Buddha to people in exchange. Followers would provide the food for the body; seunims provided the food for the soul. This was something of a mutually beneficial relationship. However, Myeong-seong and her team had embarked on a trip to collect money to build a new classroom. Begging for money, much less actually receiving the money, was not an easy thing.

Myeong-seong thought hard how to begin and decided upon Pyochungsa Temple in Milyang City as the starting point. The team traveled there in a van. The temple had purchased the van last autumn because of the great amount of food and other necessities that they had to buy for the many nuns. Most of these goods had to be purchased in Daegu City and brought from there, which is why they bought the van despite their tight budget. They hired a man named Mr. Yoon to be their driver. He was a villager who lived down the mountain and helped the temple with any work that needed a man's labor.

On the ride from Cheongdo to Milyang, Myeong-seong silently rolled her prayer beads in her hand. She was reciting Gwanseeum Bosal and Munsu Bosal (*Manjushri*) with her eyes closed. It was an everyday practice for her. However, she felt different today. The other nuns turned their gaze out the window, as it was painful to watch their beloved Master pray with desperation. Myeong-seong's anxiety was almost palpable. It was her mission to build up a solid foundation of "Education for Bhikkhunis", which went beyond merely teaching the sutras but included creating the necessary infrastructure. They now had to travel around collecting donations. Nobody had invited them, but still they had to go.

When the nuns arrived at Pyochungsa Temple, they first went to the Main Hall and offered prostrations to the Buddha. Then they bowed 108 times to the Thousand-Hands Thousand-Eyes Bodhisattva of Loving Kindness and Compassion.

'Please, Bodhisattva of Loving Kindness and Compassion, help us to build our school. Help the students to study in a better environment.'

After the prostration, they went to see the abbot. They explained their need to build more classrooms and presented their Book of Recommending Good Deeds. The abbot did not speak much. He took the book, wrote down one thousand dollars, and signed it. One thousand dollars in 1972 was a significant amount of money! Myeong-seong was delighted. She had a premonition that blessings were coming from Gwanseeum

Bosal.

Pyochungsa Temple was the starting point. They travelled around South Gyeongsang Province and Busan City to beg for alms. In the morning they went to a monk monastery and in the afternoon to a nun monastery. They would visit one temple in the morning, have lunch, then go to another one in the afternoon. Then it would be time to have dinner and sleep. That is why they visited the nuns' temple at a later time.

The team did their best to cope with the scorching heat of summer. Even though nuns were friendly, it was still not their temple. Just washing their clothes while soaked in sweat was a difficult task. However, nothing could discourage them, much less slow them down. They travelled by car and on foot, meeting with nuns and monks, continuously trying to persuade them to help out with their goals. After many days, they had completed their mission. They had raised enough funds to build a new school, which would be named the Gathering Stars Pavilion (*Hoeseongdang*).

Myeong-seong searched for a skilled Master in traditional Korean carpentry. She explained the structure of the building that she desired. She met with other workers to get them to prepare the right materials, such as lumber and roof tiles. After a while, the Master brought a floor plan for the school. It was a building with seven classrooms. Now, the building could begin.

For Myeong-seong, the day would start with teaching in

four different classes, then calligraphy and Japanese in the afternoon. Her schedule was interrupted by her frequent visits to the building site to make sure that things were going smoothly. She was going to supervise it so that the workers would create the best building possible. Her goals were to build a beautiful, sturdy, and practical school. Those were her three principles. She would routinely visit the workers and check that those principles were being upheld. She poured all of her energy into this project. It was a precious and divine undertaking. She could not allow for any mishaps, considering how important it was to respect the goodwill of the donors.

After many months, the building was finally constructed. It was time to name it. A contest was held to come up with the best name, and the nuns agreed on the name Gathering Clouds Pavilion. However, after contemplating that name, deep in thought, Myeong-seong changed it to Gathering Stars Pavilion.

"Stars shine bright in the night sky. Each of you have to go out in the world and become like a star." The students kept her words in their hearts; they would become a mirror in which they would always reflect themselves.

Just as the construction was completed, Myeong-seong's body started to send distress signals. Her back and her legs hurt. It was difficult for her to walk and even sit. The pain got worse and worse. She went to the hospital and was given medication. She took pills three times a day and got injections frequently.

However, she saw little improvement. All the while, she still had to continue teaching her four morning lectures all on her own and do other tasks in the afternoon.

When the pain was extreme, she could not even sit. Sometimes she lied down in front of the students in order to keep teaching. She did not want to interrupt the lesson. The pain got worse. Without some fundamental solution, it would be impossible to continue teaching. Another crisis had befallen Unmun. Myeong-seong and the students came together to discuss a solution. They agreed to pray to the Medicine Buddha (*Yaksayeorae*). Myeong-seong responded, "Let me go to Seoul to pray to the Medicine Buddha in Seunggasa Temple."

The students helped her with her trip. Two assistants would accompany her. As she was leaving, she reminded the students, "Keep studying. Be diligent without me. Please listen to the class leaders."

She boarded the van. As the car rolled out of sight, many students were crying. They knew why she was sick. They knew why she had worked herself into that condition. From that day on, whenever any student prayed in the Buddha Hall, she would earnestly wish for her teacher's recovery. "Please help our teacher heal so that she can return to us."

Myeong-seong had to lie down in the car as she travelled to Seoul. She could not even sit up straight. But that didn't stop her from praying. She rolled the beads in her hand and kept her focus. Reciting Gwanseeum Bosal, the Bodhisattva of Compassion, was a part of her life; she had done it since childhood. She could not even remember since when, but it had become her daily routine to recite the name Gwanseeum Bosal 1,080 times a day. However, the intention of her prayers had not always been the same. When she was little, she mainly had prayed to Gwanseeum Bosal to ask the Bosal to provide her with what she lacked. Now, she prayed that she could spread the compassion of Gwanseeum Bosal. Great compassion is the fundamental virtue of a disciple of the Buddha.

There was a reason why Myeong-seong had developed a special affection toward Gwanseeum Bosal. When she was in Gangneung Girl's High School, she had heard about the story of Gwanseeum Bosal's past life. A layperson had asked a monk why Gwanseeum Bosal had one thousand hands and eyes. The monk replied,

"Eons and eons ago, during the time of the Thousand Light King Peaceful Residing Buddha, Avalokiteshvara (*Gwanseeum Bosal*) was a Bodhisattva of Initial Ground. For a bodhisattva to become fully enlightened, he or she had to advance through fifty-two stages. The Bodhisattva of Initial Ground is one who has reached the forty-first stage.

The Thousand Light King Buddha was preaching the Mantra of No Obstruction and Great Compassion as he spoke to Avalokiteshvara. 'Good man, remember and carry this Mantra by heart so that you can help all suffering beings when the time of evil comes in the future.'

Avalokiteshvara received the Mantra with utmost dedication. As soon as he did that, he leapt from Initial Ground to Eighth Ground. His mind was filled with delight. Avalokiteshvara took a vow. 'I vow to benefit and comfort all beings in current and future worlds. May I have a thousand eyes and hands to look after them.' That moment, his body transformed to have one thousand hands and eyes of compassion.

The number one thousand actually signifies infinity, or the number of perfection. This means that Avalokiteshvara is perfect in his actions to save all beings. He lacks nothing. His power is limitless."

Listening to the monk's explanation, the person asked again, "Was the Avalokiteshvara at the forty-first stage from his birth?"

The monk replied,

"If you read Jataka Tales, you will see numerous stories of Shakyamuni Buddha's past lives. In Avalokiteshvara's Cause of Birth Sutra (*Gwaneum Bonyeonkyeong*) as well, there are many stories of Avalokiteshvara's past lives. The reason why these sutras record the past lives of the Buddhas is because the Buddha himself attained Buddhahood only after completing vow after vow through countless reincarnations. Here is a story of Avalokiteshvara from when he was little.

Once upon a time in southern India, there lived a couple.

Jangna was an elder and Manasara was his wife. They had two daughters called Jori and Sokri. Jori was seven and Sokri was five years old when their mother suddenly passed away. Unable to raise his daughters on his own, their father remarried. His new wife, however, was very evil, and would abuse the daughters whenever their father wasn't around.

Their father had no idea that his wife was such a person. He went on long trips to do business in a neighbouring country, believing that his daughters were in good hands with their new mother. However, as soon as the husband left, the wife took the two girls and abandoned them on an uninhabited island where they would die from hunger, thirst, and fear. When they were about to die, Jori tightly held her little sister's hand and spoke, 'In this world, there are many people who are abandoned just like us. There are those who are hungry, thirsty, fearful, and lonely. Let us attain great powers in our next life so that we can save all of them.'

After making this vow, Jori died. Each time they were re-born, the sisters continued to cultivate themselves. They grew their powers as they dedicated themselves to their vows. After becoming goddesses who protect the beings of the three worlds, Jori finally became Gwanseeum Bosal and Sokri became Daeseji Bosal (*Mahāsthāmaprāpta bodhisattva*). Gwanseeum Bosal symbolizes compassion, and Daeseji Bosal wisdom. The two sit beside Amita Buddha of the Pure Land. Gwanseeum Bosal is on the left of Amita Buddha, and Daeseji is on the right."

Myeong-seong was reminiscing about her affinity with Gwanseeum Bosal when she also remembered her connection to Munsu Bosal (*Manjushri*). Ever since arriving at Unmun, Myeong-seong had recited Munsu Bosal 1,080 times daily. Being the Head Instructor, she believed that she needed the wisdom of Munsu Bosal. That is why she always prayed to him, so that she may gain the power to use wisdom freely. Wisdom was definitely one of the most important virtues that a disciple of Buddha and a teacher of students could have.

Munsu also reminded Myeong-seong of a story from her youth. One day, when she was in middle school in Pyeongchang City, she was coming home from Sangwonsa Temple. She met a monk who was headed to the city, so the two walked together. The monk was speaking casually with the girl when he suddenly stopped in front of a site, known as *Gwandae Geoli* (Crown and Belt Hanger), and exclaimed loudly.

"Here is where Munsu Bosal appeared in the form of a child. Put all of your heart into your prayers to Munsu Bosal. You might be blessed to see him one day."

This is how the story goes. King Sejo was the second son of King Sejong. He was the seventh king of the Joseon Kingdom. His nephew Danjong had originally become the king. Being an ambitious man, Sejo dethroned Danjong, sent him into exile to Yeongwol, and later killed him by giving him poison. He also killed or demoted many officials who had been loyal to Danjong. The most well-known of these were the "Six Dead Loyal Officials." Sejo became king through much heavy bloodshed. After becoming the king, he started to suffer from a terrible skin disease. Eczema spread and pus would flow out of his body. He took all kinds of medicine, but still saw no signs of improvement. Sejo came to believe that he was being punished for his wrong deeds. He started to visit the prominent Buddhist temples around the country to pray to Buddha for repentance. After leaving Mount Geumgang, Sejo arrived at Sangwonsa Temple in Mount Odae. His whole body was so itchy that he could not bear it. He ordered his attendants to go away so that he could take a bath in the creek. He took off his crown and belt, hanging them on a tree and entered the water.

The water was cool, but he could not reach his back where it was really itchy. Then he spied a boy-monk walking by in the forest. He called on the boy and asked him to rub his back for him. The boy-monk rubbed the king's back with sincerity. After a while, the boy said that he was finished. Without turning around, King Sejo said, "Do not tell anyone that you have rubbed the back of a king."

The boy-monk laughed and replied, "Do not tell anyone that the Bodhisattva of Wisdom (*Munsu Bosal*) rubbed your back."

The king was so surprised that he turned around immediately, however, the boy was nowhere to be seen. After that mysterious encounter, he was healed of the skin disease.

The king later ordered a statue be made of the exact shape of the Munsu Bosal whom he had met. That Munsu is sitting in Sangwonsa Temple. The site is called Crown and Belt Hanger because that is where the king had hung his items.

When the monk finished telling Im-ho (Myeong-seong) the story, he added, "There are fifty thousand Munsu Bosal boys in this mountain. I hope you meet one too."

Im-ho remembered the statue of the Munsu boy in Sangwonsa Temple. She felt as if she would meet Munsu one day. She asked the monk, "Have you met one?" But by then, the monk had already continued on his way.

As she lay on her side in the car, Myeong-seong thought about the stories of the Bodhisattvas of Compassion and Wisdom. Then she started to pray to the Medicine Buddha. Right now, her health was the most pressing issue. Without her health, she would not be able to do anything. She desperately prayed to the Medicine Buddha.

"*Namu bagabaje bisalsaruro byeokyuriballa bagallasaya dataadaya arahaje sammyaksambuddaya eksyata om bisalseo bisalseo bisalsa sammolaje sabaha.*"

She kept reciting the mantra until she had arrived in Seoul. Myeong-seong had decided to go to pray to the Medicine Buddha of Seunggasa Temple because of a story she had heard from another monk, years ago. The Medicine Buddha had vowed to save all sick beings. Many sick people who had prayed in this temple had been healed. There was an old lady who was cured of a chronic illness. Grateful, she donated money to the temple so they could renovate the building. That is how Myeong-seong learned that you should pray to the Medicine Buddha when you are sick. Now that she was poor of health, she wanted dearly to pray to this Buddha.

Su-tae Seunim lived in the 8th century, during the reign of King Gyeongdeok of the Shilla Dynasty. He dedicated himself to practicing self-cultivation in many great mountains so that he could gain powers to help people far and wide. Despite his years of practice, he hadn't gained anything. Twenty years passed, then thirty. Disappointed, Su-tae returned to his home village at the bottom of Samgak Mountain. He intended to spend his remaining days there. It had been forty years since he had become a monk. When he arrived at his home, he found that his nephew was taking care of the house. It was his home, but neither his parents nor siblings lived there anymore. Becoming emotional, Su-tae opened his mouth.

"I am a monk passing by. Can I sleep in your house for one night? It is dark outside."

His nephew didn't seem to recognize him. He said, "Of course, welcome. My uncle is also a monk."

After eating dinner, Su-tae went to sleep. In his dream, a strange monk with pronounced cheekbones and wearing a bandana appeared in front of him. The monk kept motioning for Su-tae to follow him when Su-tae suddenly woke up. He thought about how strange the dream was. He tried to analyze its meaning but could not figure it out. He stayed awake throughout the rest of the night. In the morning, he asked his nephew whether there were any temples nearby.

"There is one in the mountain across from our house," he answered.

As soon as Su-tae finished his breakfast and thanked his nephew for the hospitality, he set off for the temple. He found it without much difficulty, and immediately offered three bows to Buddha. As he came out of the shrine, he spotted an old monk threshing sesame seeds. Su-tae bowed politely and asked him about the strange monk who he had seen in his dream. The old monk replied without hesitation, "If he was wearing a bandana and had huge cheekbones, that must be Seungga Seunim."

"Who is he? And in which temple does he reside?"

"He is in Jangan."

"Jangan? As in China?"

"Yes. He is staying in Cheonboksa Temple in Jangan City. He is originally said to have come from India. He wanted to help people far and wide so he came to China. He has supernatural powers that grant people's wishes, as if he was holding a magical pearl in his hand."

Su-tae felt like he had been struck by lightning. Helping people far and wide! Was that not his own dream that he had been seeking for decades? That was the vow that he had made. "Please tell me more. How did venerable Seungga help people?"

"Just as I said. He seems to hold a magical pearl, a cintamani, in his hand. He can perform miracles. Once, there was a major drought and fire was spreading across the mountains. Everything, including crops, were burnt. People were starving and unrest was mounting. Sensing imminent danger, the emperor went to Cheonboksa Temple to see Seungga. The emperor knelt down in front of Seungga, repenting for his lack of virtue and begging for rain to come. Seungga took a bottle of water and sprinkled water towards the sky. All of a sudden, it began pouring rain, bringing relief across the nation. Another time, a strange disease was spreading throughout the country. Dead bodies were scattered everywhere like autumn leaves. Seungga again poured water from his bottle. Then, as if being washed away by water, the disease disappeared. Now the Chinese people worship him as a Living Buddha."

Su-tae was completely captivated by the story. He asked, "The water bottle that Seungga holds, is that the nectar of immortality (*amrita*)?"

"I cannot say. It could be, since so many regard him as the Living Buddha. He wears the bandana on his head during the day. When he is alone in his room at night, he takes it off. Then, from the crown of his head, which was indented, a mysterious aroma would rise to fill up the room."

"For sure, he sounds like a Living Buddha to me. Why do you think Seungga called to me? In my dream, it was him who waved his hand for me to follow him."

"I have no idea." The old monk resumed threshing the sesame. Su-tae bowed deeply in appreciation and turned away.

As Su-tae was coming out of the temple, a blue bird flew past him. After watching the bird absent-mindedly, Su-tae thought perhaps the bird wanted him to follow it. So he did, chasing after the bird. He followed it up the mountain. When he grew tired, he sat on a rock to rest. As he did this, the bird would stay perched on a branch as if to wait for him. Su-tae was certain that the bird was guiding him somewhere. After a while, the bird flew over to a large rock and sat there. Feeling something, the monk searched around the rock and discovered a small cave underneath. He bent down and entered it. To his surprise, there was clean, pure water flowing from the rock.

Su-tae put down his sack, took out his dipper, and drank the water. Then he heard a voice, "That water will save many people's lives."

Su-tae nearly jumped in surprise. He turned around to see the same monk he had seen in his dream. The monk was sitting near the wall.

"Ah! You are the venerable Seungga!" When Su-tae tried to head towards him, Seungga suddenly vanished. A mysterious aroma filled the cave, as if to offer proof that Seungga had been there.

'I should carve a sitting statue of Seungga right here. I shall make one that looks exactly like how he was sitting.' Su-tae Seunim made a sitting statue of Seungga, exactly as he had seen him in the cave. He built a temple there and named it Seunggasa Temple. People later called the statue the "Medicine Buddha of Seungga Cave." The mountain peak where it was became known as "Seungga Peak."

Just as Seungga had predicted, the water from the cave saved many lives over a thousand years, through the different kingdoms of Silla, Goryeo, and Joseon. Queen Soheon, the wife of King Sejong, was also brought back from certain death after drinking this water.

Situated on top of Mount Seungga, the path leading to Seunggasa Temple was very steep. It was a tough journey, even for able-bodied men. You can imagine how difficult it was for Myeong-seong to reach there with her weakened body. Her back and legs were in such pain that she had taught classes lying down. With the help of her assistant nun, Mr. Yoon, and other passing hikers, she finally made it to Seunggasa Temple. She then began three days of prayer.

She knelt down in front of the statue of the Medicine Buddha, and spoke of her resolve. "O Medicine Buddha, I have so much to do. I just cannot work with this pain in my body. You can use my body to do the work of Buddha, but please take away the pain."

She prayed with all her heart. On the final night of her three-day prayer, she had a dream. She was about to give a Dharma talk when the Medicine Buddha, donning his bandana, appeared. "Teach once you have a bigger audience."

It was a strange dream. Nevertheless, she finished praying and went back down the mountain. She had to be supported on both sides when she went up, but she was able to walk by herself on her way down. After coming down, she went straight to Mandeoksa Temple. It was the forty-ninth day of the funeral ceremony for the elder monk Bo-hyeon. The abbot of Mandeoksa Temple greeted her and handed her a tape recorder. The abbot asked Myeong-seong to record the five sutras. These were the Flower Garland Sutra, Lotus Sutra, Complete Enlightenment Sutra, Avalokiteshvara Sutra, and the Diamond Sutra. While she was speaking, suddenly, the thought of desks went through her head. After she finished the recording, she murmured to herself, "It would be so nice if we could have desks in Gathering Stars Pavilion. Is there no one who could give me that?"

Coincidentally, one of the students from Unmun was also at Mandeok. She overheard her teacher saying this, and went to her Master in Mandeok to convey what Myeong-seong had said. The Master was happy to fulfil Myeong-seong's wish. That is how Gathering Stars Pavilion became furnished with desks for all the students. In addition to restoring her health, the Medicine Buddha had thrown some desks into the deal.

As autumn arrived back at Unmun, the students had more communal labour to do. The monsoon rains had just passed and the weeds were as tall as people. The vegetable fields needed working hands, but the students were getting tired. They would seek any opportunity to avoid work and sneak out without their teacher knowing.

One day, the students from the senior class had visited the neighboring village where they secretly bought two bags of eggs. They were young and active, and it was difficult for them to get by only on vegetables. The temptation of boiled eggs was too much to resist. Five students escaped to the mountain with the eggs. They had a secret hiding spot where they enjoyed getting a break from all the rules. There, they would cook pancakes and eat steamed corn and potatoes. This added an element of fun to their otherwise mundane monastic life.

"You go make the fire. I will get some water," said one of the nuns to her friend as she took down her pot from the tree.

"Sure. I am so excited just imagining eating these white potatoes."

The students merrily prepared the cooking. Since nuns were supposed be vegetarians, they referred to the eggs as "white potatoes." They munched down the white potatoes, enjoying themselves thoroughly. After cleaning everything up so that nobody would notice what had happened, they headed back to the temple. They knew that their friends were working in the vegetable field. They had to sneak back and join them without being noticed. However, luck was not on their side. Myeong-seong was out working alongside her students. As she rose to stretch her back, she spotted the five students coming down from the mountain.

"Why are those students walking like scared cats?" Myeong-seong said. Everybody's eyes landed on the rule-breakers.

"Humans are not cats. You should straighten your back when you walk," Myeong-seong added. Then she went straight back to working. After the work was finished, Myeong-seong returned to her room beside the office. The students who had eaten the white potatoes followed her to beg for forgiveness.

Myeong-seong was staring up at the swallows in the ceiling rafters. She talked to them, "Why do you birds not listen to me? You are just like my students."

The birds were pooping everywhere in Myeong-seong's room. She had laid out a newspaper underneath their nest for them to poop on but they didn't heed her wishes. A pair of swallows had returned to the temple last spring and selected Myeong-seong's ceiling rafters as their home. They laid eggs in their nest from which hatched five babies. The baby swallows grew bigger every day, until one day they began to fly around. That is when they started to scatter droppings all over the room. Myeong-seong had put out newspaper for them but they couldn't be bothered with using it.

Witnessing this scene, one of the students giggled, unable to contain her laughter. That was when Myeong-seong noticed that the students were present. Another student quickly volunteered to clean up the droppings. She took off her towel from around her neck and wiped the floor clean. Then, the nuns stood together in front of Myeong-seong.

"We want to repent for skipping the communal labour. Please forgive us." They bowed three times and knelt down before her.

"You are not swallows, are you?" asked Myeong-seong.

"No, we are not."

"If you understand then, you are dismissed."

"Yes, teacher." The students bowed three times again and left the room. They were surprised to have avoided any punishment or scolding. They looked at each other. "Are we not the same as the swallows?"

"Did the sutra not say that every single thing has a Buddha nature? In that case, we are the same."

"Those pooping swallows should come join our class. Haha!"

Myeong-seong had come to the Buddhist college of Unmun in 1970. She was of the firm conviction that if a teacher was to teach, the teacher had to be well-educated first. Conditions were extremely difficult, but she continued her pursuit of knowledge and completed her doctoral program at Dongguk University in 1974. Even after coming to run the school at Unmun, she did not give up on her own studies. It was only in 1998, however, twenty-four years later, that she finally received her PhD degree with her thesis on the Three Transformational Consciousnesses. This demonstrates perfectly how deeply dedicated she was to teaching and to her pupils throughout her long life.

Four years after Myeong-seong had arrived at Unmun, its Buddhist College was becoming more firmly established. Myeong-seong had built the school up from scratch, teaching the entire curriculum all by herself and developing the whole system. In the process, she had sacrificed her health. Her mind was also exhausted. After completing her doctoral program, she traveled to Southeast Asia for rest and refreshment.

The Thai Royal Temple of Wat Benchamabophit had sent an invitation to Gwang-u and Myeong-seong Seunims. The Royal Temple had invited them because, the year before, the abbot of that temple had met them during his visit to Korea. For Myeong-seong, the timing of this trip could not have been better. She would have a chance to enjoy a very much deserved rest and also see for herself the Buddhism of Southeast Asia, which is thought to have preserved its early form.

1975, the year that Gwang-u and Myeong-seong left for Southeast Asia, was a memorable year for Korean Buddhists for two reasons. The first reason was that the Buddha's birthday had been designated as a national holiday. The second was that the Commission for Photo-printing the Goryeo Tripitaka had been established within Dongguk University in order to scan the eighty thousand woodblocks. This project later continued onto the translation of the Tripitaka, in which Myeong-seong also participated. The part she was responsible for was Abhidharma-nyāyānusāra.

The designation of the Buddha's birthday as a national holiday owed much to the work of the executive chief of the Korean Buddhist Jogye Order at that time, Cheong-dam Seunim, who was supported by the will of the masses. However, Korean Buddhists should not forget the very important contributions made by lawyer Taeyeong Yong.

Chapter 07

A Dharma Lantern that does not go out

Invited by the Royal Wat Benchamabophit Temple, Gwang-u and Myeong-seong went on a tour of Southeast Asia. The purpose of their trip was to study ancient Buddhism. In 1975, South Koreans were not permitted to travel abroad freely. The trip that the two nuns were taking was something extraordinary. It was probably the first ever overseas trip taken by Buddhist nuns. They were excited to arrive in Thailand, a Buddhist country. They were curious about the new culture. Their host, along with a representative from the Korean embassy, came to the airport to greet them. From that day on, the two stayed in the Royal Temple while visiting numerous other famous places. The temples in Thailand were majestic and colourful. The most incredible thing, however, was that despite being a Buddhist nation, there were no bhikkhunis in Thailand. There were female practitioners, known as *dasa sil matas* (*maechi*), but they were not equal to the male monks. They were neither officially ordained nor received formal precepts. Gwang-u and Myeong-seong were quite disappointed by this fact.

After their tour of Thailand, they traveled to Indonesia and Singapore. Then they continued on to Europe to visit Germany, the United Kingdom, France, Switzerland, and Italy. After that, they went to the US, spending three months touring around the whole country. In total, the trip took about half a year. In each country they visited, staff from the Korean embassy greeted them and took care of them. They were even occasionally attended to by ambassadors. In each country, they were warmly welcomed by Korean immigrants and fellow Buddhists. In Asia, the main sites of attraction were the Buddhist temples, whereas in Europe, they were the cathedrals. The cathedrals they saw were magnificent and beautiful. The outer form of these places of worship may have been different, but the human will that was embodied within them seemed somehow similar.

When Myeong-seong was about to return to Korea, she sent letters to her students in Unmun and all the other related agencies. She wrote that after coming back to Korea, she would not be returning to the Buddhist College, as she intended to participate in a Seon meditation retreat or engage in prayer for a certain period of time. Myeong-seong wanted to have some time of her own. She wanted to dedicate herself to her cultivation. That was her wish.

On their way back, Myeong-seong would chat with Gwang-u about what they had seen and experienced during their trip. The issue of greatest interest and disappointment to them was that there were no bhikkhuni orders in Southeast

Asia, where Buddhism was the national religion.

In the earliest days of Buddhism, the sangha consisted only of bhikkhus. When Gautama Buddha visited his hometown of Kapilavastu, after his enlightenment, his aunt Mahapajapati came to him after hearing of his teachings. She asked him to accept her as his disciple. She had been the one who raised him after his mother Maya had passed away only seven days after his birth. Gautama Buddha is said to have refused her at first, but Mahapajapati begged him three times, after which he finally relented. When she became a nun, she was joined by five hundred women from the Shakya clan. This was the beginning of the sangha becoming split into monks and nuns.

The nuns were diligent in their cultivation practice. It is recorded in the Ekottaragama-sutra that ninety-three nuns became arahats during the time of Buddha. The same sutra notes that fifty bhikkhunis were each so exceptional in various abilities such as asceticism, wisdom, clairvoyance, and precepts that the Buddha praised them as follows.

"My first bhikkhuni disciple, Mahapajapati, has cultivated herself for a long time and is respected by the king. There is Khema, the foremost scholar on Great Wisdom; Uppalavanna, foremost in realization; Gautami, foremost in holiness; Sakula, foremost in clairvoyance; Sama, foremost in Samadhi; Paduransana, foremost in preaching; Patacara, the foremost holder of the Vinaya; Sigalakamatra, foremost in 'attainment through faith'; Choiseungui is without fear of the four calamities; Bhadra Kapila, foremost in remembering past-lives; Hyemado, respected for her pure face; Sonya, foremost in teaching the right path to heathens; Dharmadina is the foremost missionary and teacher. Udara is not ashamed of wearing rags; Gwangmyeong is peaceful in all senses and mind. Seondu always acts according to the Dharma. Over one thousand bhikkhunis are skilled at making stanzas to praise the Buddha. Gubi hears a lot and spreads knowledge wide and always treats people with blessings and wisdom."

You can almost hear the Buddha's own voice, calling the names of his individual disciples and recognizing the level of their attainment. It is amazing that ninety-three nuns attained arahat-ship during Buddha's time.

King Ashoka was the first to unify India. He became a Buddhist and governed the nation with Dharma. His son, prince Mahinda, was a bhikkhu and his daughter, princess Sanghamitra, was a bhikkhuni. The king sent them to Sri Lanka to deliver the teachings of Buddhism. Because of this, Sri Lankan Buddhism became very influential. Later, Sri Lankan bhikkhunis would participate as the Ten Teachers in the ordination of Chinese bhikkhunis.

Around the 11th century, with the invasion of the Kola

clan from southern India, Buddhism was nearly annihilated. After that, bhikkhu sangha was reestablished but bhikkhuni sangha was not. Theravada Buddhism from Sri Lanka reached Myanmar in the 5th century but had changed to Tantric Buddhism. In the 11th century, Theravada was revitalized in Myanmar, which was the only country in Southeast Asia known to have had a bhikkhuni order. That too, however, vanished during the 13th century.

Tantric Buddhism entered Thailand in the 8th century where it became popular. Later, Theravada was transmitted from Myanmar and again from Sri Lanka in the 13th century. When the Thai people invaded Cambodia and Laos late in that century, they brought Theravada along with them.

Unfortunately, bhikkhuni sangha is nowhere to be found in these countries. There are, however, female practitioners called maechis, who, after receiving the ten precepts from a bhikkhu master, don white or pink robes. There are neither bhikkhuni nor laypeople. They are somewhat akin to novice nuns (śrāmaṇerī or *samini* in Korean).

Bhikkhu Bochang of the Liang Dynasty in China wrote The Record of Bhikkhunis in 517. According to that book, the first bhikkhuni in China was Jing Jian. There had been another before her, during the Han dynasty, a woman from Luoyang named Aban. However, Aban had become a bhikkhuni on her own, without an ordaining ceremony; a situation similar to that of Sassi in Korea, who was the sister of Morye. So, it would be correct to say that the first bhikkhuni in China was Jing Jian. The Record of Bhikkhunis documents over one hundred Chinese nuns. Astonishingly, it records in detail the stories of their youth, their family life before becoming a nun, which sutras, vinayas, and abhidharmas they studied, what they wrote and how they preached. A few centuries later, Zhen Hua (909-947) wrote a sequel to the book that records information on over two hundred Chinese bhikkhunis. Fifteen of them came from aristocratic families and achieved great things after being ordained.

Buddhism was first brought to Korea during the Three Kingdoms period around the fourth century. It is thought that bhikkhuni sangha was established around that period. During the Silla dynasty, the first bhikkhuni is said to be Sassi, however, like Aban from the Han dynasty, Sassi became a nun on her own. When King Beobheung grew old, he went to Heungnyunsa Temple, shaved his head, and wore robes. He became a bhikkhu, using Beob-gong as his Dharma name. His wife, Bodo, followed him. She founded Yeongheungsa Temple and became a bhikkhuni, using Myo-beop as her Dharma name. Some see Myo-beop as Korea's first bhikkhuni. Another king, King Jinheung, also became bhikkhu Beob-un in his later years. His wife Sado entered Yeongheungsa Temple and became bhikkhuni Myo-ju. Ji-so, wife of the famous general who led the unification of the three kingdoms, Yu-sin Kim, also became a bhikkhuni. Such records indicate that the Silla people believed that becoming a Buddhist practitioner was among the most noble of lives one could lead.

One rather intriguing fact is that in Silla, the bhikkhuni sangha was considered above the bhikkhus. The hierarchy was organized as follows: Daeguktong-Guktong (Seungtong)-Doyu-narang (Supreme Leader of nuns)-Daedoyuna (Supreme Leader of monks)-Daeseoseong- and so forth. In this hierarchy, the Supreme Leader of nuns was ranked higher than the Supreme Leader of monks.

A number of Japanese historical records describe how active Korean nuns were during the Three Kingdoms period. According to these historical texts, King Wideok, the 27th king of Baekje, sent a group of Buddhist seunims to Japan to offer the teachings of Buddhism in 577 CE. In this group of seunims were nuns, including Seon-sin, Seon-jang and Hye-seon, who became the founders of Japan's bhikkhuni sangha. After shaving their heads under the guidance of monk Hye-pyeon of Goguryeo, they went to the Baekje kingdom around 588 CE and studied for three years, receiving the bhikkhuni precepts before returning to Japan. This is because Baekje had a double sangha system, with ten monk teachers and ten nun teachers. In 655 CE, during King Uija's reign, a bhikkhuni named Beob-myeong went to Japan and healed patients by reciting the Vimalakirti Sutra. It is believed that this is why the Vimalakirti group later became so influential in Japan.

Bhikkhunis from Silla kingdom also went to Japan to teach. I-won built a pavilion in Prime Minister Daebananma's house by Mount Jwabo, where she taught Japanese aristocratic women.

Bhikkhunis from all three kingdoms went to Japan to spread Buddhism. This proves how active nuns were in Korea. There are no records of it, but it is believed they also travelled to China. Many monks had gone to China to study. Nuns would have surely done the same.

Goryeo was a Buddhist country. Bhikkhuni monasteries were operated within the government system. The Karma-Cleansing Centre (*Jeongeopwon*) and Peace and Safety Centre (*Anilwon*) were temples for the women of the royal family and aristocracy. Naturally, the seunims of the temples were nuns.

In the 8th year of the reign of King Hyeonjong, a decree was announced that prohibited women from becoming nuns. Such an action actually gives credence to the fact that there were many women who had joined the monasteries. Korea continued to have many bhikkhunis until the late Goryeo dynasty. Myodeok was the bhikkhuni who provided the funding necessary to publish the world's oldest extant books printed with movable metal type, "Jikji" and "Speeches of Monk Baekun." She was a disciple of Master Naong's school and belonged to the Karma-Cleansing Centre.

During the Joseon dynasty, Confucianism was promoted and Buddhism was suppressed. Despite this official stance, many ladies of the royal families and aristocracy still supported Buddhism. Again, it was the bhikkhunis who played a vital role in the preservation of Buddhism.

When the Joseon dynasty moved the nation's capital to Hanyang (present-day Seoul), bhikkhuni temples were relocated as well. Cheongnyongsa Temple, the very place where Myeongseong had resided and started a school, was formerly Karma-Cleansing Temple. Queen Munjeong established Jasuwon and Insuwon, where five thousand bhikkhunis are said to have gathered. However, due to the attacks and criticism coming from Confucian scholars, the temples had to undergo repeated cycles of being shut-down and reopened. The prohibition of nuns from entering the palace area in 1623 by King Injo significantly diminished Karma-Cleansing Temple. Finally, in 1660, in the second year of King Hyeonjong, both Jasowon and Insuwon were permanently closed.

Such trends during the Joseon dynasty undermined bhikkhuni activities, but many nuns ended up moving out of Seoul, going deep into the mountains to practice self-cultivation. English author and geographer Isabella Bird Bishop writes in her book, Korea and Her Neighbors (1898), that in Jangansa Temple in Geumgang Mountain, there were over 120 nuns, ranging from children to an 87-year-old woman. We can assume that other major temples of a similar size would have had a similar number of nuns.

To be sure, the Joseon kingdom was an extremely hostile environment. Nonetheless, nuns strove to keep the flame of the Dharma lantern burning so that it could be passed down to future generations. Because of this unwavering effort, the Three Great Bhikkhunis – Geum-gwang, Hye-ok, and Su-ok – arose during Japanese colonial rule. They added fuel to the fire and transmitted the Dharma so that it continues to burn today.

Returning from her overseas trip in 1977, Myeong-seong went to Cheongnyongsa Temple in Seoul. She did not return to Unmun, having already informed them that she would not be returning to teach, and would instead join in a meditation retreat or engage in prayer. Myeong-seong had found another instructor to replace her, so she had few qualms about leaving the school. She wanted to have some time of her own for her own self-cultivation. She had been teaching from the age of twenty-six at the Buddhist College in Seonamsa Temple. After also teaching at Cheongnyong, then at Unmun, she had reached the age of forty-eight. She desperately yearned for some time of her own to devote to her own practice.

Two days after Myeong-seong arrived in Cheongnyong, more than thirty students from Unmun rushed to the temple. Hearing that Myeong-seong had arrived, they shouted and clapped with joy, and immediately rented a bus and drove all the way to Seoul. Many students cried when they saw Myeong-seong and begged her to return to Unmun to teach them. Myeong-seong could not accept that this time, because she desperately needed a turning point in her life as a practitioner. The students and Myeong-seong argued over many hours, but Myeong-seong would not be swayed. Unable to convince her, the students returned to Unmun. Two days later, a treasurer seunim came to Myeong-seong. She was a disciple of Gwang-u, who had travelled for six months with Myeong-seong. She told Myeong-seong, "Your luggage has arrived at the Port of Busan. It is in Customs right now. Come with me to go pick it up."

Without a hint of suspicion, Myeong-seong hopped into the van. But when the car passed Daegu, it turned towards Gyeongsang. Even then, Myeong-seong thought that this could have been an alternative route to Busan. Still, something seemed strange, so she asked, "Why are you not going to Busan? This is the way to Gyeongsang."

The treasurer nun did not answer, pretending she was asleep. Myeong-seong realized that she had been kidnapped and was being taken to Unmun. She alternatively scolded and coaxed the nun, but she would not budge. She continued sleeping, or pretended to do so. At the end of the day, Myeong-seong was back in Unmun.

Many things had happened at the temple. There had been a wild fire that somehow released a rock which hit a studentnun. Tragically, the woman ended up dying from the wound. The abbess that had held the position when Myeong-seong left for her trip had quit the post due to issues with the contract. The next abbess, Hye-an Seunim, Myeong-seong's Dharma sister, also left the post before long.

Things were pretty messed up in the temple. Of course, the college was not operating normally. That is why, when the students heard of Myeong-seong's return, they had been so overjoyed. When they failed to convince her, they plotted her kidnapping. Once she saw the situation at the temple and heard the pleas from the students, she felt a sense of duty. If she did not tend to the school, it would surely fall into ruin.

In 1978, the abbot of Donghwasa Temple called upon Myeong-seong. Donghwa was the head temple of Unmun. It was customary for head temples to call upon Myeong-seong. She went to Donghwasa Temple with her assistant. The abbot of Donghwa was Seo-un Seunim. As soon as Myeong-seong sat down, Seo-un opened his mouth, "I really think you should take up the role of abbess, too."

The offer was so abrupt. "What do you mean? I cannot become an abbess. I don't have any experience. Teaching alone is too much for me." Myeong-seong firmly decline the offer. However, Seo-un was adamant about convincing her.

"Nobody has experience at first. You will learn as you do the job."

"No, I really cannot do this. It is outside my abilities." After making it clear that she did not want the position, she hurried back to Unmun. However, a few days later, she received a letter. It was from Donghwasa Temple, and it appointed her as the Abbess of Unmunsa Temple. Myeong-seong was confounded. She summoned the managing seunims and told them what had happened. To her surprise, everybody suddenly lit up and began clapping their hands and yelling.

"That is such great news! You must become the abbess, of course. You can run the school however you wish."

All her staff seunims suggested that Myeong-seong should accept the position. Unmun College had been a separate entity within Unmunsa Temple. This meant that the abbess and head instructor had different roles. If one person took on both roles, the potential for conflict would be removed. Myeong-seong thought about this and decided to accept it. There were so many things to do to establish a strong foundation for the college, and having to constantly coordinate with another abbess could complicate that process. So, that is how Myeong-seong became the first seunim to simultaneously hold both titles of abbess and head instructor.

Chapter 08

Be truthful
in all things

"Be truthful in all things. Be sincere in whatever you do. If you do your best with utmost sincerity, there is nothing you cannot do. Because that mind is the original mind of the universe, the mind of the Buddha. In big or small affairs, you must observe yourself and check whether you are truthful, putting your heart into it with sincerity. If you feel no embarrassment about what you have done, you have been truthful. Other people might not acknowledge your effort, or you may fail at what you try to do, but that should not cause you to question yourself in the least. Reflect only yourself upon your own mirror of the pure mind. If you have been truthful and sincere, then you have done all you can. Now, what is the most thing important here?" Myeong-seong asked her students.

"The mirror of the pure mind," they replied.

"Look at yourself in the mirror. Are you putting all of your sincerity and truthfulness in your studies?"

"No!" Someone yelled out.

"Who just said 'no' in such a loud voice? Raise your hand."

The student raised her hand.

"Should we reward her or punish her?"

"She should be rewarded."

"Why?"

"Because her mirror of the pure mind is clear."

"Okay. The student with the clear mirror, please come forward."

Shyly, the student came forward.

"I will reward you with this. From now on, study with the utmost sincerity and truthfulness."

Myeong-seong gave her a fountain pen. The other students gasped in envy. At the time, such fountain pens were very rare, particularly ones made in other countries. If you were a student, you longed to have a fountain pen. Along with the fountain pen she had bought overseas, Myeong-seong also gave the student her own work of calligraphy that said, "Be truthful in all things."

When Myeong-seong finished with the Flower Garland class, an architect was waiting for her. She went with the architect to her office.

"Hello. I brought the blueprints you asked for."

"Thank you." Myeong-seong looked at the blueprints. It was for a 1,200 square foot bathhouse. She looked at every small detail, asking about anything she was unsure of, and correcting everything she wanted to improve. She picked the colour of the tiles herself. Then she gave the go-ahead for the construction to proceed. The construction cost around seven thousand dollars, but with over one hundred nuns sharing a living space together, Myeong-seong believed that it was essential that the school have a bathhouse.

The construction began in February, before the weather became hot. The year was 1978. It was the first construction project she had undertaken after becoming abbess. If she had not been the abbess, there might have been disagreement about whether to build a bathhouse. It was probably best that Myeong-seong had become the abbess as it allowed her to run the school more efficiently. When the bathhouse was finally finished, the students were jubilant. More than one hundred people were using it, but there was a system for scheduling who could use it when. The students from different classes would wash at different times and days. For the nuns, being able to wash themselves clean with hot water was a much-appreciated gift.

In 1979, the number of applicants began to grow exponentially. Unmun Monastic College was taking root and becoming established, right at a time when nuns were becoming increasingly thirsty for more education. In fact, schools for nuns, such as Unmun, were spreading throughout the country. They provided an education to many women and contributed to the notion that nuns should be educated. Masters scrambled to send their disciples to these schools.

As the number of students rapidly grew, constructing new buildings become more and more of a priority. Myeong-seong decided to relocate the Flower Garland class into a separate new building, and had a design drawn up. She had organized the construction of the Gathering Stars Pavilion, but that was merely a lecture hall. The Novice Nun class and Four Collection class had their lessons in the Gathering Stars Pavilion, but still ate and slept in the Main Buddha Hall. Having everyone gathered there made the Main Buddha Hall extremely overcrowded. As the most senior class, the Flower Garland class seunims were beyond uncomfortable. Wanting to remedy this, Myeong-seong decided to give the Flower Garland class their own space. She began the construction of the Pavilion of Profound Lectures (*Seolhyeondang*). With an area of 2,000 square feet, the construction costs amounted to approximately forty thousand dollars. This was in 1979, and South Korea was industrializing. While temples were economically better off than before, forty thousand dollars was still a considerable sum of money.

Myeong-seong again prepared a book of donations and began traveling to collect alms. She visited the temples and monks who she knew, or she sent the book of donations via post. The students also participated, asking their Masters and temples, and gathering what money they could. After combining their hearts and their efforts, the funds had been raised. They bought the lumber and stored it in the Pavilion of Eternity. Machines and chainsaws were brought in to begin the carpentry work.

The sounds of buzzing machines filled the Pavilion of Eternity. In mid-May, it started raining heavier than usual for spring. The Hall of Judgment (*Myeongbujeon*) started to leak. Then, the Hall of Avalokiteshvara, the Pavilion of Eternity, and the Hall of the Cosmic Buddha all began showing signs of leaking. All of these old buildings needed maintenance. Myeong-seong decided to start with the Hall of Judgment. She invited experts and asked them to renovate the roof tiles before the coming of the monsoon rains.

The most important part of a journey is the destination. You cannot walk a path without knowing where you are going. It is the same with education. If you do not have a clear idea of what kind of person you want to develop, there can be no education.

Myeong-seong explained her goals for education in three parts:

"The first is one's purpose and vows. A Buddhist nun is a renunciate. One should have a clear purpose for why she became a nun. It wasn't for comfort, pleasure or a lifestyle of plenty. It wasn't for fame or material possessions. Nuns only desire to follow the bright wisdom of the Lord Buddha.

In this case, what should we do? The first thing is to have a clear purpose and clear vows. If a practitioner does not have solid, immovable vows, it would be like building a house without any blueprints. It would be like weeding without having sown any seeds. Nothing is gained by this. Living life as a practitioner is not easy. You need to stay strong and persevere. This is a painful path. But the path is not without rewards. You must go and seize your goal. Make your purpose clear, and vow to work toward that goal.

The second is to practice without retreat. If you already have your vows, what you are left with is practice. You must practice self-cultivation. The last words left by the Lord Buddha was, "Do not be lazy. Be diligent in your cultivation." Do not put off until tomorrow what you can do today. You cannot progress without diligence. When you hear the wooden block (*moktak*) struck at 3 am, rise immediately, go to the morning worship, read the sutras, and meditate. Be faithful and present throughout your daily routines. Sometimes laziness can creep in; sometimes you might get depressed or bored or doubtful, but you have to overcome this. Overcoming the negative mind within you is more difficult than defeating an army of a thousand warriors. Whenever you feel laziness rising up inside you, imagine that you are at war with an army of a thousand warriors. It is not an easy battle. You must fight with all your power. You must work hard to cultivate yourself without retreat.

The third is to communicate and spread the teachings. Why do we make vows; why do we cultivate ourselves? It is to spread the Buddha's teaching throughout the world. Why do we choose a life of purpose? It is to spread the Buddha's teachings. There are many things for nuns to do at Unmun. There are clubs for a variety of activities: preaching, faithful living, culture, physical activities, broadcasting, singing, etc. The students involved in each club should always be thinking about how to better spread the teaching of the Dharma. If you do not pass on what was passed down to you, you are not returning what you have received from the Buddha. Such a person cannot be called a Buddhist."

Having purpose and vows, practicing self-cultivation without retreat, and communicating and spreading the teachings. These were the three pillars of Myeong-seong's life.

During the summer break of 1979, students from the preaching club invited elementary school students to the temple and organized a Summer Buddhist School. Planting the seeds of Buddha's teachings in the hearts of children was the first implementation of "communicating and spreading the teachings."

In September, the sky grew bluer and the sunlight shined more clearly. Myeong-seong resumed the renovation of the Hall of Avalokiteshvara that had been halted during the monsoon rain. She installed the new roof tiles and erected the pillars again. The building had been neglected for a long time, and a lot of money was needed for repairs. When the Hall of Avalokiteshvara was nearly finished, Myeong-seong began replacing the roof tiles on the Pavilion of Eternity.

There were stacks of wood piled up in the Pavilion of Eternity because there was always some construction and repairs going on. The constant ear-piercing sound of machines made it difficult for people to hear one another. Having to go on with their work and lives while dealing with the noise and construction was starting to get on people's nerves.

The roof of the Pavilion of Eternity was very wide, and more than ten people were working on it at once. The workers carried in mud and new roof tiles, removed the old broken roof tiles, and then used the mud to lay the new roof tiles.

One day, the roofing work was almost finished and only the ridge of the roof needed to be replaced, when suddenly there was a great crackling noise, as if thunder had crashed. The roof of the Pavilion of Eternity had collapsed unexpectedly. The workers inside the building ran out. Ten workers who were on the roof also climbed down the ladder. As soon as the workers gathered together, they called out everyone's name to check that everybody was safe. There were about twenty workers; some cutting wood on the ground, some had been up on the roof. It was a miracle that all had escaped unscathed.

Myeong-seong was nearby at the time, preparing medicinal herbs with students. She saw the roof collapse, and thanked Gwanseum Bosal that no one had been hurt.

Early the next morning, television, radio and newspapers reported the assassination of President Junghee Park. It was October 25, 1979. It seemed a mysterious coincidence that the roof of the Pavilion of Eternity had collapsed on the day the country's

President was assassinated.

Now, six thousand dollars of labour and materials was buried in the soil. All of that money had been spent in vain. Myeong-seong needed even more money now as she renovated and repaired aging buildings. Knowing that she needed to do something, she went to meet the governor of North Gyeongsang Province. The governor listened to how the roof had collapsed, and then he offered to help. "Our province will pay for the repairs. The Pavilion of Eternity is an old building that should be protected as a cultural heritage."

The governor gave his promise, and not long after, he sent Myeong-seong the needed money. After the repairs to the Pavilion of Eternity's roof was complete, there was still money left over. Myeong-seong decided to construct a bell tower with the remaining money. She had repaired a fabulous bell but did not yet have a tower in which to hang it. The collapse of the Pavilion of Eternity's roof was, it turned out, a blessing in disguise, leading as it did to the construction of the bell tower. Even to this today, the Pavilion of Eternity and the bell tower stand together like brother and sister.

Myeong-seong was asked to write an essay for a Buddhist magazine, Dharma Wheel (*Beomnyun*), and she submitted an essay titled "Problems in Education in Bhikkhuni Schools."

Myeong-seong's book, Rules and Decorum for Novice

Nuns, was published by Boryeonkak in 1981. She had a particular interest in the precepts. Becoming a renunciate was among the most courageous things one could do. You renounce the secular life, choosing to live as a practitioner. The precepts were what was most urgently required to live as a practitioner. Whether one followed the precepts or not was the best indicator of whether one was living the life of a practitioner. Myeong-seong always told her students to live by the precepts. The precepts did not exist to restrict you, on the other hand, they protected and guarded you. They are what allows practitioners to live with dignity.

When Myeong-seong first laid her eyes on the book Rules and Decorum for Novice Monks that had been published by Il-ta Seunim, she immediately vowed to publish a book for novice nuns. She gathered her research, got some assistance from people around her, and published the book. She was thrilled to finally be able to present a set of guidelines for those who had just become nuns.

The mountains were ablaze with the red of autumn leaves. Mount Hogeo was settling into autumn. Myeong-seong summoned the head seunims for tea.

"There is not a proper guesthouse in our temple. Even when senior seunims visit, there isn't a place for them to stay. What do you say we build a house across the bridge? We can name it the Bamboo Forest House (*Jungnimheon*)."

"That is a wonderful idea. It would be nice to have a clean guestroom for important visitors."

Whenever Myeong-seong had suggested a plan to her staff, they would almost always be against it. They would either think that it wasn't so important or that it would be too expensive. This time, however, was different.

"How come you don't object this time?"

"Because we all agree with you."

"Well, then. Let's begin."

Myeong-seong already had a plan in mind. She knew exactly where the house should be located, from when she had asked Mr. Yoon's help in finding some good trees. A few years ago, an old seunim who was also a *fengshui* expert had come to Unmun. The old monk looked around Unmunsa Temple and pointed to the empty space across the bridge. "That place is a propitious site. You should build a house there." As soon as Myeong-seong heard this, she knew she had to build it there.

Construction began in October of 1981. That is how the Bamboo Forest House came to be. The house was not very big, with an area of only 710 square feet.

Myeong-seong believed that bhikkhu and bhikkhunis were both disciples of the Buddha and that they should be treated equal. She thought that her teaching lineage should be passed on from a bhikkhuni. In 1983, she held a Dharma-transmission ceremony in which she would receive the Dharma from Su-ok

Seunim. Su-ok was a nun for whom Myeong-seong had great respect. Since it was after her passing, Myeong-seong set up Su-ok's spirit tablet to conduct the ceremony.

Myeong-seong had first been permitted to teach at Seon-am College by Seong-neung Seunim in 1958. A very famous lecturer at Tongdosa, Haeinsa, and Gaesimsa Temple, Seong-neung had been a disciple of Han-yeong Park. However, because Seong-neung was a bhikkhu, Myeong-seong had always aspired to receive the Dharma from a bhikkhuni. It was her belief that she should create a tradition where a nun could pass on the permission to teach to other nuns.

Hwasandang Su-ok, Geumgwangdang Geum-nyong, and Jeongamdang Hye-ok are the three giants in Korea's modern bhikkhuni history. These three protected the modern bhikkhuni system, and were the foundation from which sprang great scholar-nuns, including Gwang-u, Myeong-seong of Unmun Monastic College, Myo-eom of Bongnyeong Monastic College, Myo-seon of Samseon Monastic College, and Il-cho of Donghak Monastic College.

Su-ok was born in Jinhae, South Gyeongsang Province, in November of 1902. She went to Sudeoksa Temple's Gyeonseong Hermitage when she was sixteen and became a nun. Her teacher there was Myoridang Beob-hui Seunim. She took her Novice Nun class and Four Collections class from Gogyeong Seunim of Haeinsa Temple College. In 1929, she finished the Four Sutras and Flower Garland Sutra class under Dae-eun Tae-heup Kim in Seoul. She then studied the precepts and vinayas from monk Yong-seong Baek. She returned to Gyeonseong Hermitage at Sudeoksa Temple where Man-gong and Beob-hui Seunims resided. There, she meditated for the next five years, thereby accomplishing all three studies of sutra, vinaya, and dhana.

However, Su-ok was not satisfied. She went to Japan in 1937 and studied in a Nichiren temple. She then spent three years studying in Mino Nishū Gakurin, which belonged to the Linji School. Such a trajectory, ambitiously studying overseas, was unimaginable for a nun at that time. After returning from Japan, Su-ok began teaching at a Buddhist college at Namjangsa Temple in Sangju. For a nun to become an instructor at a Buddhist college was unprecedented. The nuns who learned directly from Su-ok included Byeok-an, Gwang-u, Myo-seon, In-sun, Deok-su, Mun-su, Ja-ho, and Tae-ho of the Four Collections class; Bo-in, Su-yeon, and Hye-ryeon of the Novice Nun class. Byeok-an, Gwang-u, and Ji-hyeong completed the Flower Garland Sutra class but, immediately after that, the college shut itself down in order to prevent the Japanese authorities from forcing the students into sexual slavery for the Japanese military.

Su-ok had twenty-nine disciples in Namjangsa Temple. These included Gwang-u, Tae-gu, Byeok-an, Bo-in, Ji-hyeong, Deok-su, Su-yeon, Tae-ho, Hye-ryeon, Myo-hi, In-sun, Mun-su, Ja-ho, Beob-gwan, Beob-jun, Hye-myeong, Se-deung, Jeong-o, Yeong-deok, Myo-gwan, Ji-yeon, Dae-won, Deok-hyeon, Seonghwan, Beob-in, Myeong-won, Gyeong-sun, Ja-eun, and Ji-taek. These nuns later rose to play a pivotal role in Korea's modern Buddhism.

Su-ok Seunim was teaching many disciples but felt that her own self-cultivation was still lacking. She again went to Gyeonseong Hermitage and practiced arduously for seven more years. Finally, in 1945, her moment of enlightenment came. She wrote of her experience in Chinese character poems and shared them with Gyeong-bong Seunim, who was greatly revered as an enlightened one.

After liberation from Japanese colonial rule, Su-ok moved to Seoul, where she stayed at Bomunsa Temple, opened a bhik-khuni college, and taught students. Many of the bhikkhunis who studied here during this time also became important figures in the history of Korean nuns. The college was shut down when the Korean War broke out in 1950. Su-ok went to Naewonsa Temple, tucked away on Mount Cheonseong in South Gyeongsang Province. Staying there for ten years, she built up Naewon from a dilapidated temple into the greatest Seon Centre in the country. In 1954, after the purification of the Jogye Order, she was elected as leader of the bhikkhunis. She was then elected as a member of the Central Committee of the Jogye Order in 1955. Su-ok entered nirvana on February 7, 1966, aged 65, with a Dharma age of 48.

A Dharma-transmission ceremony was held on February 7, 1983, the anniversary of her passing. Wol-ha Seunim of Tongdosa Temple gave Myeong-seong a stanza from Su-ok's book of poetry, Flower Mountain Collection:

The comfort of my mind is unmovable, like a mountain
The honour and disgrace of the outside world are of no sur-
prise
Silently reading the sutras, the meaning becomes self-evi-
dent
All worldly right and wrong have nothing to do with me

Myeong-seong replied:

Appreciating the words you left word by word, this humble
disciple looks back at how she has lived. My admiration for
you was inexhaustible while you were living, but I was nev-
er able to express it properly. Today, on your 18th memorial
day, I get to receive Dharma transmission before your spirit,
and I cannot describe how much I feel sorrowful and empty.
As a student who is more trivial than a firefly, I feel greatly
sorry and ashamed to receive your sublime Dharma as high
as Mt. Cheonseongsan.

However, you assuredly gave permission to me, and I too
want to hold up your intent. I will try to read what you had
in mind, and dedicate my whole being to spread the ocean
of the Buddha's teachings. As a small token of my sincerity,

I took the liberty to republish Hwasanjip, the collection of your precious words. I will share them with those who long for you, and pray with palms joined that you return to this world in no time and become an eternal light for all beings.

Respectfully and offering incense,
Your Dharma disciple, Myeong-seong

Through this ceremony, Myeong-seong became a Dharma disciple of Su-ok Seunim. It had long been her aspiration that the Dharma be transmitted by a bhikkhuni. And so, Myeong-seong created the tradition where a bhikkhuni can transmit the Dharma to a fellow bhikkhuni.

Spring rain sprinkled down. It was not pouring heavily, but still uncomfortable to work outside. Myeong-seong cancelled the afternoon communal work and made the students recite the sutra they had read that morning. The air rang with the sound of the sutras being read by each class. It was pleasant to her ears. Smiling, she stepped outside to take a walk.

Myeong-seong crossed a creek with an umbrella in hand. She passed by three or four abandoned houses which were in disrepair but had not yet been demolished. There were persimmon, cherry, and pear trees on this land, which Myeong-seong had reclaimed from the village for the temple.

During the 500 years of the Joseon dynasty, Buddhism

had declined into a state of desolation. Most of the land that had been given to the temples during the Silla and Goryeo dynasties had been taken and occupied by villagers. They farmed on the land and also settled on it. The temples without resident monks were first to be occupied. Even in temples where monks lived, as their status was not recognized by the government, it was difficult for them to bring their claims against the occupiers. This was same for Unmunsa Temple.

When Myeong-seong first arrived at Unmun, there were about ten houses remaining on the other side of the creek. Some of the houses were abandoned, but some were occupied during the spring. Villagers would come in the spring to farm on the land. They believed that it was their land, even though it formally belonged to the temple.

Myeong-seong took this fact very seriously. Determined to solve this problem, she brought it up in a meeting. The other seunims, however, had a different opinion.

"Those people have been living there for hundreds of years. We should let them continue to farm there."

"If we maintain good relations with them, it will be easier to get their help when we need to."

"We might have to file a lawsuit in order to remove them. That could be overwhelming. We might not even have clear documental evidence that the land belongs to the temple."

All of the other seunims were opposed to her idea. They were used to the status quo and accepted the fact that farmers were occupying the temple's land.

Myeong-seong was thinking about things differently. She wanted to turn Unmun Monastic College into a world-class school. The first thing the temple needed was more space. The students should not have to deal with so much inconvenience. Myeong-seong had detailed plans for where to construct which building. Creating an ideal place for studying did not mean only the construction of buildings. The surrounding environment also had to be properly designed. Myeong-seong felt the need to clean up and organize the entire surroundings.

Myeong-seong wanted the students to fully understand and agree with her plan. She wanted the students themselves to be the ones who turned Unmun Monastic College into the world's premiere school for bhikkhunis. She began inviting students to her room, one by one.

"Come over for some tea."

"Come to my room for cookies."

"Come visit my room for some candy."

"Come to my room. I'll give you a handkerchief."

Myeong-seong finally managed to convince everybody of her plan. They agreed to her idea and concurred that it was necessary to organize the surrounding land. The students themselves decided to form a committee to help implement Myeong-seong's plan.

Myeong-seong and the committee worked to organize the land that surrounded the temple. It took three years in total, from 1977 to 1979. This work began as soon as Myeong-seong had become the temple's abbess, and cost around 8,000 dollars. Some students thought that this was not a necessary process, especially if it meant spending so much money. However, if the matter had not been taken care of at that time, it would have become much more complicated later on down the road. Myeong-seong had an insight into the bigger picture, and as time went by, the other seunims came to understand her reasoning.

Nearly two hundred students were living in Unmunsa Temple, but they still did not have fully running water. It was very inconvenient for the students. Myeong-seong decided to tackle that task first. Water piping was installed three times in 1979, 1980 and 1984. She also installed lotus flower-shaped stone water basins in a few spots for students and visitors. Lights were set up outdoors so that students could walk more easily at night when going to the bathroom. Fences were mended, and parking lots were built as more visitors began coming with their cars.

Myeong-seong then went on to build an oyster mushroom farm in an area full of pine trees to the south. The mushrooms provided an excellent source of protein for the students. A compost pit was installed outside the rear fence, which produced a high quality soil amendment.

Unmunsa Temple was busy undergoing renovations under Myeong-seong's leadership. One day, Mr. In-hi Lee from Busan visited her. He was a businessman with a particular affection for Unmunsa Temple. He had donated the funds to pay for building the bathhouse and oversaw the entire construction himself. He was a devoted Buddhist who had been the president of the Busan Buddhist Laymen's Society. While talking with Myeong-seong, Mr. Lee proposed something.

"I have been watching all the work you do. I was particularly impressed at how you, as a new abbess, arranged so that the students themselves did the accounting, clerical, and auditing work. I have been thinking about this for a while. What would you say to renovating and enlarging the Sariam Hermitage where we worship Lord Naban? Many people who visit there would like to stay for a few days to pray, but they are unable to because there is no place to eat or sleep. If you agree to it, I will take the initiative to make that happen."

Mr. Lee's proposal was completely unexpected. He had been observing Myeong-seong for a few years and had come to trust her. He was deeply impressed at how she ran the monastery as an abbess, especially how she let the students directly manage all financial affairs. Myeong-seong was both the abbess and the head instructor, but she made all the students take turns doing the accounting work. Everybody in the temple knew how the money was being used. It was completely transparent.

Whenever an offering was given to the temple, Myeong-seong always divided it among the students. People frequently made donations to support the young bhikkhunis who were practicing self-cultivation. These offerings included soap, towels, socks, underwear, fruit, bread, rice cakes, and cookies. Some people donated money. Everything was doled out equally between the students. If there was not enough of a particular item to go around, it would be kept until the same thing was offered again. Then, Myeong-seong would distribute it equally. Nobody was dissatisfied with how the monastery was run. There was nothing to complain about.

Myeong-seong replied to Mr. Lee's offer. "I hadn't thought of that before. If you are able to do that, it would be greatly appreciated."

"Thank you for accepting my offer. I will discuss my plan with some experts and report back to you." Smiling, Mr. Lee left the temple. After a few days, he returned with blueprints for an expanded Sariam Hermitage. The blueprints were more ambitious than Myeong-seong had imagined. They included living quarters, a Hall of Avalokiteshvara, a kitchen, an office, and a bathroom. Every building would have electricity and tap water.

"I am not sure if you can afford a project of this scale," Myeong-seong expressed her concern.

"You have always said in your lectures that the mind creates matter. If we put our minds to it, we can do it for sure," Mr. Lee replied confidently.

"This is a very important project. Please give me a few days to think it over." Part of Myeong-seong wanted to go ahead with erecting a majestic shrine, but another part of her had doubts. A large project at the top of the mountain could be dangerous. Accidents could happen.

After Mr. Lee left, Myeong-seong summoned all of the leader seunims. She showed them the blueprints left behind by Mr. Lee and asked for their advice.

"This project is very important. Please tell me what you think."

There was a moment of silence. Then, one of them spoke out, "I think it is too dangerous. Sariam Hermitage is at the top of a mountain. We can barely carry a sack of rice up there. How would the workers be able to carry all the construction equipment up the mountain?"

The other seunims nodded in agreement. However, Myeong-seong was listening to a different voice. Something told her that it was alright to go ahead with the project. She felt that Lord Naban would protect them. She designated Hye-un Seunim as the project leader. Hye-un had been a faithful supporter of Myeong-seong since her time at Cheongnyongsa Temple, and had followed Myeong-seong to Unmun.

Mr. Lee proceeded with the plan. Assisting him was Mr. Min-jo Yoon (currently the manager of temple administration). He purchased the materials and brought them all the way up the mountain. When word got out that Sariam Hermitage was undergoing a major extension, more people visited. Everyone who came wanted to help. Visitors, guests, and students would carry anything they could.

Sariam Hermitage is situated close to the peak of Unmun Mountain. First constructed around the 10th century by Boyang Guksa, the shrine venerates Lord Naban. Lord Naban had been assigned the role of protecting and blessing all secular beings during the period between the passing of Shakyamuni Buddha and the arrival of Maitreya Buddha, or five billion six hundred and seventy million years. Lord Naban was Pindola Bharadvaja, who had achieved the fruit of arahat during Shakyamuni Buddha's time.

Sariam Hermitage was famous for answering people's prayers. Many people from all over the country came there to pray. But, because of the poor facilities, people could not eat or sleep there. People who came from far away could only pray for a short period of time before having to leave. That is why Mr. Lee wanted to build a guesthouse.

Mr. Lee proceeded with constructing the first building. He acquired concrete, iron bars, wood, and sand. He assigned a contractor named Mr. Park to bring them up the mountain. Mr. Park studied how to best carry all of the equipment and materials up the mountain. He wanted to utilize a pulley, as electricity was already available at Sariam Hermitage. Everybody, including Mr. Lee, agreed with this idea. It was just too difficult to carry everything by hand. The problem now was figuring out how to make their own pulley. They had neither the knowledge nor money for a pulley. They took the engine from a tractor and turned it into a pulley engine.

When the pulley was completed, materials that had been hauled up the mountain by hand were now being transported with the machine. Once the pulley was loaded, workers at the bottom and at the top of the mountain prayed, 'Please, let it reach the top safely. Please, do not let the rope break.' The act of construction itself became a prayer. Visitors were touched by the sincerity of the project, and word of it spread. More people wanted to help. Mr. Jeonghwan Oh from Busan gratefully donated the funds to build the living quarters.

Construction of the living quarters began in December of 1982 and was completed in 1992. The project took more than ten years to complete and was free of any accidents. Team leaders Hye-un Seunim and Seong-ho Seunim managed the finances; Mr. Yoon managed all of the on-site work. The two directors were Myeong-seong and Lord Naban.

When Sariam Hermitage was finally completed, people flocked there from all over. The money they would leave was neither too much nor too little, but was just enough to support the students with their studies. Finances were taken care of in the same method, that is, the students managed all of the money themselves. Five students would form a team and stay at Sariam Hermitage for a week. They received registrations for prayers and took care of the visitors. They presided over worshipping ceremonies. Then, after a week, they returned to the main temple with all the money and the next team would climb up the mountain.

Lord Naban continues to watch over the students of Unmunsa Temple as they cultivate their field of good fortune.

Chapter 09

Restoring the Broken Dharma Lineage

It was late autumn of 1985 and the sky was blue and clear. Myeong-seong gazed at the clouds momentarily and continued on her way toward the main hall. Today was a historic day.

As she entered the Main Buddha Hall, students and guests rose to greet her. It was the day of the Dharma transmission ceremony, where one bhikkhuni passes on her teachings to another bhikkhuni. This was a significant moment in the history of Korean Buddhism. It had been the aspiration of Myeong-seong for so long. Her wish was finally coming to fruition. Nok-won Seunim, president of the Jogye Order; In-hong Seunim, an elder bhikkhuni from Seoknamsa Temple; Yun-ho Seunim from Cheongnyongsa Temple; and Hye-chun Seunim, president of the National Bhikkhuni Association, were among the many in attendance.

The ceremony began solemnly with the chanting of the three refuges. President Seunim gave congratulatory remarks. "Today's ceremony marks the first time in the history of our nation in which a bhikkhuni will transmit her Dharma to another bhikkhuni. I offer my deepest respect and appreciation to Myeong-seong Seunim for her dedication to the education of bhikkhunis for over thirty years."

In-hong and Hye-chun Seunims also gave speeches. It was a deeply emotional atmosphere. The lamp had been lit; now it must be passed on. After more congratulatory statements from guests, Myeong-seong came forward and sat on the Dharma chair. The Hall reverberated with applause. Heung-nyun and Il-jin Seunims came forward and stood in front of her. As the symbolic act of Dharma transmission, Myeong-seong gave them both a stanza, a Dharma robe, a Dharma name, and a begging bowl. Then she spoke:

You may spend billions of aeons worshipping the Buddha
You may travel across three thousand universes as his disciple
But if you do not deliver beings with the teachings
You are not repaying what you have received

After reciting the stanza, Myeong-seong gave them the robe and Dharma names. The name Won-hae was given to Heung-nyun; Won-un to Il-jin. Myeong-seong had first arrived at Unmun in 1970. Fifteen years later, she had finally trained two disciples who were qualified to teach.

After Myeong-seong finished speaking, the two new teachers put on their new clothes. They bowed three times to their teacher, then turned around and bowed three times to the audience.

"Thank you, Teacher. We will become the good teachers that you wish us to become. We will put our heart and soul into educating bhikkhunis. Thank you to the guests, senior seunims, and students. We will work hard to sow the seeds of bhikkhuni education in this land."

The two bowed and the audience burst into applause. Myeong-seong came down from the Dharma seat with a smile on her face. Many people in the audience were crying. This was truly a historic moment, a significant achievement for bhikkhunis and for Buddhism, which would not have been possible had it not been for Myeong-seong's decades of dedication.

Thus concluded the ceremony. By receiving Dharma from Su-ok Seunim, Myeong-seong had created the roots of her own lineage. Now, she had transmitted the teachings to her two disciples. This lineage would continue without breaking. It will flower and bear fruit.

After the ceremony, Myeong-seong presented the two newly appointed teachers with a table overflowing with food. The two teachers were moved by this, and everybody enjoyed celebrating the joyous occasion.

November 25, 1985 went down in bhikkhuni history as an important and auspicious day. After that day at Unmun, Dharma transmission ceremonies continued to be held at the temple. Many bhikkhunis were appointed as teachers by Myeong-seong.

Their names are as follows:

(Name as Dharma transmitter, original Dharma name, year of Dharma transmission)

Won-hae Heungn-yun, 1985

Won-un Il-jin, 1985

Won-in Gye-ho, 1990

Won-cheon Myo-jeong, 1990

Won-myeong Jin-gwang, 1999

Won-eum Se-deung, 2003

Won-jeong Un-san, 2003

Won-gwang Yeong-deok, 2003

Won-eung Eun-kwang, 2003

Won-jo Hyo-tan, 2007

Won-myo Il-jin, 2007

Won-heo Myeong-beop, 2007

Won-deung Beop-jang, 2007

Won-dam Seo-gwang, 2014

Won-jin Won-beop, 2014

Won-yung Ji-seong, 2014

It is a great source of pride for Korean Buddhism that it revived the dual sangha system of bhikkhus and bhikkhunis. Myeong-seong's light shines even brighter for having restored this broken tradition.

One day, Myeong-seong came out of her classroom after teaching the Flower Garland Sutra to find a seunim waiting for her. She looked young, probably in her early twenties.

"I have come to see you." She bowed politely.

"It is cold. Please, follow me." Myeong-seong led the way. The young seunim looked like she had been waiting outside in the cold for a while. They headed towards Gathering Stars Pavilion.

Myeong-seong asked her assistant to prepare some tea and spoke to the guest. "Please, speak freely. Tell me why you came to see me."

Hesitating slightly, she spoke. "I was accepted by the Buddhist Studies Department at Dongguk University, but I cannot afford the tuition. My teacher is against my going to school. She says I cannot become a proper nun if I go to school."

It was clear why she had come to see Myeong-seong. Myeong-seong thought about how much money she had available. "If you enter university, will you be able to keep studying?"

"I can earn money during school breaks by praying in other temples."

"Why do you want to go to university?"

"I want to know for sure what kind of person Buddha is. I want to go abroad after I graduate. I wish to become a Buddhist scholar."

"Fortunately, I have some money to spare. Enter university and study hard. Become a Buddhist scholar as you have vowed to do."

The young seunim was in tears. "Thank you so much. When I found myself in trouble not being able to pay for tuition, someone advised me to come visit you. She told me that you helped many nuns to study. I will become a Buddhist scholar and repay you for this."

She received the envelope and put it into her bag. Then, she asked one last question, "The nuns and monks around me tell me that I have to meditate and not do anything else. Whenever I hear that, I wonder about who will actually teach the sutras to the people. Am I right or wrong?"

Myeong-seong smiled and replied, "Meditation and studying the sutras are both important. Do what you believe is important. I believe that teaching the sutras to students is important; that is why I do this."

The young nun's face lit up. "I understand. I too will do what I believe is important – studying the sutras. Thank you."

As she rose and was leaving, Myeong-seong added, "Come back if you need any more help."

This kind of incident was not rare. Myeong-seong was known for her passion for bhikkhuni education. Novice nuns who could not get their teacher's support for their studies came to Myeong-seong seeking help. If she had money, she always gave them some.

On December 10, 1985, Myeong-seong arrived in Seoul

to attend a signboard-hanging ceremony. The National Bhikk-huni Association managed to acquire an office in Jongno, Seoul. There was now a physical office for them to conduct their business.

The National Bhikkhuni Association had previously been called Udumbara Association. Udumbara Association had not been very active in the 1970s. It was revamped in 1985 under the new name and with Hye-chun Seunim appointed as the first president. The formation of this organization was another significant event that advanced the status of bhikkhunis in South Korea.

In 1986, Myeong-seong published an article titled A Study on the Philosophy of Bhikkhuni Education in the first edition of the magazine "Sudara." In her paper, Myeong-seong stressed how a specialized education was necessary for bhikkhunis which took into consideration their feminine qualities and virtues. Some of the skills that could be useful for bhikkhunis in their outreach work to the public included knowledge about tea ceremonies, temple food, calligraphy, flower arrangement, teaching children, and playing the piano.

Myeong-seong was in fact disagreeing with the majority view, which held that nuns should rid themselves of feminine qualities, becoming gender neutral. It was a widely held belief that if nuns were to become true nuns, they should no longer be women. It was common for nuns to be scolded for liking something pretty or doing something considered as feminine.

In her curriculum, Myeong-seong included not only reading the sutras, but also skills related to tea ceremonies, flower arrangement, playing the piano, foreign languages, and calligraphy, among others. She believed that studying Buddhist texts alone was not enough. It was important for nuns to know many other things, especially now that many citizens were more highly educated.

Myeong-seong was also aware that nuns could excel when their feminine qualities, such as gentleness and attention to detail, were put to good use. She believed that nuns should be trained to work in kindergartens, day cares, orphanages, nursing homes, hospitals, etc. This assertion does not sound remarkable today, but at the time it was an innovative suggestions. In some ways, Myeong-seong could be said to have been thirty years ahead of her time.

In her paper, A Study on the Philosophy of Bhikkhuni Education, Myeong-seong emphasized the following points:

1. The training of disciples and sangha education needs to be well-organized in order to produce qualified teachers and leaders.
2. The study of non-Buddhist disciplines and general knowledge is important. Foreign language study is vital. Korean Buddhism should develop more exchanges with other countries.

3. Bhikkhunis need a separate and specialized educational system. The education needs to train them to become workers who can teach Buddhism to the public and contribute through social welfare and volunteering.

4. The Jogye Order needs to support the tuition and operation expenses of Bhikkhuni universities.

Nowadays, the order sets aside a budget for education, but this was not always the case. In the past, when monks or nuns wanted to study, they had to rely on their teachers or other sponsors to help cover tuition. But Myeong-seong had raised her voice, making it clear that the Order should provide this for the seunims.

Myeong-seong had always maintained that seunims should study the disciplines that are taught in ordinary schools, and not only study Buddhist texts. Such knowledge is crucial to communicating with the general public, let alone preaching to them. Myeong-seong had incorporated psychology, philosophy, Confucianism and other studies into the curriculum.

In 1987, the Order changed the name of all Sangha schools from colleges to universities. Unmun Buddhist College also became a university, with Myeong-seong as its first president. She dove into the work of transforming the school into a real university. She organized all the rules and regulations for the school and trained top-level researchers and professors. In the same year, she was invited to Kyungpook National University to teach Ethics as a visiting lecturer. For the first time, she began teaching regular university students.

Myeong-seong even did some collaboration with the military. One day, Ms. Ji-sim Nam asked Myeong-seong if she could bring her student nuns along with her to give a Dharma talk at the Korea Military Academy. Buddhist cadets were going to hold a "Handwriting the Heart Sutra" event on Buddha's Birthday. So, Myeong-seong took a bus to go to the Academy in Seoul with students from her Flower Garland class. There were over one hundred cadets in attendance at the handwriting ceremony. Myeong-seong explained the meaning behind the handwriting ceremony and presided over it. She brought all the handwritten sutras back with her to the temple. Later, she would put them inside the Buddha statue when she built the Main Hall. This had two meanings. First, Unmunsa Temple is where Won-gwang Guksa taught his Five Precepts for the Secular World to the two Hwarang warriors – Gwi-san and Chu-hang. In other words, Unmun was the site where patriotism and the warrior spirit merged with Buddhism. Second, Myeong-seong wanted to imbue the statue of the Buddha with the young and pure energy of the cadets. The following year, Myeong-seong invited cadets from the Korea Military Academy to visit Unmun, and they established a sister-school relationship. She made a point to try and guide the cadets so that they would maintain their interest in Buddhism.

At a military training centre in Nonsan, Myeong-seong presided over a Transmission of Precepts ceremony where she gave precepts to 3,500 soldiers. This ceremony had been held four times, and it was the first time that a bhikkhuni had presided over it. She will continue to do this work for as long as she is able to.

The evening wind grew chilly. As Myeong-seong was leaving the dining hall, the Secretary Seunim came to deliver a letter. It was from Yeong-dam Seunim.

"The weather is beginning to turn cold. We wish to send our regards to you and all the student-nuns. Thanks to you, the nuns here at Naewonsa Temple are practicing cultivation without difficulties. Yesterday was the winter solstice. We gathered to eat red bean soup, then we took a bath and shaved our heads. Since today is your birthday, we decided to climb up the mountain and, facing the direction of Unmunsa Temple, we put our hands together and bowed. We shouted, 'Myeong-seong Seunim! Happy Birthday! Live long and happily!' We talked about you and sent our love. (Omitted)"

Myeong-seong smiled. The letter was from some of the graduates of Unmun who had gone to live in Naewonsa Temple.

This brought back a memory from a few years back. As Unmunsa Temple was becoming famous for rebuilding bhikkhuni education, a broadcasting station wanted to make a documentary on the life of the student-nuns of Unmun. At first, Myeong-seong was against the idea, but after listening to the producer's repeated explanation, she was persuaded. She realized that a good documentary could help ordinary people better understand bhikkhunis. She invited all the leader seunims to hold a meeting about it. There was unanimous opposition. They did not want their daily lives to be aired nationwide. Many seunims were uncomfortable with their faces being on television.

Myeong-seong once again implemented her particular method of persuasion, inviting the seunims one by one to her room for tea, cookies, candy, and handkerchiefs. She continued to invite them over and over until they agreed.

"As you wish, Seunim," they finally gave in.

But then, something unexpected happened. The entire Four Sutras class vanished from the temple. The students had been complaining about the planned shooting. One of them had convinced the entire class and they had all escaped together.

Myeong-seong waited at first. She thought they would return by sunset, but they didn't. She waited until nighttime. They still didn't return. They didn't show up to the morning ritual the next day either. One day passed. Two days, then three days passed, but they still did not show up. Now, the problem had gone beyond the television shooting, the daily cycle of the temple was entirely disrupted.

Finally, Myeong-seong decided to look for them. She

found out that they were all staying at a temple in Gyeongsan. She went straight to that temple, where the forty-plus student-nuns were surprised to see her. As she sat down in the room, they all rose and bowed three times. Myeong-seong asked:

"Are you eating well?"

"No."

"Are you sleeping well?"

"No."

"Are you peaceful in mind?"

"No."

"I will wait for you at a Chinese restaurant. Mr. Yoon will tell you where."

"Are you going to treat us to Chinese noodles?" The students' faces lit up.

"After eating noodles, come back to Unmun, if you haven't forgotten the way."

"Yes, Teacher. We will."

That is how she resolved the student strike with Chinese noodles. She did not ask a single question about who the leader was. She smiled thinking about this and folded the letter from Naewonsa Temple. She knew that, among the seunims who had shouted from the top of the mountain towards Unmunsa Temple, the leader of the strike had been there together with them.

Myeong-seong put on her knapsack and came out of her room. Her assistant nun immediately snatched the sack and carried it for her. A few seunims were waiting for her outside of her room, looking anxious and sad. One of them spoke, "Why don't you leave when the weather becomes warmer?"

"It doesn't matter. I'm in the car anyway. Please go back in. It's cold out. Don't follow me."

However, when Myeong-seong got in the car, everyone else boarded as well. Mr. Yoon drove the car out of the temple and through the pine tree forest. Nobody spoke.

"Stop the car here please, Mr. Yoon. We've come too far. Everybody, please get out and go back."

"No. Please, let us accompany you to One Pillar Gate."

Mr. Yoon restarted the car. Once again, silence filled the air. When they finally arrived at One Pillar Gate, the seunims stepped out of the vehicle, one by one. They gave their parting greetings.

"Please take care."

"Don't catch a cold. Don't overwork yourself."

"See you soon."

"You take good care too, Mr. Yoon."

"Please go back. It's freezing," Myeong-seong waved at them again, urging them to return. Mr. Yoon started the car. He drove fast so that they wouldn't have to wait in the cold any longer.

Myeong-seong had decided to do some fund-raising during the winter break. There were too many students to deal with. Applications flooded in, but even after whittling them down, they still ended up with over 120 students in the Novice Nun class and Four Collections class. Myeong-seong had constructed the Pavilion of Profound Lectures for the Flower Garland class, but the Main Buddha Hall was still overflowing. Myeong-seong always felt sorry that she could not accommodate all the young seunims who wanted to study at Unmun. Some students were already enrolled at Unmun but had nowhere to stay. They had to commute from other temples in the vicinity, such as Bukdae, Cheongsin, and Naewon. Wanting to embrace them all and not turn them away, she started to go on fundraising tours. In Sangha universities, students don't merely study together, they also eat and sleep together. This required a lot of space.

Myeong-seong invited an architect and asked him to prepare blueprints for the buildings that she had commissioned. A few months later, the designer returned with blueprints for accommodations for the Novice Nun class and Four Collections class. It was a very large wooden house, with an area of 9,900 square feet.

Myeong-seong wanted her own room, also. When she first came to Unmun, she had stayed in a small room next to the office. When the Gathering Stars Pavilion was built, she occupied a small room in the corner. Now, she needed an independent room for herself. It was inconvenient for both her and her students to stay in the same space. She also had many visitors and guests to greet. The architect brought plans for a building with an area of 960 square feet that was both her sleeping space and a guesthouse.

The overall cost of the construction was five hundred thousand dollars. That was half a million dollars in the year 1988. It was impossible for Unmun to afford that amount, but Myeong-seong could not give up on the construction, as that would be the same as giving up on the students.

And so, Myeong-seong decided to embark on another fundraising journey. She had done it once when she built the Gathering Stars Pavilion, and again after she had become the abbess when she built the Pavilion of Profound Lectures. It was not an easy task. Asking for money was very difficult, especially when she went to temples where she didn't know anyone. It was also physically grueling to be constantly on the road, and uncomfortable to eat and sleep in other temples, especially now that she was reaching the age of seventy.

She decided to visit Woljeongsa Temple in Gangwon Province first. She chose that temple because she wanted to begin the tour after prostrating in front of the holy relics enshrined at the Shrine for Sakyamuni Buddha's Sarira.

Myeong-seong became emotional when she arrived at Pyeongchang, Gangwon. This is where she had spent her girlhood. As a middle school student, she had delved into the books her father had given her. She would frequently visit Sangwonsa Temple where Han-am Seunim gave her candy and told her to recite Avalokiteshvara.

She started climbing up toward Buddha's Relic Palace (*Jeokmyeolbogung*). It was cold outside, but the sky was pure and clean. When she arrived at the palace, she did 108 prostrations to the Buddha. She prayed that this fundraising would be successful so that the Buddha's disciples could study in better conditions.

Myeong-seong travelled to Gangwon, Gyeonggi, Seoul, Chungcheon, Gyeongsang, and finished at Busan. She visited Unmun every once in a while, but most of the winter was spent on the road, raising money for the construction of the school.

The night Myeong-seong returned from the trip, two of her molar teeth fell out. Nobody knew about this, and she made sure to tell no one. She didn't want anyone to know that the trip had been that taxing on her.

In June of 1989, Blue Wind Quarters (*Cheongpungnyo*) was completed as planned. The Novice Nun class and Four Collections class moved into the spacious building to study. Now, the Novice Nun class and Four Collections class was at Blue Wind Quarters, the Four Sutras class was at the Main Buddha Hall, and the Flower Garland class was at the Pavilion of Profound Lectures. Unmun Sangha University had solidified its position as the top bhikkhuni educational institute.

When the construction of Blue Wind Quarters was nearing its end, Myeong-seong commenced with the construction of the House of Six Virtues (*Yukhwadang*), to be used as an office. A proper office was greatly needed as a space to conduct meetings, manage incoming and outgoing materials, greet guests, and as a place for nuns who were on duty or came to teach. The building had an area of 4,700 square feet. Myeong-seong simultaneously extended Gathering Stars Pavilion by adding two storage rooms in which to keep education materials. This construction ended up costing another four hundred thousand dollars. This was almost as much as Blue Wind Quarters.

When Myeong-seong was not teaching, she would hold her beads and pray to Manjushuri, Avalokiteshvara and the Medicine Buddha. She trusted that the Buddhas and Bodhisattvas would protect the Sangha University. In her spare time, she always stayed at the construction site to oversee the process. She already had an expert's eye and was paying so much attention to the construction that nobody would dare slack off on the job. That is how the House of Six Virtues joined the buildings of Unmun.

Pihadang was built for Myeong-seong. It was built where Hwaseokjuk had originally stood. Pihadang was a small wooden structure with an area of 1,000 square feet. It contained a room for Myeong-seong, a guest room, a room for an assistant nun, a kitchen, and a bathroom. After twenty years of living at Unmun, Myeong-seong finally had a room for herself.

Proper accounting was the most important part of these projects. In her book-keeping, Seongho Seunim made an incredible effort to keep their finances transparent and efficient.

In 1988, the Seoul City government built a Youth Centre

in Mokdong and entrusted the management to the National Bhikkhuni Association of the Korean Jogye Buddhist Order. In 1989, Gwang-u Seunim was appointed as president and Myeong-seong as the chairperson of the steering committee. They worked hard to strengthen the mind and body of the youth in Yangcheon district. Myeong-u Seunim became the next president, while Myeong-seong continued to contribute as head of the steering committee. All in all, she worked in that position for ten years.

On April 16, 1989, Hye-chun Seunim was elected as president, and Myeong-seong as vice president at the general assembly of the National Bhikkhuni Association. Myeong-seong was also elected as a member of the Central Committee of the Order and took part in its affairs.

This was all at the age of sixty. She had built up the foundation of Korean bhikkhunis from scratch. She created and wrote the history; she is a central figure in the history of Korean bhikkhunis.

Chapter 10

Blessings come only to those who are ready

Huge flakes of snow were falling on Unmunsa Temple. Seunims were bustling around in preparation for a joyful ceremony to be held that day. Myeong-seong's disciples were presenting her with a publication of her collected papers. Guests came from far and wide, filling up the temple. They all praised the accomplishments of Myeong-seong, who had built Unmun into a magnificent and majestic fully functioning temple with many new and restored buildings. Its university trained many seunims every year. It had become a pillar of Korean bhikkhuni education. Unmun also produced bhikkhuni teachers who conducted further research into Buddhism or taught Buddhist studies to non-Buddhists. For Myeong-seong to have published her research as a scholar on top of having done all of that seemed a superhuman feat.

The guests hailed from many different places including the Headquarters of the Order and Dongguk University. Unmun graduates and students added to the crowd. The ceremony began with the Three Refuges, followed by congratulatory remarks from the guests. Finally, Myeong-seong's disciples came forward to present the published collection of her papers to her, reading:

"We bow to the Buddhas and Bodhisattvas that are always present in all the ten directions of the past, the present, and the future. Time passes by quickly for those who work with dedication. Our Teacher, who has devoted her life to education, has now reached the age of sixty. Once again, we realize how all things truly are transient.

We have learned much from our Teacher. We are now cultivating hard in meditation, preaching to the people, or studying Buddhism. Our Teacher has always told us to be truthful to the moment. We are walking our paths as practitioners with this teaching in our hearts.

We have long pondered how to express our gratitude toward our Teacher. We had originally planned on making a collection of our own papers, which could have been a meaningful gift to present to our Teacher on her sixtieth birthday. However, we worried that our knowledge and views were too shallow in comparison with the work of our Teacher, so we decided to publish that collection at a future date. Instead, we have gathered all the papers written by our Teacher into a single collection. It is an excellent testimony to the sincere life that our Teacher has lived, truthful to her vow, never once wavering in her faith.

When we consulted our Teacher about this, she told us that the papers had been written a long time ago and needed much correction. But she graciously embraced our suggestion and revised all the papers herself. We were both honoured and thrilled to watch these thirty-year-old papers emerge from her drawers, every page a record of the truthful and sincere life that she has lived.

These papers are the living history of our Teacher. They were written as far back as 1958, when she was given the Dharma from Seong-neung Seunim at Seonamsa Temple, in South Jeolla Province. Some were completed during the time she was teaching at Cheongnyongsa Temple and working on her Ph.D. at Dongguk University. For us, they are precious lights and gems. We knew that she had had no intention of doing so, but we thought it was important that these old papers be taken from their drawers and organized into a book. It gives us great pleasure knowing that her precious work will now be available to the public.

We all remember how Professor Dong-hwa Kim had asked Myeong-seong to stay at Dongguk University to teach, but she turned him down and instead came to Unmun to teach bhikkhunis. That was her vow, and that vow has made Unmun what it is today.

We thank all those who helped and encouraged us along the way, including Ji-gwan Seunim, Il-ta Seunim, Ok-bong Seunim, Il-dang Seunim, Cheong-myeong Chang-soon Lim, Professor Hyang-san Jeong-hwan Byeon, Yeo-cho Eun-hyeon Kim, San-jeon Il-ho Yoon, and Dr. Byeong-ho Lee. We also would like to thank Beop-jeong Seunim for reviewing the papers, and

Bulkwang Publishers for publishing this book.

Once again, we congratulate our Teacher on her sixtieth birthday. May your teachings continue to shine on this world of suffering."

The audience erupted into a thunderous applause, and Myeong-seong gave a response to her disciples. Many renowned scholars, calligraphers, and artists had sent their artwork to congratulate her.

In fact, Myeong-seong's actual sixtieth birthday had been the year before this event. Myeong-seong had refused any kind of celebration, and had ultimately disappeared two days before the planned party. Her disciples were unable to have the event. The following year, however, the disciples were victorious, convincing their Teacher to approve the event and presenting her with the publication of her papers.

The following are the titles of the papers that Myeong-seong had written since her thirties. They were written during her studies at Dongguk University while doing her bachelor's, master's, and doctoral programs.

1. A Study on the Consciousness-Only: Focused on Vasubandhu's Yogâcāra Theory
2. The Dharma Realm Perspectives of Dushun of Tang China

3. A Study on the Huayan Ten Stages

4. An Investigation on the Absolute in Its Causative Condition

5. The Concept of Ten Stages from the Viewpoint of Consciousness-Only

6. A Brief Review on the Five Period Classification of the Teachings from the 4th Chapter of the Lotus Sutra, "Belief and Understanding"

7. An Investigation on the Four Divisions of the Tiantai Teaching

8. Types of Seon and Their Philosophical Implications

9. A Study on the Five Teachings of Huayan

10. A Study on the Ten Ontological Positions of Huayan

11. The Three Major Scripturalists in the Early Era of the Sixth Patriarch

12. On Dependent Arising of the Storehouse Consciousness (Ālaya-vijñāna)

13. A Study on the Dependent Arising of the Dharma Realm

14. The Standing of Huiyuan of Lushan in His Influence on Chinese Buddhist History

15. A Brief Review on the Mahāyāna Saṃgraha Śāstra

16. Buddhism in the Era of the Eastern Jin Dynasty

17. The Storehouse Consciousness as Explained in the Mahāyāna Saṃgraha Śāstra

18. Ganhwa Seon and Mozhao Chan [Phrase-Investigating

Meditation and Silent Illumination Meditation]
19. A Brief Review on the Sutra of Perfect Enlightenment
20. The Establishment of the Jogye Order
21. A Conceptual Investigation of Monastic Education
22. Unmunsa Temple, Residence of Seon Master Iryeon

It is amazing that, amidst her relentlessly busy schedule, she managed to write so many papers. While she was writing Alaya vijñāna: Focusing on Vasuvandu's Consciousness-Only Doctrine for her master's degree, she read between forty to fifty Japanese books – Japan was the leader in research on Consciousness-Only Buddhism – devoting over ten hours a day to the work. She used to talk about how, on multiple occasions, she would touch her head to make sure that it was in the right place.

On the day of the dedication ceremony, Myeong-seong also held an exhibition of her calligraphy artworks. She used the event to raise funds for the Beopgye (Dharmadatu) scholarship, which took its name from Myeong-seong's Dharma alias. As of 2015, this scholarship has given out 200 thousand dollars in support of students.

One day, when Myeong-seong was teaching sutras in a postgraduate course, a student from the office came to her. "Teacher, the governor is here to see you."

Myeong-seong was startled. Why would the governor visit without giving prior notification?

"Should I take him to Pihadang?" the student suggested.

"Yes, please," answered Myeong-seong.

After telling her students to work on interpreting the text, Myeong-seong went to Pihadang. Soon, the governor entered along with his entourage. The governor explained why he had come, "We have some important guests here from the Ministry of Education. I wondered where I should take them and decided to bring them here. The temple has grown so much I barely recognized it."

Governor U-hyeon Kim smiled as he said this. He had visited the temple some years back.

"Thank you for coming all the way to our temple," Myeong-seong replied.

Her assistant nun entered with tea and snacks. "These are pine pollen cookies. This is persimmon leaf tea. We made them here in our temple."

The guests marvelled at the special treat presented to them. Governor Kim remarked, "Every time I come here, it feels like paradise. Everything is so beautiful and organized."

"I am allowed to feel that way because I'm Buddhist. But Governor, you are Christian," joked a senior official from the Ministry of Education.

Time passed by quickly as Myeong-seong and her guests enjoyed the tea and conversation. Again, the assistant nun came to Myeong-seong and asked in a low voice, "Should we prepare dinner for them?"

"Yes, let's do that please," answered Myeong-seong.

The guests were excited by the unexpected development in their itinerary and seemed eager to try temple food. After dinner, they sat down for tea again. That was when Governor Kim asked, "I am impressed at how fast Unmun is growing. Is there anything we can do to help?"

Never at a lack for projects she wanted to work on, Myeong-seong answered immediately. "There is some abandoned farmland across the creek that belongs to our temple. Could you please help prepare the land to make it suitable for farming? That would help to resolve our food issue."

"That doesn't sound terribly difficult. I'll look into it as soon as I get back. We love the presence of a temple like Unmun in our province."

A few days later, an official from the province came to look into the matter. Not long after, tractors and bulldozers came to the field and cleared it for farming. The work began in December of 1991 and finished in August of the following year. The place was called Janggun Pyeong (General's Field), and consisted of about thirty-five acres. This completely solved the food issue for the temple. They could now become fully self-sufficient.

This might not have been possible had Myeong-seong not claimed that land ten years ago from the local farmers. It was as if she was preparing to receive heaven's blessings. Governor Kim also built two bridges over the creek, so that people from the temple could access the farmland.

If Myeong-seong had not been always thinking about the temple's work and her projects, she would not have been prepared to answer the governor's question. Blessings come to those who are ready, to those who truly seek them. If she had not made this request, Unmun might never have acquired some thirty-five acres of farmland, space for a forest reserve, and two bridges.

Myeong-seong did not only focus on expanding the temple's size, she started to really focus on beautifying the existing facilities. She planted trees and flowers, put benches in appropriate places, and set up stone water basins. Importantly, she focused a lot of attention on the arboretum. She visited many different arboretums to learn about them. She met with professors to seek their advice. That was around the time when the provincial government sent a notice to Unmunsa Temple. The government wanted the temple to plant trees on its property.

Myeong-seong consulted with a professor of forestry and decided to plant pine nut trees. Upon the decision, she applied to the provincial government for support. That is how Unmun's mountain was reforested. The trees would be put to good use in the future. The government helped further by developing the creek sides to prevent flooding and erosion. They reinforced the embankment and dug out the sand.

March of 1991 was a memorable month. Unmun began

the construction of its Main Hall (*Daeungbojeon*) where the Lord Buddha would be seated. Until then, Unmun's main hall was the Hall of the Cosmic Buddha (*Birojeon*). However, that hall was very old and small. Myeong-seong had long desired to build a Main Hall that would enshrine the Three Buddhas (Shakyamuni Buddha, Dipamkara, and Maitreya Buddha) and the Four Bodhisattvas (Manjushuri, Samantabhadra, Avalokiteshvara, and Mahasthama-prapta). She wanted it to be 4,410 square feet in area to be able to accommodate all the members of the Sangha. She had even picked which tree to use as the main pillar and prepared the roof tiles. She assigned Mr. Yeonghun Shin as the construction's general director. Mr. Shin was a good friend of Myeong-seong who, as a member of the National Cultural Heritage Committee, was qualified to restore cultural assets and national treasures.

All of the construction projects initiated and completed by Myeong-seong had one thing in common: the needs of the student-nuns came first, no matter what. She built their classroom first, then their living space. Only after twenty years, did she prepare a small room for herself and construct the Main Hall. Some might argue that the Main Hall, which consecrates the Buddhas, should have been completed first. However, would the Lord Buddha have wanted his shrine to be built before the nuns had proper facilities to study in?

Student-nuns were the future, and their needs should come before anything else. That was a solemn principle held by

Myeong-seong. Only after Unmun had completed the facilities necessary for education did it move on to working on the Buddha's Main Hall. Myeong-seong tended to every detail: carving the statue, drawing the Buddhist portraits, painting the wood, decorating the hall, etc. She sought out experts for each job. After four years, the Buddha's Main Hall was completed in December of 1994. The 4,410 square feet building cost around two million dollars.

In 1993, the Parliament of the World's Religions was held in Chicago. It was a centennial celebration of a previous event held in the same city in 1893. Myeong-seong was invited as a representative of Korean Buddhism. It was her first time to participate in an official international event with religious leaders from many countries. The event was organized by Christians, but they did not monopolize the process. Participants shared the understanding that it is not possible for a single country or religion to address the complicated issues of the present-day world.

The main point of discussion was how different religions should communicate and cooperate with each other in order to solve the challenges that faced humanity. After a heated debate, over five hundred leaders from more than forty different religions adopted a declaration titled, "Towards a Global Ethic: An Initial Declaration." It was meaningful that leaders from different faiths came together to seek a solution to the common problems that ailed humanity. As it concluded, the parliament agreed to hold the same event every five years.

Myeong-seong had the opportunity to rethink the role of a religious leader. She broadened her views by meeting people from many different traditions. She realized that humanity's problems are religion's problems; that religion had to engage in the struggle to find answers.

During the summer break of 1995, Myeong-seong visited Cambodia along with Jin-gwang Seunim and the writer Ji-sim Nam. Jin-gwang was Myeong-seong's formal Dharma disciple; Ms. Nam was her lay disciple. She was visiting Cambodia for a simple reason. She had heard that Cambodia had traditionally been a Buddhist country, but that Buddhism in the country had been seriously degraded due to a long period of colonialism and civil war. Lacking resources, monks there were unable to pursue their studies. It would cost a mere thirty dollars per month to support one monk. Myeong-seong knew of a Won Buddhist master who donated sixty dollars a month to sponsor the education of two monks.

Thirty dollars a month was not very much money, but Myeong-seong wanted to see the situation with her own eyes. It was about three years after Pol Pot had lost power. After studying in France, Pol Pot pursued his fantasy of creating an agrarian socialist society by murdering anybody who he perceived as the enemy of agriculture and socialism. Such people included businessmen, capitalists, industrial workers, liberalists, scholars, monks and many others. Around three million people were killed out of a total population of eight million. Six thousand monks were slaughtered and temples were burnt. Some temples were spared so that they could be used as animal feed houses.

Buddhism, in its traditional form, was pretty much lost. However, after Hun Sen came to power, many people wanted to become monks. While the number of aspirant monks increased exponentially, the country had no resources to educate them. Myeong-seong's team visited the Supreme Patriarch Tep Vong and heard about the country's tragic history first hand. Even the Supreme Patriarch's monastery on the banks of the Mekong River, boasting an elementary school, high school, and Sangha university, was destitute and dilapidated.

Students sat on the ground and wrote in the soil. There were no pens, pencils, or paper. The chalkboards were so worn they were turning white like chalk. The situation reminded Myeong-seong of the post-war period in Korea. Myeong-seong gave the monastery all the money she had brought so that they could use it for the school. She continued to help them after coming back to Korea. She funded the digging of wells for them and also helped them build a dam that allowed more stable farming conditions for over five thousand rice farmers.

When Seol-jo Seunim of Bulguksa Temple heard about this, he also began donating one thousand dollars every month. After three years, thirty-three monks from Cambodia Central Sangha University were able to complete their education.

Chapter 11

The most beautiful bond

Myeong-seong always carried herself with dignity. Her movement, appearance, and speech all had the air of a practitioner. She always had beads in her hand, reciting Manjushuri, Avalokiteshvara, and Medicine Buddha prayers at least one thousand times everyday. She did calligraphy whenever she had time. She had learned it from the greatest masters in Korea – Il-jung and Yeo-cho. She taught this art to her students as well. After writing calligraphy, she would not throw the paper away but collect and turn them into artwork. She called this "paper art." She would rub and twist the paper into threads which were used to make fabulous handicrafts.

Myeong-seong liked to collect flowers and leaves from places she would visit, whether in Korea or abroad. She dried them and put them into a book. She certainly enjoyed collecting rare plants, but part of it was just an appreciation of small and pretty things. She was also good at knitting. She would knit scarfs, gloves, and hats, which she would give out to others. She had an appreciation for beauty; she would give out pretty things as gifts. Clearly, she had a feminine and soft side that was visible to anyone.

However, when she pursued her work, her driving force was stronger than any man. She continuously planned and built for over thirty years; none of the construction projects were carried out without her close oversight. She was always there on-site, overseeing, caring, and checking on things. She had an expert's eye. That is why, no matter how tough the workers were, they never questioned Myeong-seong.

Furthermore, not for a moment was she idle with her studies. She was a teacher and a scholar. If she did not work continuously to improve her studies, it would not have been easy for her to teach others.

Every night, before going to sleep, Myeong-seong always meditated for an hour. She would practice Seon with a Koan. Her work and life did not allow her to cultivate intensively at a Seon Centre, so she focused on her practice even harder when she was able to.

Interestingly, she enjoyed watching television dramas. It helped her to understand the lives of laypeople. Understanding the secular world was no different from understanding the divine world, for the secular and divine were not actually separate. She particularly liked historical dramas, which gave her some degree of insight into history, however indirect, and helped her to understand the world more. She was also fond of documentaries.

It is amazing to see her excel at the highest level in whatever she does, whereas ordinary people struggle to excel in even a single field. She lives her life accumulating endless merits; then giving them all away.

In 1964, she translated a Japanese book into Korean: The Main Principles of the Abhidharmakośakārikā, written by Kajikawa Kendō. It was published in Korea by Bulkwang. Two years later, she translated Essentials of Consciousness-Only Buddhism by Katō Satoshijun and published it through Unmun Publishing.

Abhidharmakośakārikā is the foundation of Theravada Buddhism. Yogacara is the basis for Mahayana Buddhism. Myeong-seong believed that these two books were most needed to help guide her students.

In 1995, she translated Abhidharma-nyāyānusāra in the Korean Tripitaka. The book was published by the Sutra Translation Centre of Dongguk University. She was the first bhikkhuni to translate a sutra in the Tripitaka.

In 1998, she became the President of the Graduate School of Unmun Sangha University, which had been established by the Jogye Order. She felt the need for a graduate school to train real experts. Among the students who graduated from Unmun Sangha University, those who wanted to continue with their studies entered the graduate school. Myeong-seong invited outside experts, both laypeople and seunims, to come and teach along with her. Unmun is the first temple to have formed its own graduate school.

Graduate school students received a small amount of money. It was unlike other schools, where students had to pay for tuition on their own. This shows how dedicated Myeong-seong was towards developing the graduate school. She sincerely wished to see many bhikkhuni Buddhist scholars.

In 1998, Myeong-seong finally acquired her doctoral degree from Dongguk University. Her dissertation was titled Three Transforming Consciousnesses: Based on Discourses on the Perfection of Consciousness-Only. It was 24 years after she had completed her graduate course at Dongguk. She was 69 years old. She had spent the past twenty-four years living and working for others, while holding on to the thought that she would one day finish her own personal studies. Many disciples, followers, laypeople, and seunims came to Dongguk University to congratulate her.

In the same year, she completed the Three Basket Library (Samjangwon), a name which meant that it contained books on the three different studies of sutras (discourse), vinaya (discipline), and abhidharma (doctrine). The Three Basket Library had over twenty thousand books and one hundred and fifty chairs, along with research rooms for scholars to use. The building was two stories high with an area of 7,545 square feet. It was the temple's second largest structure after Blue Wind Quarters. Built in the traditional Korean way, it cost 3.5 million dollars. The next building to be raised was the House of Meditative Bliss

(*Seonyeoldang*), which finally concluded the decades-long construction of Unmun. The monastery was now fully equipped with all the necessary facilities.

Myeong-seong had come to Unmun at the age of forty. By the age of seventy, she had built thirty-nine buildings and repaired ten. Unmunsa Temple, a historical yet abandoned site, had transformed into a world-class bhikkhuni education centre boasting Unmun Sangha University and its Graduate School. Myeong-seong praises the Buddhas and Bodhisattvas for making such accomplishments possible.

In autumn of 2000, to commemorate the seventy-first birthday of their Teacher, Myeong-seong's students published "A Collection of Essays on Buddhism to Commemorate the Seventieth Birthday of Myeong-seong" and dedicated it to her. Contributors to this collection of essays included not only her students, but also many Buddhist scholars. Guests came from all over. Her friends, students, disciples, scholars, and laypeople from various occupations all came together to congratulate and pay respect to Myeong-seong and her life's work.

The ceremony took place in the Pavilion of Eternity. After finishing the Three Refuges and a Buddhist ritual, Jin-gwang Seunim read out loud:

"Last spring, we formed a publication committee to celebrate the work of our teacher and commemorate it in our humble way. We decided to dedicate an essay collection to her. Many students who learned directly from our teacher, as well as other scholars who wished to congratulate her, sent us their precious papers. Some people also sent calligraphy and paintings. (Omitted)"

As Jin-gwang had mentioned, in addition to her students and seunims, many Buddhist scholars, calligraphers, and artists eagerly participated to send their love. Myeong-seong had friendships with many, and many of them trusted and respected her.

Yeo-cho Eun-hyun Kim sent a work of calligraphy, Wol-un Seunim sent a poem, and Professor Seoggu Song offered a congratulatory message. Many Buddhist scholars such as Yeong-tae Kim, Karma Lekshe Tsomo, Jeong-bae Mok, Yeong-ja Lee, and Pyeong-nae Lee contributed essays of their own.

The landscape where Unmunsa Temple is located itself inspires comparisons with the Pure Land. The mountain, the creek, the forest, and the valleys were all pristine. Mount Unmun had been well-managed. In addition to the temple, Myeong-seong paid special attention to taking care of the mountain. She made sure that the temple became a steward of the forest. She planted trees in empty spaces and thinned out dense areas, pruning when necessary. The whole of Mount Unmun had been transformed into a majestic garden. In 2000, she was recognized for this work by the government and awarded the Environment Minister's Special Award.

When she turned seventy-two, the Dongguk University Alumni Association elected her as vice president. This generated new affinities within the secular world. Her activities were far from limited to the Buddhist world.

In the same year, the Sri Lankan government presented Myeong-seong with the Sasana Kirthi Sri award, which was given to those who have contributed greatly to the development of Buddhism.

As bhikkhunis acquired greater education and status, the Jogye Order prepared a separate ordination platform in which bhikkhunis could ordain other bhikkhunis. Jeong-haeng Se-unim presided over the ceremony. The witnessing teachers were In-hong, Myo-eom, Gwang-u, Hye-un, Tae-gu, Tae-gyeong, Myeong-seong, Ji-won, and Jeong-hun. Myeong-seong was the instructor (acarya) for conduct and teachings. In 2001, a platform for the full ordination of bhikkhunis was established. Myeong-seong passed on the precepts to ordaining bhikkhunis. Bhikkhunis had come a long way and had struggled hard to advance their status. Now, along with bhikkhus, they were one of the two pillars of Korean Buddhism. Many bhikkhunis had invested so much effort and Myeong-seong had certainly been a major part of this.

On November 20, 2003, Myeong-seong was elected as president of the National Bhikkhuni Association. The first president had been Eun-yeong Seunim, then Cheon-il, Ji-myeong, while Hye-chun and Gwang-u both served two terms each. This made Myeong-seong the eighth president.

In November of 1985, at a meeting in Banyasa Temple, Busan, the association had first discussed the need for an office building. Ten years later, in September, 1995, at the Mokdong Youth Centre, they had discussed their land use in Suseo district and how they could strengthen the association. They had been preparing for an office building for ten years. Hye-chun Seunim was instrumental in this project. She went all over in search of the proper site. During her tiresome journey, whenever she met people who empathized with her mission, she would sing 'Solveig's Song' as she rested her weary legs.

After three years, on September 10, 1998, construction finally began in Suseodong, Seoul, on a two acre site. The construction costs were provided by the Headquarters and with donations from followers. The building was three stories tall with two basement floors. It had a main hall, special rooms for activities, a cafeteria, rooms for sleeping, and a parking lot. It cost about one million dollars to construct. The sixth and seventh president, Gwang-u Seunim, worked hard to raise the money. The largest contributor to building the association's office was

Dae-haeng Seunim of the Hanmaum Seon Centre. Had it not been for her generous donation (0.8 million dollars), the construction would have been much more difficult.

Hye-chun prepared the site and Gwang-u built the office. Now, it was Myeong-seong's turn to get it up and running. As the eighth president, Myeong-seong poured all of her energy into bringing life to the association. First of all, she had to secure the association's finances. She encouraged her followers and other Buddhists to donate. She asked for donations of statues: Past Buddha, Present Buddha, Future Buddha, assistant Bodhisattvas, thousand shapes of transforming Buddhas, etc.

She used her personal money to open a small shop that sold Buddhist items, books, and tea. Every time she visited, she bought hundreds of prayer beads to help the shop make ends meet. She would give these out to anyone who came to see her. If you visited her, you never left empty-handed.

Myeong-seong presided over a Dharma ceremony at Beomnyongsa Temple, which was located inside the Bhikkhuni Association's building. She held classes on calligraphy, pottery, Buddhist painting, and tea ceremonies so that the community could benefit from the temple. Seon-jae Seunim's class on Temple Food was a big hit. Many Buddhists wanted to learn how to prepare food as they did in temples. Myeong-seong had a great affection for the calligraphy class. She went to Insa Dong to purchase calligraphy supplies for new students, remembering how she had yearned for such things when she was just learning calligraphy.

Myeong-seong came to Seoul twice a month to attend to Bhikkhuni Association matters. She would hold leader meetings to resolve any pressing issues. It was not easy for her at her age to visit Seoul twice a month, but she gave all she had to her two sacred duties, running Unmunsa Temple and the National Bhikkhuni Association. The Association's finances also became completely transparent due to her method of entrusting it to clerical officers. It was not long before both the National Bhikkhuni Association and Beomnyongsa Temple were running smoothly.

In 2003, the Munsu Seon Centre (*Munsuseonwon*) opened at Unmunsa Temple. The Seon Centre was located on the way up to the Sariam Hermitage where large pine trees grew and azaleas blossomed. Myeong-seong had for a long time yearned to open a Seon Centre, as she knew the importance of both doctrinal and meditational studies. It was open to all bhikkhunis, whether graduates of Unmun or from other temples. Hye-un Seunim, who had successfully led the construction of the Sariam Hermitage, was put in charge of the Seon Centre. Hye-un had assisted Myeong-seong since her time at Cheongnyong; the two had been collaborating for nearly their entire lives.

On February 29, 2004, Gwan-eung Seunim, at that time an elder at Jikjisa Temple, entered nirvana. He was ninety-four years old and had been a monk for seventy-five years. Buddhist monks and nuns are sworn to renounce everything. For Myeong-seong, Gwan-eung was officially her teacher only, however, fatherly love ran deep between them. Gwan-eung's funeral took place at 11 am on March 3, at the Hall of Abundant Virtue (*Mandeokjeon*) in Jikjisa Temple.

Gwan-eung was both the greatest scholar and Seon master of his time. He had graduated from the monastic college at Yujeomsa Temple in Geumgang Mountain, Hyehwa College, and Ryukoku University in Japan. He had also completed six years of intense meditation at Gateless Gate (*Mumunkuan*). As a master of both doctrine and meditation, he transmitted his Dharma to ten disciples. Numerous seunims and followers flocked to Jikjisa Temple upon his death. The last day of February had a hint of spring's warmth, and the number of mourners who had gathered was a testament to how many people were indebted to Gwaneung.

Myeong-seong remembered how Gwan-eung had given her books about heroes and heroines, and *The Truth of Life*, advising her to read them ten times each. This was meant to teach her, to prepare her. He had visited her when she was a postulant at Mireugam Hermitage in Dasolsa Temple to teach her Self-Admonition for Beginners. Gwan-eung had told her to go and study under Un-heo Seunim, and had given her a letter to pass on to him. On the day he left after finishing the lecture, she had cried for so long while watching him leave. This time, she was watching him leave for good.

She also remembered when Gwan-eung came out from his six years of meditation at Gateless Gate in Cheonchuk Mountain. He had entered Gateless Gate when he turned sixty. When he opened the door, in his sixties, over one thousand Buddhists were gathered there to greet him, full of respect and tears. She had felt such immense pride. She was in the back, behind the crowd, but watching her father, she was filled with pride.

When Myeong-seong went abroad for the first time, she received a letter from her father while she was in Chicago. At that point, she had finished her tour of Southeast Asia and Europe.

Dear Myeong-seong,

I was worried that you might have left New York already, so I am resending the letter to Chicago. I wish for your safety in your long journey. I received your letter sent from Thailand, but it arrived more than ten days after you had sent it. I also replied late, having just returned after an outing. I calculated that my letter would arrive in New York more than twenty days after the date sent, so I decided to send this to Chicago.

I am pleased to hear that your travels to many countries have been smooth and safe. Take care of your health. Make sure to observe and remember everything so that you learn as much as possible.

It seems that Unmunsa Temple has invited Jamin temporar-

ily; they invited me to come to a completion ceremony for the ritual painting of the seven saints on February 17 in the lunar calendar. I would like to go there but will have to see. Again, I pray for your wellness and safety throughout your journey.

March 13, 1976
from Bojangsa Temple, Gwan-eung

It is clear that Myeong-seong had kept Gwan-eung informed about her itinerary. Gwan-eung knew her address in Chicago. He had first sent a letter to New York, but then sent it again to Chicago in case his daughter might not receive it.

Chapter 12

Buddha's Daughter

One year after Myeong-seong had become president of the Korean Bhikkhuni Association, the Eighth Sakyadhita International Conference on Buddhist Women was held in Seoul, Korea. Sakyadhita means "daughter of the Buddha." Established in February of 1987 in Bodh Gaya, India, it is the largest Buddhist women's organization in the world. The organization has been working hard to improve the rights of Buddhist women. The conference is held every two years, rotating in turns among the member countries. There are forty-five countries, with around 1,900 members participating. Membership includes both nuns and Buddhist laywomen.

The 8th Sakyadhita International Conference on Buddhist Women ran from June 27 through July 2, 2004. It was held at Joong-Ang Sangha University and organized by the Korean Bhikkhuni Association. The conference's theme was "Discipline and Practice of Buddhist Women: Present and Past."

Myeong-seong was designated as a co-chairperson along with Tsomo, the president of Sakyadhita. Bon-gak Seunim, a professor of Joong-Ang Sangha University, was the head of the steering committee. Tenzin Palmo, who had meditated in a cave for twelve years, was greatly revered by all. The majority of the Korean bhikkhunis attended this eighth conference. Many Buddhist women also took part. The event overflowed with participants; about twenty thousand people attended over the whole period. There were numerous seminars and group discussions focusing on the past and present state of education of Buddhist women, and what they should be doing to prepare for the future.

Numerous volunteers came together to cook food, clean the area, organize things, guide the guests, and more. It was one of the most successful Sakyadhita conferences. To the delight of attendees, Buddhists from different countries offered cultural performances. The conference was a meaningful event where all participants shared in-depth discussions on the education of Buddhist women. It was also an important opportunity for letting the world know of the progress made by Korean bhikkhunis.

Many bhikkhunis and upasikas from Korea and abroad also came to the academic conference. For six days, experts in the field engaged in serious discussions. After the debate, all attendees, scholars and even the performers went on a tour of Korean temples. The tour was part of the event. During the six days, Joong-Ang Sangha University continued to hold programs for guests, including a Buddhist service, a Sutra recital, a Seon experience, a tea ceremony, screenings of videos on Korean Buddhism, Korean handcrafts, a display of Korean robes, traditional paper art, and photographs. Indeed, the eighth Sakyadhita conference was remembered by all as a heartfelt success.

The event proved how far Korean bhikkhunis had come. In the late fifties, there was no such thing as bhikkhuni education. Gwang-u, Myo-eom, and Myeong-seong were the pioneer bhikkhunis who had to go to bhikkhu schools in order to learn. Less than fifty years later, Korean bhikkhunis had grown enough to host an international conference. They produced many nuns, experts, and scholars. It was nothing short of a miracle.

This was all possible due to the endless dedication of so many bhikkhunis. They had devoted themselves to the education of their disciples, to the future of Korean bhikkhunis. Myeong-seong was truly a living history, and a testimony to their struggle.

– **Myeong-seong founds the "Dharma Wheel Scholarship"**

In 2006, Myeong-seong held a calligraphy exhibition at Beomnyeonsa Temple where she displayed all of the artwork she had done throughout her entire life. She wanted to establish a scholarship for bhikkhunis. Myeong-seong had begun studying calligraphy under masters Il-jung and Yeo-cho in the early seventies, while she was enrolled at Dongguk University. After over thirty years, she gave away her lifetime's work for the education of younger bhikkhunis. The exhibition was full of visitors. Many monks, nuns, and Buddhists came to watch and support.

Upon her inauguration as the president of the Korean Bhikkhuni Association, Myeong-seong emphasized the importance of scholarships as a means to produce talented nuns for the future. She managed to raise five hundred thousand dollars through the exhibition. This was added to the donations of two hundred thousand dollars from director seunims and others. In 2010, with seven hundred thousand dollars, she founded the "Dharma Wheel (*Beomnyun*) Bhikkhuni Scholarship".

The purpose was the same as that of the "Dharmadatu (*Beopgye*) Scholarship." Myeong-seong always believed that advancing the status of bhikkhunis was possible through the power of education. It was her aspiration to found both the "Dharma Wheel" and "Dharmadatu" within her lifetime. They were pure acts of dāna, for she had built the foundation for the scholarship by giving away her lifelong works of calligraphy and paper art.

— Myeong-seong received by the Thai princess as an equal to a bhikkhu

For four days, starting from May 7, 2006, Myeong-seong attended the Vesak Day ceremony hosted by Mahachulalongkorn University, Thailand, together with approximately one hundred other people from Korea. Many in the delegation were from the Korean Bhikkhuni Association, but seunims and scholars from Dongguk University attended also. Vesak Day is a United Nations-designated Buddhist holiday that celebrates the full moon of May, the birth and enlightenment of Buddha, and his parinirvana. Buddhists of the world come together to hold a Dharma conference to spread the teachings and wishes for world peace.

Over four thousand Buddhists from forty-seven countries gathered at Mahachulalongkorn University, the top school in Thailand. They were divided into seven social spheres, such as education and culture, and heatedly debated how to further develop Buddhism. Myeong-seong read the congratulatory message out loud. Jeong-yul Seunim sang a song at the opening that was wildly received by the delegations from different countries. Seon-jae's Korean temple food was also popular among the participants.

On the third day, May 9, when delegations from all of the countries visited the Royal Emerald Temple, Myeong-seong was the only bhikkhuni to join a team of visitors paying homage to princess of Thailand. Myeong-seong received gifts along with the other bhikkhus. This meant that Thai Buddhism recognized Korean bhikkhunis as equals of bhikkhus. On the last day, when Myeong-seong met with the Patriarch of Thailand, she emphasized that Thailand, a country with a rich Buddhist heritage, must establish a bhikkhuni sangha. She promised that the Korean Bhikkhuni Association would assist with this endeavor if it were to proceed.

A Forum on the History of Korean Bhikkhunis

On June 1, 2006, a forum was held on the traditional

practices of Korean bhikkhunis. There were presentations and discussions on the topic, covering from the Three Kingdoms period to modern times. They looked into the history of bhikkhunis, Seon Centres and Theory schools, and the life of bhikkhunis. Papers presented at the forum were collected and published under the title "The Cultivation and Life of Korean Bhikkhunis." Myeong-seong wrote the preface:

> *In June 2006, a forum on 'The Cultivation and Life of Korean Bhikkhunis' was held by the Korean Bhikkhuni Association. The forum looked into the cultivation of bhikkhunis since the arrival of Buddhism in the country. Participants confirmed how the devoted practice of the great bhikkhunis from each era contributed to the spread and development of Buddhism. It provided us an opportunity for renewed determination and vows.*
>
> *Many papers were presented at the forum which highlighted the life and role played by bhikkhunis. They have been organized and put into this book. We hope the noble practice of our predecessors sheds light upon the bhikkhunis of our times and guides them along their path. This book should not be an end but rather a beginning to continue the work of supporting our bhikkhunis so that they can become beacons to guide all Buddhists.*

This book introduced to the public the vivid lives of bhikkhunis from the Three Kingdoms era and Goryeo and Joseon dynasties. The book also introduced the bhikkhunis of our time, such as Beob-hui, Il-yeop, Hye-ok, Su-ok, Bon-gong, In-hong, Bongnyeokwan, and Jeong-haeng. It explained how the lineage of bhikkhunis has continued to flow like a river since the arrival of Buddhism. Historically, heroic bhikkhunis would appear from time to time to advance the status of bhikkhunis.

This job continued after the publication of the first book, culminating in a second book after three years. Book two described the lives of bhikkhunis like Jin-o, Kwe-yu, Wol-hye, Se-deung, Beob-il, Hye-chun, Man-seong, and Jang-il, among others. The work continues to this day.

_ **Congratulatory message at the 10th World Religious Leaders' Conference**

The 10th World Religious Leaders' Conference was held in Korea from June 8 to 14, 2006. The Society for Enhancing Manhae's Dream organized the event. Thirty-five religious leaders from eight religious organizations and eighteen countries took part. Korean representatives from many different religions – Buddhism, Catholicism, Protestantism, Cheondoism, Won Buddhism, Anglicanism, and Daesoon Jinrihoe – gathered to discuss how religion can resolve the conflict and tension present in our world and bring forth reconciliation and peace.

The organizer tried to invite the Dalai Lama but was unable to due to political reasons. Nonetheless, the Dalai Lama sent a message which was read out loud. Myeong-seong also sent a message:

> *Along with the Korean bhikkhunis and female Buddhists of the world, I congratulate the successful opening of the 2006 World Religious Leaders' Conference. The theme of this conference is reconciliation, peace, and sustainability. As female Buddhists in Korea and around the world who have contemplated their roles in the reconciliation between religions and world peace, this is a meaningful and grateful event.*
>
> *Bhikkhunis of the world, including the Korea Bhikkhuni Association, have continued to seek ways to bring about reconciliation and peace in this world. The Sakyadhita Association, founded in India in 1987, is the largest female Buddhist organization in the world. Sakyadita has members in forty-five countries and holds a biennial conference. After the first conference in Bodh Gaya, India, in 1987, the eighth conference was held in Seoul, South Korea, in 2004 under the theme Discipline and Practice of Buddhist Women: Present and Past.*
>
> *Tsomo, the president of Sakyadhita, said at the Seoul conference that she was impressed at how Korean Buddhist women were leading the world in advancing the status of Buddhist women. In Cave in the Snow: a Western woman's quest for enlightenment, Tenjin Palmo commented, "The*

more than seven thousand bhikkhunis in Korea are a model for bhikkhunis around the world."

Just a few decades ago, there had been no monastic colleges for bhikkhunis in Korea. Now there are five located in Donghak (Gongju), Unmun (Cheongdo), Cheongam (Gimcheon), Bongnyeong (Suwon), and Samseon (Seoul). Here, nuns teach nuns. Of eighty-seven meditation centres, thirty-two are for bhikkhunis. This is unique to Korea. For sure, Korean nuns are leading the way in showing the direction in which bhikkhunis should move forward.

In addition to nuns, the role of laywomen is also important for reconciliation and world peace. In Korean, the word for wife means the sun inside the house. All wives must have wisdom when raising children and managing household affairs. Women's compassion needs to expand to revealing Buddha's philosophy of equality. Those women who make a happy family can also make a happy world. Home is where you cultivate, it is paradise and heaven.

Goethe said that religion is more about walking than talking. Action is important, not just words. Why does the world suffer from terrorism, war, division, poverty, starvation, and disease? It is not because we do not know the cause; it is because we do not take any action. Religious leaders need to awaken the politicians who are leading the nation in a wrong direction. They need to teach indifferent people to have compassion for their suffering neighbors.

That is why each and every one of you who have attended today's conference is precious.

Creating a forest of merit with the Lotus Sutra, the flower of Mahayana

The Korean Bhikkhuni Association held a "Lotus Sutra Forest Seminar" for eight months at Beomnyongsa Temple. Thirty-two bhikkhuni teachers taught the sutra at 11 am every Sunday as a symbol of the Thirty-two Responsive Manifestations of Avalokiteshvara. It was the first time that bhikkhunis had given lectures on the Lotus Sutra. This would not have been possible had they not achieved a higher status than before.

Myeong-seong gave the introductory lecture; the Education Director of the Korean Bhikkhuni Association, Il-beop Seunim, taught the Ways and Means; the Dean of Donghaksa Temple, Il-cho, taught the Parables; the Dean of Unmun Sangha University, Il-jin, taught Faith and Understanding; the Director of Social Affairs at the Korean Bhikshuni Association, Gwang-ok, taught the Parable of the Plants; the Dean of Sangha University at Bongnyeongsa Temple, Do-hye, taught Assurances of Becoming a Buddha; the abbess of Yumasa Temple, Il-ji, taught The Magic City; the Dean of Cheongamsa Temple at Sangha University, Ji-hyeong, taught Assurances for 500 Arhats; Se-deung of Heungansa Temple taught Assurances for Trainees and Adepts; the Director of Administration of the Korea Bhikkhuni Association, Seong-jeong, taught Teacher of the Dharma;

Professor Hae-ju of Dongguk University taught the Treasure Stupa; Dae-u from Hanhwasa Temple taught the Devadatta; Imdae of Gwaneumsa Temple taught Encouragement to Uphold the Stupa; Seong-beop of Mangwolsa Temple taught Peace and Contentment; the abbess of Jingwansa Temple, Gye-ho, taught Springing Up from the Earth; the Director of Regulations of the Bhikkhuni Association, Seung-hye, taught the Eternal Lifespan of the Tathagata; Professor Bon-gak of Joong-Ang Sangha University taught Merits and Virtues of Enlightenment; Professor Gye-hwan of Dongguk University taught Merits and Virtues of Joyful Acceptance; Professor Neung-in of Joong-Ang Sangha University taught Merits and Virtues obtained by a Teacher of the Dharma; Professor Myo-ju of Dongguk University taught The Bodhisattva Sadāparibhūta; Hye-gyeon of Daeboksa Temple taught The Spiritual Power of the Tathagata; the abbess of Jijang Hermitage Seon Centre, Jeong-an, taught The Passing of the Commission; the previous cultural director of the Jogye Order, Tak-yeon, taught The Bodhisattva Bhaiṣajyarāja; the current abbess of Unmunsa Temple, Jin-gwang, taught The Bodhisattva Gadgadasvara; Sang-deok taught The Bodhisattva Avalokiteśvara; Hyo-tan taught Dhāraṇī; Hye-won taught King Wonderfully Adorned; Il-yeon taught Encouragement of the Bodhisattva Samantabhadra; Su-gyeong taught Virtuous Act of Sutra of Infinity (Muryanguigyeong); Un-won taught Teaching of Dharma; Beob-jo taught Ten Virtues; and on the final day, the previous president of the Korea Bhikkhuni Association, Gwang-u, returned all merits to sentient beings.

Some of the bhikkhunis mentioned above have doctorate degrees, and some are professors who teach bhikkhus and bhikkhunis at Dongguk University and Joong-Ang Sangha University. When Myeong-seong entered Dongguk University in 1961, the school had just two bhikkhunis – Gwang-u and Wol-song. This demonstrates the amazing development that has taken place in less than fifty years.

_ **Discussion with the Dalai Lama on the Vinaya and Ordination Lineages**

The International Congress on Buddhist Women's Role in the Sangha: Bhikkhuni Vinaya and Ordination Lineages took place from July 18 to 20, 2007, and was organized by Studienstiftung für Buddhismus (Foundation for Buddhist Studies) in co-operation with the Asia-Africa-Institute of the University of Hamburg. It was a meeting of internationally recognized Buddhist scholars specializing in monastic discipline and history, as well as practitioners.

This international event aimed at restoring bhikkhuni ordination lineage in Tibetan Buddhism. The Dalai Lama attended the congress and expressed his support for its goals. Below were the topics of discussion:

1. The status of women in Buddhism
2. The debate surrounding the full ordination of women in Buddhism

3. Procedures for the full ordination of women
4. The meaning of full ordination of women in Buddhist society
5. Possibilities for reviving ordination lineages in Buddhism based on equity between the two sexes

Over forty people attended from Korea, including Myeong-seong, who was the president of the Korean Bhikkhuni Association. Myeong-seong gave an opening address on The Role of Bhikkhunis in the Twenty-First Century. Four different seunims and scholars introduced the current status of Korean bhikkhunis. The dean of Bongnyeong Sangha University, Myoeom, presented on the structure and curriculum of the Diamond Vinaya school; Professor Hae-ju of Dongguk University spoke of the dual sangha system and the Four-part Vinaya of the Jogye Order; Professor Hyangsoon Yi of the University of Georgia talked about general issues facing bhikkhuni sanghas during the Joseon dynasty; and Seok-dam from the University of Virginia presented on the rehabilitation of dual sanghas for Korean bhikkhuni.

On the last day of July 20, Hye-won Seunim, planning director at the Korean Bhikkhuni Association and president of the Buddhist Culture Institute of Dongguk University, gave a speech about the big role that Korean bhikkhuni sangha could play in reviving bhikkhuni sangha in Tibet.

It is miraculous that Korean bhikkhunis were able to raise their voices and contribute to such an important international event. This feat would not have been possible just fifty years before.

Below is an excerpt from the presentation given by Myeong-seong:

I am very happy to meet you all. Buddhism began in India 2,550 years ago with Shakyamuni Buddha, but it has now spread throughout the world, allowing people outside of traditional Buddhist regions to also have access to the knowledge. As a result, we now see more western nuns. This has brought changes to the sangha, and we have had a chance to reflect upon the history and achievement of bhikkhunis. However, it is most important that we define the role of bhikkhunis in the twenty-first century.

Buddhism is special among the religions of the world in that it gives equal possibility of full enlightenment to both men and women. The Lord Buddha established a bhikkhuni sangha not only to teach us about gender equality, but also because it is essential. I believe the Lord Buddha wanted us to accept and respect bhikkhunis as an essential part of the Three Jewels. Unfortunately, however, discriminatory cultural customs have clouded Buddha's original intention and we have deviated from gender equality. This has restricted the bhikkhunis from performing their mission of seeking en-

lightenment and delivering sentient beings. (Omitted)

I am not saying that we bhikkhunis should attempt to solve all the problems of the world. There are many bhikkhunis who are already practicing compassion through local societies or international non-governmental organizations. My point is that bhikkhunis should be able to inspire people with their strong faith and expert knowledge as spiritual leaders of humankind.

To that end, the first thing we should do is to rehabilitate bhikkhuni sanghas where Buddhism exists. Women make up half of the world's population. Equal opportunity must be given to women so that they are able to realize their religious aspirations. The tradition of ordination is alive in China, Korea, Taiwan, and Vietnam. Recently, Sri Lanka has successfully revived bhikkhuni ordination. However, it is not so in Theravadan Buddhism and in Tibet. There are differences in the ordination procedure between Mahayana and Theravadan Buddhism. When we open our hearts to converse with truthful intent, I believe these differences can be resolved.

Second, we need exclusive places of cultivation for women. Bhikkhunis need an environment where they can concentrate on study and enlightenment. We need more venues dedicated to their education. There is a lot of difficulty in building and maintaining such facilities. This work should not solely rely on donations, but the women need to solve *it directly, themselves. We need to have courage. This courage comes from the very faith and confidence that made us choose to surrender to the Three Jewels of Buddha, Dharma, and Sangha. Allow me to tell you my story.*

Unmunsa Temple is over 1,400 years old. The monastic college was founded fifty years ago. We faced so many problems after establishing the school. You need extraordinary determination to overcome such difficulties, but we rose to the challenge and built up our school. Currently, in Korea, there are four more Sangha universities just like Unmun that are dedicated to teaching novice nuns. Unmunsa Temple also built a Seon or Meditation Centre. In Korea, thirty-four out of ninety-seven Seon Centres belong to bhikkhunis. Five out of fifteen sangha universities belong to bhikkhunis. We even have three schools that research bhikkhuni vinayas. (Omitted)

To realize such goals, we need to build an international network to help each other. For bhikkhunis to be able to practice compassion, we need to first rid ourselves of our inner obstacles. If a system is obstructing us, we need to fix it. The support and cooperation of bhikkhu sangha is absolutely crucial. That is why I believe that the Buddha established the dual sanghas of bhikkhus and bhikkhunis. Now is the time that we bhikkhunis should appear as the thirty-two manifestations of Avalokiteshvara to act. The whole world awaits our wisdom and compassion. (Omitted)

When I attended Vesak Day in Thailand last year, it felt wrong to me that a Buddhist country like Thailand should not have a bhikkhuni sangha. I pleaded to the Thai Patriarch to help build a bhikkhuni sangha. I sincerely wish that a bhikkhuni sangha can be built, not only in Thailand, but in other Southeast Asian nations as well. Thank you for listening.

The audience applauded after Myeong-seong's opening address. Senior monks from various nations sat to the right of the Dalai Lama, while nuns sat to his left. Representing the Korean Bhikkhuni Association, Myeong-seong sat right next to the Dalai Lama, where she was able to speak to him.

"Bhikkhus and bhikkhunis are like two wings of a bird, two wheels of a wagon. Missing one, the bird cannot fly; the wagon cannot move forward. The sutras also clearly mention the four components of bhikkhu, bhikkhuni, upasika, and upasaka. It is absurd that, except for Korea, Taiwan, and Vietnam, no other country has bhikkhuni sanghas."

She added that if Tibet established a bhikkhuni sangha, Korean bhikkhunis would lend their full support.

MOU with Qinghua University, Beijing

On September 5, 2007, Unmun Sangha University concluded a memorandum of understanding for academic exchanges with Qinghua University. Myeong-seong, dean of Unmun

University, and Meilang Chang, director for international affairs at Qinghua, signed the agreement. The following is the content of the MOU.

1. Exchanges between students
2. Exchanges between professors and researchers
3. Giving priority to graduates of Unmun if they desire to enter Qinghua
4. Exchanges of academic journals and materials
5. Rotational hosting of international events

This opened up the door for graduates of Unmun to enter China's Qinghua University.

Highest Dharma rank for a nun

In autumn of 2007, Myeong-seong was given the Dharma rank of Enlightened Teacher (*Myeongsa*) by the Jogye Order of Korean Buddhism. Jogye Headquarters held the ceremony at 11 am on October 23, 2007, at the Hall of Great Peace and Light (*Daejeoggwangjeon*), Haeinsa Temple. Seven bhikkhunis - Hye-un, Jeong-hwa, Gwang-u, Jeong-hun, Myo-eom, Ji-won, and Myeong-seong - received their certificates of Dharma rank and robes from Patriarch Beob-jeon. The Enlightened Teacher rank is the highest among bhikkhunis and is the equivalent of Great Patriarch Teacher (*Daejongsa*) for bhikkhus.

The ceremony began with five rings of the bell. The Chairperson of Dharma rank read a statement to the Buddha, receivers of the rank offered flowers and made vows. The president of the Jogye Order gave a symbol of compassion to each individual. Myeong-seong responded by saying that she would receive this as an encouragement to practice cultivation even better.

Myeong-seong became an elder of the bhikkhunis. She was aged seventy-eight.

Outstanding Women in Buddhism Award

In early spring of 2008, Myeong-seong went to Thailand with some close friend nuns and a clerical nun. The United Nations-designated International Women's Day celebration was taking place in Bangkok, Thailand. Myeong-seong was given the "Outstanding Women in Buddhism Award."

The event opened on March 6th and lasted until the 9th. Myeong-seong gave speeches on the following topics:

1. The merits of nurturing the bhikkhuni sangha
2. The importance of determining the legal status of bhikkhunis and laws concerning bhikkhuni sangha education
3. How maechis and bhikkhunis can co-exist

Here is an excerpt from her speech on the importance of determining the legal status of bhikkhunis and laws concerning bhikkhuni sangha education:

Traditions are not built in a day. The four groups of bhikkhu, bhikkhuni, upasaka, and upasika were established during the time of the Lord Buddha. Many bhikkhunis have attained fruit through cultivation. The bhikkhuni tradition has continued to be passed down, but unfortunately, it was severed in regions of southern Theravadan Buddhism. In regions of northern Buddhism like Korea and Taiwan, bhikkhuni sangha is strong. I am delighted that countries like Thailand, Vietnam, and Tibet are making efforts to revive bhikkhuni sangha.

I first became interested in the issue of bhikkhuni sangha in regions of "Southern Buddhism" in 2004 at the eighth Sakyadhita conference in Seoul. After that, I looked into this issue on Vesak Day in Thailand, the ninth Sakyadhita conference in Malaysia, and the first international conference on the role of Buddhist women in 2007 in Germany, which His Holiness the Dalai Lama himself attended. Bhikkhuni sangha in "Southern Buddhism" has become a major issue at any international Buddhism conference. I am deeply interested in this matter and I pray everyday that bhikkhuni sangha become revived in "Southern Buddhism." (Omitted) Not recognizing bhikkhuni sangha is against the spirit of the Buddha. The whole world is crying for gender equality. For some reason, bhikkhuni sangha has vanished in the south, but we have to recognize that there are more and more nuns all over the world. Buddha's teachings are welcomed not only in Asia, but throughout the whole world. Humanity has begun its journey toward enlightenment. If anyone wishes to join the Buddha's sangha and practice cultivation, we should help them. We should protect them and give them the proper status, and work toward the harmony of sanghas. The reinstitution of bhikkhuni sanghas in Southern and Tibetan Buddhism was mentioned in many different ways during the conference in Hamburg, Germany. The example of Korea could offer a good model for Thailand and other Southeast Asian nations. In Korea, we successfully revived the dual sangha full ordination system in the 1970s and it continues to this day. Historically, in Korea, Buddhism was at times influential but at times it was oppressed by the state, especially from 1392 to 1945. At that time, the existence of bhikkhunis could be barely felt.

However, after liberation in 1945 and modernization, we managed to reestablish dual sanghas. This meant that a nun could be ordained by three bhikkhuni teachers and seven witnesses and then, within the same day, be ordained again by three bhikkhu teachers and seven witnesses. This follows the bhikkhuni vinaya. The reestablishment of this system is the fruit of hard work by many senior bhikkhus. Bhikkhunis have worked hard to elevate their status, making great efforts in education and cultivation.

Through this process, bhikkhunis were able to advance their status and finally accomplish the dual sangha system. This would not have been possible were it not for the open attitude of the bhikkhu sangha. I express my deepest respect and gratitude to the Korean bhikkhu sangha.

The first thing we did was to educate the nuns. We built

schools and cultivation centres. We expanded our social activities. Many bhikkhunis are active in a variety of fields, doing their part to contribute. Unmunsa Temple, for example, where I reside, built Unmun Sangha University in 1958, the Munsu Seon Centre in 2000, and the Bohyeon Vinaya school in 2008. (Omitted)

Dearest friends from Thai sanghas! Let us gather our wisdom so that all of us may be enlightened within the teachings of Buddha. Truth is not far away. It is inside us, close to us. Thank you.

Myeong-seong was becoming an international leader in Buddhism, representing Buddhist women in particular. This was when she was seventy-nine.

– **Honorary professorship from the president of a university in Thailand**

On September 7, 2008, the Main Hall of Unmunsa Temple was bustling with people. Important guests from Mahachulalongkornrajavidyalaya University, including the school's president, had come to Korea to bestow Myeong-seong with an honorary doctorate.

The university had originally contacted Myeong-seong, asking her to come and receive the degree. Feeling that she did not deserve the award, Myeong-seong refused. The next thing she knew, people from the university had arrived at Unmunsa

Temple to present her with the degree. This kind of action was the first in the history of the university.

Addressing those in attendance, President Dhamma Kosajan said the following:

"I have heard a lot about how Korean bhikkhunis are very active all over the world. I sincerely hope that Thailand will follow the example of Korea and establish its own bhikkhuni sangha. This would be a great advancement for Thai Buddhism."

Then, he added, "This is the first time that university officials have travelled abroad to offer an honorary doctorate! Knowing the great achievements of Myeong-seong Seunim, we did not hesitate to come here."

For such words to come from the mouth of a bhikkhu from a country that does not recognize bhikkhuni sanghas is an extraordinary thing. The university had taken surprising measures to express their praise and support for Myeong-seong. This was a greatly honourable event, not only for her, but for the whole Korean bhikkhuni sangha.

Myeong-seong responded, "I refused so many times because I do not deserve such an honourable degree. I will accept it as a reminder to urge me to work harder to spread Buddhist teachings and teach the future generation."

More than ten monks with important positions in the school had come from Thailand. While staying in Korea, they concluded a memorandum of understanding on exchanges and cooperation between the two universities of Mahachulalongkorn and Unmun. Abbess Jin-seong Seunim was enthusiastic. Un-san Seunim, in charge of education affairs, visited Mahachulalongkornrajavidyalaya University, joined the International Association of Buddhist Universities (IABU) and finalized the MOU.

— **Academic Memorandum of Understanding with Hanazono University, Kyoto, Japan**

Myeong-seong signed an MOU with President Abe Kosan of Kyoto Hanazono University on February 24, 2009. The university was founded by the Linji School in Japan. The two universities agreed to exchanges, not only academically, but also in terms of students and professors.

With the help of this MOU, graduates of Unmun Sangha University could directly enter the Master's program at Hanazono, despite not having a formal Bachelor's degree. Another feature was that this benefit extended to graduates of Unmun as well. This was different from an exchange student program. The Japanese school was recognizing Unmun students as formal international students. Unmunsa Temple entered into agreements with Chinese, Thai, and Japanese universities. This opened the door wide for Korean bhikkhunis to study abroad.

When Myeong-seong turned eighty, she had been teaching at Unmun for forty years. To celebrate her eightieth and fortieth anniversary, Myeong-seong's students, graduates, followers, disciples, friends, and laypeople who admired her all gathered at the temple. Her birthday is November 15 of the lunar calendar, at the height of winter.

In commemoration of her birthday, three books – Frangrance of Silver Magnolia Flowers; Like the Smile of Flowers, Like the Tears of Birds; Live in the Truth in Everything – were published and dedicated to her. The dedication ceremony took place at 2 pm on September 27, 2010.

Fragrance of Silver Magnolia Flowers was written by Seo-gwang Seunim, a student and disciple of Myeong-seong. She recorded the many faces of Myeong-seong – practitioner, scholar, teacher, administrator, and leader. Seo-gwang had become a nun with Myeong-seong as her Teacher after finishing graduate school at Ehwa Women's University. Going to the US, she acquired her master's degree in religious psychology and doctorate in transpersonal psychology. She established the Korean Meditation and Psychological Counselling Institute where she actively holds workshops and seminars on transpersonal psychology, Buddhism, Seon counselling, meditative healing, and similar subjects. She teaches at Dongguk University in addition to many other organizations.

Like the Smile of a Flower, Like the Tears of a Bird is a collection of 148 letters that Myeong-seong had received from various people dating as far back as the 1950s. The letters are from monks, nuns, and laypeople. They include letters from seunims such as Seong-neung, Un-heo, Dae-eun, Gwan-eung, Gwang-deok, Sung-san, Wol-un, Beob-jeong, and Ji-gwan. The book also has letters from pastor Su-hwan Kim, father Seok-hi Park, friar Yohan Yu, and sister Jemmarusi Kim. Letters from Myeong-seong's disciples, students, and lay followers help illuminate the life of this great bhikkhuni.

Live in the Truth in Everything is a collection of Myeong-seong's Dharma teachings. It contains speeches and talks given by her in many different events and gatherings. It effectively explains the philosophy and values of Myeong-seong. There are a total of forty speeches and talks, divided into six chapters: the Path to Liberation, Young Path-seekers, Life and Action of a Bodhisattva, Light of Wisdom and an Eternal Life, Lotus Sutra, Generating the Mind and Reaching Enlightenment.

The dedication ceremony took place in the Pavilion of Eternity. It marked both her eightieth birthday and her fortieth year at Unmun. People there asked her what the key to her success was.

"Most people's lives are led by greed. However, Buddhas and Bodhisattvas live a life pursuing their vows. Think of Amita Buddha's forty-eight vows, the Medicine Buddha's twelve vows, Tathagata's ten vows, Samantabhadra's ten vows, Four Great Vows, and the like."

"There are many kinds of forces in this universe. The strongest of all is the power of a vow. A dedicated, devoted mind can achieve anything."

"Taking a vow is like planting a seed. Vows will be accomplished just as a seed will sprout. A bell will never ring if you do not strike it. No vow, no achievement. Do not have doubts. Take a vow and devote yourself to it. You can do anything. That is how the universe is."

"Cultivation is no more than living a sincere life."

These words demonstrate the attitude of Myeong-seong herself in living her life. They are how she perceived this universe and the meaning of life.

In 2016, she turned eighty-seven. Residing in Unmun, she has taught two-thousand graduates, sixteen instructors, and over forty researchers. More than twenty bhikkhunis obtained PhDs. Many are professors teaching in Dongguk University or Sangha universities. Along with the Sangha University, Unmun opened the Munsu Seon Centre and Bohyeon Vinaya Centre. Unmun has almost reached the scale of a Great Monastery. Unmunsa Temple is not only the top bhikkhuni education centre in Korea; it is the top bhikkhuni education centre in the world. Myeong-seong also founded two scholarships – the Dharmadatu scholarship and the Dharma wheel scholarship. Myeong-seong has over thirty nun disciples and over forty lay disciples.

As of 2019, her nun disciples are as follows:

Su-gwang, Yu-gwang, Do-gwang, Hye-gwang, Myo-gwang, Seon-gwang, Jin-gwang, Yeon-gwang, Jeong-gwang, Mi-gwang, Bo-gwang, Un-gwang, Ju-gwang, Hyeon-gwang, Wol-gwang, Ja-gwang, Ji-gwang, Song-gwang, Hi-gwang, Il-gwang,

Eun-gwang, Won-gwang, Seo-gwang, Yeo-gwang, Yun-gwang, In-gwang, Se-gwang, Deung-gwang, Hyang-gwang, Sim-gwang, Jae-gwang, Mun-gwang (thirty-two as of 2019)

_ **As of 2019, her lay disciples are as follows:**

Seon-ok Han (Seondeokhaeng, deceased), Nog-gyeong Yun (Banyahaeng), Seong-suk Hong (Hongnyeonhwa), Ji-sim Nam (Yeoryang), Sun-gon Park (Mue), Seon-hyeong An (Cheongnyeonhwa), Taek-suk Kim (Myoryeonhwa), Geum-ja Jeong (Beomnyeonhwa), Bok-ja Lee (Yeonhwasim), Yun-jeong Choi (Baengnyeonhwa), Chun-ho Jo (Mue, deceased), Wi-ju Son (Bodeokhwa), Bohyeonhaeng, Seon-mi Park (Seonmihwa), Myeong-sun Lee (Cheongjeongsim), Eun-suk Choi (Jagwang-hwa), Seonhyeji, Sun Nam (Yeouiju), Ran Lee (Sunhyesim), Dong-geun Bae (Seongwol), U-gi Jin (Yeoncheon), Su-ho Lee, Myeong-jin Jeon (Beophwasim), Seon-suk Lee (Muguhaeng), Eun-yeong Kim, Gin-eum Han (Bohwanghwa), Sun-yeong Lee (Jieumseong, deceased), Jong-su Kim (Yeonhwasim), Beom-nyeonhwa, Il-un Lee (Boriseong), Yeoryeonhwa, Yeong-no Kim (Hyeonsu), Hyeon-dam (Heorak), Su-ja Park, Seung-hu Kim (Mujin), Man-seok Kim (Mui), Myeong-ju Jang (Musang), Byeong-ju Jeong (Muchak), Sun-ho Hong (Muryeom), Seong-jae Gang (Muju), Geum-sik Choi (Muryang), Seong-gu Hwang (Hwahyeon), Sang-hyeon Kim (Cheongun), Su-yeong Yun, Myeong-sun Choi (Wonmanhaeng) (forty-five as of 2019)

Myeong-seong had said thus, "Unmunsa Temple gives me food and shelter, I have no need for money. So, I saved any money that I received and put it to good use. Money is a wicked thing; if you keep it for a long time, you want to hold on to it. I try to get rid of it within three days by deciding where to use the money before I get it."

Myeong-seong always tried to give whatever she had away. When a temple or a seunim was raising funds, she would help generously – for she had gone begging for alms herself and understood its difficulties. She particularly made sure to donate to senior nuns who were having their sixtieth, seventieth, or eightieth birthdays. Myeong-seong frequently gave scholarships to students separately from those given out by her two foundations.

Myeong-seong has accomplished the tasks that she set out to do. She built up the framework of Unmunsa Temple, Sangha University, and the National Bhikkhuni Association. Now it was up to the future generation to shape and breathe new life into them. Her role, her job was completed. The last aspiration that she had was to help Buddhist countries such as Tibet, Thailand, Myanmar, Laos, and Cambodia set up bhikkhuni sanghas. It is uncertain whether this can be accomplished within her lifetime.

If Asian Buddhist countries started recognizing a separate sangha of bhikkhunis, that will influence Europe and the Americas. How Buddhism will unfold for women remains to be seen. May the Buddhas and Bodhisattvas guide us.

Chapter 13

Forest of Merits, Hill of Flower Garlands

At 11 am on May 8, 2015, the sound of a bell rang out throughout Unmunsa Temple. Heung-nyun Seunim had passed away. People hurriedly gathered at Three Basket Library (*Samjangwon*) where Myeong-seong and other teacher nuns were sitting around the body and reciting the mantra of light. The crowd quickly joined in:

"*Om amogha bairochana mahamudra mani padma jeubara prabarltaya hum.*"

Just a few days had passed since Myeong-seong went to see Heung-nyun Seunim at Dongguk Hospital in Ilsan. She was very ill, but her mind was clear. Myeong-seong held her hand and recited the mantra of light one hundred and eight times, praying that she take refuge in the great light of the truth. Leaving the room, Myeong-seong went to see the doctor.

"I wish to take the patient to the temple. She looks very ill."

The doctor replied, "I understand your feelings, but I can't send a patient to a temple where there is no medical equipment.

It could also cause her much stress."

Myeong-seong understood the doctor's point and left the hospital. She asked several times that the hospital call her should anything happen. On her way back to the temple, she got a phone call. Heung-nyun's condition was critical, so the hospital was sending her to the temple in an ambulance. It felt as if a cold dagger traveled through her heart. On her way back, Myeong-seong kept turning her prayer beads. The ambulance had arrived before her. Heung-nyun was brought to her room in Three Basket Library. Myeong-seong stayed with her. Heung-nyun was able to spend two more nights in the temple surrounded by people who loved and respected her.

Since a few years before, Myeong-seong had wanted to install a crematorium behind the arboretum, but this project stayed on the back burner because there were so many other things to be done. However, because of the sudden deterioration in Heung-nyun's health, they quickly finished preparing the grounds for the crematorium.

Along with Il-jin, Heung-nyun had been Myeong-seong's first generation disciple. She was the first to have received the transmission of the post of lecturer (*Jeon-gang*). Whenever Myeong-seong went out to perform a duty, either Heung-nyun, Il-jin or Gye-ho would always accompany her. For forty-five years, she lived together with Myeong-seong in Unmun. She started as a student, then became an instructor, then the abbess, and finally, the dean. Myeong-seong and she did everything together and had been through it all together. Still, she departed this world before Myeong-seong.

Only a month after Heung-nyun's passing, on June 19, Hye-un Seunim, Head of the Munsu Seon Centre, entered nirvana. She had been Myeong-seong's student at Cheongnyong. Six years younger than Myeong-seong, they had lived together for fifty-five years. She had had the utmost respect for her teacher; she would wash her garments, clean her room, and treat her with the utmost respect. When Myeong-seong first came to Unmun, Hye-un was with her. She took charge of the difficult construction of Sariam Hermitage for thirteen years. Were it not for Hye-un, Sariam Hermitage would not have existed in its current form. After finishing construction of Sariam Hermitage, Hye-un returned to Unmun and took on the roles of abbess and head of the Munsu Seon Centre before passing away. She was sick for a long time. Her death was not unforeseen, but painful nonetheless.

Seondeokhaeng and Mu-e (Professor Chun-ho Jo) had also passed a few years earlier. Myeong-seong had known them both for many decades. Although they were laypeople, Myeong-seong's heart ached just as much as when she separated with her nun disciples. In the case of the Buddha as well, two of his great disciples – Sariputra and Moggallāna – died earlier than him. When the Buddha learned of the passing of Sariputra, he did not eat for three days. One can only imagine his sorrow. Some people believe that the Buddha felt no happiness and no grief, but that does not seem correct. He was not attached to emotions, but he would still have felt with great sensitivity the pain of others and himself.

Myeong-seong maintained a calm exterior, but on the inside, she missed them dearly. Her grief had been particularly profound when her mother, Jeonggaksim, had passed away. For nearly all of her life, Myeong-seong had been away from her mother's side, but she was determined to stay by her at the hour of her passing. When Myeong-seong arrived, her mother's daughter-in-law had gone out to buy some things. Her mother passed away not long after Myeong-seong arrived. Myeong-seong closed only one of her mother's eyes. She wanted the daughter-in-law to shut the other. Her brother and his wife had taken care of her mother for so long; she wanted them to say farewell in their own way.

Myeong-seong's mother had left behind ten thousand dollars for her. No matter how great a bhikkhuni Myeong-seong had become, to her mother, she was always her daughter. Between the successes, beyond the glory, her mother saw and felt the loneliness and hardship that her child had endured. Myeong-seong was deeply moved, but still, she gave the money to her brother.

"She seems to have transcended life and death," nuns around Myeong-seong would say about her.

Myeong-seong would not possess two of anything; as

soon as she had a surplus of any item, she would give it away. She gave away blankets, clothes, winter jackets, books, tea, incense, pottery, and money. She only has two outer clothes and two inner clothes.

Myeong-seong's assistant nun also commented, "You'd think that she would be very proud and attached to everything she has done, but she is not. She seems to completely erase from her mind any work that has been finished."

Myeong-seong always said that one percent is giving out orders, and ninety-nine percent is checking. That is how she did her work. Of course, for the people who are the targets of this "ninety-nine percent checking," it could be unbelievably tiring. People might think that Myeong-seong is too much of a perfectionist, too attached to the small details. In fact, she gives all her energy to checking the 99%, and when she thinks all is good, she forgets it and moves on. That is another secret to her being able to accomplish so much.

Currently, Myeong-seong's official titles are elder of Unmunsa Temple and Dean of the Graduate School of Unmun Sangha University. She teaches the Lotus Sutra to seventeen graduate students once a week. She focuses the most on writing the Flower Garland Sutra. The Flower Garland Sutra is the top of the eighty-four thousand sutras taught by the Buddha. According to Professor Gangnam Oh of the University of Regina, Canada, scholars around the world have reached the conclusion that humanity will not be able to create any theory which surpasses the

Flower Garland Sutra.

Starting a few years ago, Myeong-seong has devoted herself to writing the Flower Garland Sutra. She writes it one or two hours every day. If her situation allows, she writes even longer. For Myeong-seong, writing the Flower Garland Sutra is an act of communicating with all the Buddhas and Bodhisattvas of the universe; it is reaching out to their world.

Another source of Myeong-seong's happiness is taking care of trees. Unmunsa Temple has two arboretums on its land. One is the Bodhi Forest (*Borisu*) at Janggunpyeong, and the other is Hwarang Hill behind the Main Hall. The arboretum was created with the soil that was dug out when constructing Unmun dam. It is said that the mountains of Unmun are like generals; they need small hills to support them. That is why Myeong-seong purchased hundreds of trucks of soil from the dam construction and built hills to create an arboretum. Numerous flowers bloom and fall here. Visitors are welcomed by beautiful trees bearing name tags. These parks provide pleasure to many people.

Once the forest park became more popular, the temple held a contest to name the two arboretums. That is how they got the names. "Bodhi Forest" comes from the song of Unmunsa Temple.

Deep in Mount Hogeo where the energy of one thousand

years has collected

We take our vows with the sincere heart of a Bodhisattva

Wisdom has become a light that cleanses ignorance

This is the temple of Unmun, seat of truth

The hill of silver magnolias is full of sweet aroma

The mind is cultivated where the Bodhi trees grow

This song is where the name "Bodhi Forest" came from. There are over ten Bodhi trees in the arboretum.

The name Hwarang Garden was given in memory of Won-gwang Guksa, who gave his 'five precepts for hwarang' to the two hwarangs, Gwi-san and Chu-hang. Hwarangs were an elite class of young warriors from Silla kingdom who played a central role in uniting the three kingdoms.

Myeong-seong greatly enjoys giving prayer beads to children. Whenever a child comes to see her, or when she sees children in the street, she gives them beads to put on their wrists. Even when she is out in the market, when she sees a child, she would head after the girl or boy. Other onlooking seunims would comment, "Does it not look like a large child following a small child?"

Unmunsa Temple is itself a fantastic garden. Among the impressive trees are a five-hundred-year-old pine tree and four-hundred-year-old ginkgo tree. Numerous other trees and flowers were planted by Myeong-seong. This land, now blooming with hundreds of different flowers, had formerly been just vacant land. Different life forms came together to create a living world. They give their respective light to decorate Flower Garland Hill.

Myeong-seong had devoted her life to creating the world of Flower Garlands within this world. The space called Unmunsa Temple is where she put all of her energy into building this. She raised buildings, formed gardens, planted trees and flowers, and taught students. Every single student would go out into the world and build another world of Flower Garlands of her own, taking us one step closer to the utopian new world to which all Buddhists aspire.

Myeong-seong continues with her work. It never stops. Her effort is reflected directly into the world of Flower Garlands. It is never complete. It is her attitude of life to dedicate everything to decorating the Flower Garlands.

How could one person achieve so much in one lifetime? How is it possible? To this question, Jin-gwang Seunim, Myeong-seong's disciple and abbess of Unmunsa Temple, replies:

I believe she receives blessings due to her attitude towards life. When the Munsu Seon Centre was finished, some of us went there together with Myeong-seong. Myeong-seong would pick up the rusted nails and wires and put them into a bucket. Hye-un Seunim asked her why she would collect the rusted metal. Myeong-seong said that they might be rusted now, but they can be reborn in a steel mill.

I have seen so many of such aspects of Myeong-seong since I was a student nun in Unmun. I am used to it. She would even collect small pieces of wood. Nothing is wasted. When I saw her pick up those things, I would think to myself that she is actually picking up merits. It reminds me of a story.

"One day, king Udanaya offered five hundred robes to the Buddha. Ananda thanked him and was about to leave when the king asked, 'I thought you were practitioners who lead a life without greed. What will you do with five hundred robes?' Anada replied, 'I will not keep these for myself. There are many people among the hundreds and thousands of disciples of Buddha whose robes are worn. I will give these to them.'

'What will you do with the worn robes?'

'We will clean them and use them as blankets.'

'What do you do when the blankets wear out?'

'We make them into pillow covers.'

'What do you do with the used pillow covers?'

'We use them to make cushions.'

'What do you do with used cushions?'

'We use them as rags to clean our feet.'

'What do you do with the used rags?'

'We use them to wipe the floor.'

'What do you do when the rags wear out?'
'We shred them and mix with mud to make walls.'
King Udayana was moved by this explanation and came to
respect the Buddha's sangha even more."

Jin-gwang Seunim came to Unmunsa Temple as a student,
became an instructor, and is now an abbess. She is the disciple of
Myeong-seong who has been with her for life. In her view, merit
is derived from the way Myeong-seong lives, the attitude that
she has toward life. Those who live a life of generating merits
and then ultimately return them to the people are called "saints."

Doing good deeds and returning the good fruits were two
wings of Myeong-seong's life.

Beop-gye Myeong-seong Seunim

Myeong-seong was born in 1930 in Sangju, North Gyeongsang Province. She entered the Buddhist path in 1952 under Seon-haeng as her teacher, at Gugiram Hermitage, Haeinsa Temple. In 1958, Seong-neung at Seonamsa Temple approved her as teacher and transmitted the Dharma. She taught in monastic colleges at Seonam and Cheongnyongsa Temples before coming to Unmunsa Temple in 1970. She became the abbess and dean of Unmunsa and has taught over 2,000 graduates and 16 disciples who received her Dharma. She built over forty buildings on the temple grounds, successfully developing it into the leading education centre for bhikkhunis. She is currently the Most Eminent Elder of Unmunsa Temple and Dean of the Graduate School of Unmun Sangha University. As president of the Korean Bhikkhuni Association, she has devoted her life to advancing the status of bhikkhunis.

"If you wish to teach others, teach yourself first." "This place here where we live is where we shall cultivate." These are her teachings, in which her everyday life is united with her practice of cultivation. Her motto is to be faithful to every moment.

She majored in Buddhism Studies at Dongguk University, obtaining Master's and Doctoral degrees from the same school. Her published texts include A Study on Alaya Vijñāna, Study on Three Transforming Consciousnesses, Collection of Buddhism Studies and Introduction to the Flower Garland. She translated The Main Principles of the Abhidharmakośakārikā, Essentials of Consciousness-Only Buddhism, and Abhidharma-nyāyānusāra. She edited Rules and Decorum for Novice Nuns and Prefaces of the Sutras, among others.

Chronology

1930	Born in Sangju, North Gyeongsang Province as the eldest daughter of Jae-yeong Jeon and O-jong Jeon
1948	Graduated from Gangneung Girl's High School
1949	Teacher at Gangdong Elementary School, Gangneung
1952	Began monastic life under Seon-haeng at Gugiram Hermitage, Haeinsa Temple, Hapcheon City
	Received the precepts of a novice nun from Preceptor Dong-san
1956	Graduated from the Four Sutras class at the monastic college of Donghaksa Temple
1958	Graduated from the Flower Garland class at the monastic college of Seonamsa Temple, Seungju City, South Jeolla Province
	Received lectureship transmission from Seong-neung
	Taught at the college for three years
1961-1970	Taught at Cheongnyongsa Temple, Seoul
1964	Graduated with a Bachelors in Buddhist studies, Dongguk University
1964	Received Special Prize in the 1st Dongguk Calligraphy Contest
1965	Received Special Prize in the 2nd Dongguk Calligraphy Contest
1966	Recognized at the Korean National Arts Exhibition in the calligraphy division, received the Dongguk presidential award for calligraphy
1967	Received the precepts of a full nun (bhikkhuni) from Ja-un at Gamno Platform, Haeinsa Temple
1970	Received Master's degree from Dongguk University with research on alaya-vijnana
1970-1989	Councilwoman of the 3rd, 4th, 5th, 8th, and 9th Central Council of the Korean Buddhist Jogye Order
1970	Head instructor of the monastic college at Unmunsa Temple, Cheongdo County

1974	Completed Doctoral program in Buddhist studies, Dongguk University
1975	Appointed as Korea director at the World Buddhist Friendship Association
1975-1976	Toured Southeast Asian Buddhist nations, Europe and America (six months)
1977-1998	Dean of Unmun Sangha University and the 8th, 9th, 10th, 11th, and 12th abbess of Unmunsa Temple
1980-2000	Reciting preceptor and instructional preceptor for the Bhikkhuni ordination platform
1987	Became Dean as "Unmun Sangha College" was renamed "Unmun Sangha University"
1988-1989	Lecturer of National Ethics, College of Education, Kyungpook University
1989-2002	Chairperson on the working committee for the Seoul Mokdong Youth Centre and Yangcheon Gymnasium
1989-2003	Vice president of the Korean Bhikkhuni Association
1990	Pilgrimage to sacred Buddhist sites in China (32 days)
1991	Recipient of the 4th Dharma Propagation Award
1993	Attended the Parliament of the World's Religions in Chicago
1995	Visited Cambodia and Thailand to help international refugees
1997	President of the graduate school of Unmun Sangha University
1998	Acquired PhD at Dongguk University
2000	Special Award from the Environment Minister
2001	Appointed teacher of precepts for full ordination of the Jogye Order
	Received the Sasana Kirthi Sri Award by Sri Lanka
2003	Served as preceptor for the bhikkhuni ordination platform
	Appointed the 8th president of the Korean Bhikkhuni Association, Jogye Order
	Established the Beopgye (Dharmadatu) scholarship

2004	Korean president for the 8th Sakyadhita International Conference on Buddhist Women
	Received the Social Contribution Award from the Ilmaek Foundation
2005	Calligraphy Exhibition (to raise scholarship funds for the National Bhikkhuni Association)
2007	Inaugurated as the 9th president of the Korean Bhikkhuni Association
	Given the Dharma title "Enlightened Teacher" (*Myeongsa*) by the Jogye Order
	Signed an academic exchange pact between Unmun Monastic College and Qinghua University in Beijing
2008	Received the Outstanding Women in Buddhism Award on UN International Women's Day
	Received an honorary doctorate from Mahachulalongkornrajavidyalaya University, Thailand
2009	Attended the Commemoration of Bhikkhuni Heogyeong of Queen Jeongsun (Congratulatory remarks)
2010	Appointed President of the Chinese Buddhist Text Graduate School
	Attended the Taiwan Offering to Monks and Nuns Ceremony (Congratulatory remarks)
2011	Received the 9th Daewon Award in Dharma Propagation of Sangha
2013	Established the Dharma Wheel (*Beomnyun*) scholarship
	Inaugurated as Most Eminent Elder of Unmunsa Temple
2016	Appointed Chairperson of the Senior Bhikkhuni Council of the Jogye Order
	Established the Beopgye Literature Award

(As of September 2016)

Conferred the title of Enlightened Teacher (*Myeongsa*) (2007)

Teacher at an elementary school (1949)

Graduation from the monastic college of Cheongnyongsa Temple (1961)

On top of Mount Sorak together with students from Unmunsa Temple (1970)

With Yun-ho and Il-ta Seunim at Cheongnyongsa Temple (1961)

Master's degree ceremony at Dongguk University (1970)

Doctoral degree ceremony at Dongguk University (1998)

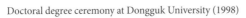

Speaking as a doctrine teacher at the ordination platform of Beomeosa Temple

A scene from her class

Formal monastic meal (*Balugongyang*)

Graduation at Unmun Sangha University

Teaching in Gathering Stars Pavilion

Writing calligraphy

Arm-wrestling

Playing ping pong

With Ja-ho Seunim

With Il-jin and Gye-ho, two disciples who received Myeong-seong's Dharma

Teaching at the Seon Practice Centre (*Seonhagwon*) (1959)

Giving an award during a children's summer Buddhism camp

Pilgrimage to the sacred site of Borobudur, Indonesia with Gwang-u (1975)

Pilgrimage to Jetavana, India (1975)

Pilgrimage to Bagan, Myanmar (1975)

Pilgrimage to the Temple of the Emerald Buddha, Thailand (1975)

15th Bhikkhuni single platform ordination ceremony (1995)

48th graduation at Unmunsa Temple (2012)

32nd Bhikkhuni single platform ordination ceremony (2012)

Outstanding Women in Buddhism Award from the United Nations (2008)

Gwan-eung during Hyehwa College days

Receiving the Dharma from the late Su-ok (1983)

With author Ji-sim Nam

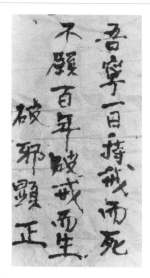

Letter written in blood in protest of the screening of the movie Bhikkhuni

Composed by Ji-gwan and written by Myeong-seong (Epitaph of Su-ok, Naewonsa Temple)

Composed by Un-heo and written by Myeong-seong (Historical record, Seobongsa Temple, Daegu)

Planting rice with students (1970s)

Threshing soybeans

Conferring the precepts to soldiers at Hoguk Army Training Centre (2016)

With seunims who participated in the precept conferring ceremony (2016)

With Korea Military Academy cadets (2016)

Offering the collection of essays on her seventieth birthday (2000)

With Tenjin Palmo (2004)

Outdoor class

Buddhist service at the Main Buddha Hall

Stone pillars at Unmunsa Temple of Mount Hogeo and Unmun Sangha University

Returning from Buddhist service

Novice nuns walking around the Stone of Setting in Motion of the Wheel of the Dharma
after receiving the offering of robes

Buddhist bell and drum

Unmunsa Temple in Mount Hogeo, Cheongdo County,
North Gyeongsang Province, Republic of Korea

MYEONG-SEONG
SEUNIM:
THE BRIGHT STAR ABOVE UNMUNSA TEMPLE

First Edition   June 21, 2019
Written by   Ji-sim Nam
Translated by   Rei Yoon & Seung Suk Lee
Edited by   Jeff Lazar
Book design by   Koodamm
Published by   Bulkwang Publishing
                 3F, 45-13, Ujeongguk-ro, Jongno-gu, Seoul, Korea
                 Tel: +82-2-420-3200
                 www.bulkwang.co.kr

ISBN 978-89-7479-661-7 (03810)

Printed in the Republic of South Korea